Office

Crush

a novel by **John Musgrove**

Published by Quarter Mile Press

Richmond, Virginia

Published by Quarter Mile Press

Richmond, Virginia

Copyright © 2023 by John Musgrove

ISBN 979-8-88722-075-8

All Rights Reserved.

Also available as an Ebook and an Audiobook at your favorite retailers.

eBook: 979-8-88722-091-8

Audiobook: 79-8-88722-076-5

Connect with the author at www.QuarterMilePress.com

Interior design and layout by Clifton Edwards

Edited by Cathy Plageman

Other Books by John Musgrove

Reticent Richmond Series is a hundred-year saga of one family's influence on the queer culture of Richmond, from Reconstruction through the dawning of Civil Rights for LGBTQ people.

1: Ginter's Pope – June 2022

The richest man in Reconstruction Virginia led an incomplete life until he found a younger man to love him.

- Paperback: 979-8-98612-990-7
- eBook: 979-8-88722-098-7
- Audiobook: 979-8-88722-099-4

2: Mary's Grace –September 2023

A wealthy heiress that chose love over societal expectations, and service to her community instead of a life in leisure.

- Paperback: 979-8-88722-083-3
- eBook: 979-8-88722-084-0
- Audiobook: 979-8-88722-085-7

3: Garland's Legacy – expected Spring, 2024

A widower reflects on her lifelong career in education, her own patronage of the arts, and her support for the underground LesBiGay culture of Richmond before.

4: George's Race – expected in 2025

The first sponsor of Ferrari racing in America discovers that men in motorsports are more exciting than a settled domestic life.

About the Author

John works as an Information Security Specialist for the Federal Reserve Bank of Richmond. Side duties include recruiting at LGBTQ events for new employees, volunteering at local nonprofits, as well as being a champion of Privacy and Security practices.

On their first date in 1986, John moved in with Clifton. They have not been apart since. They married when the Commonwealth of Virginia stopped fighting to keep exclusionary laws on the books in the Fall of 2014. The only thing that changed was the jokes they tell: *"THIS is marital bliss? I don't remember that in the brochure!"*

They have traveled to more than fifty countries on six continents. Pictures from many of their trips are posted on FLICKR at the link below.

Find John on the web: http://quartermilepress.com/

To Admire or Avoid?

It was another rainy spring day. The gray clouds matched my mood, and I couldn't get enough coffee to kick myself into gear. I sat down at the conference room table, apprehensive about the meeting. The group had a good rapport, and everyone agreed on the deliverables. The issue for me was not work, it was the chairman.

Jerome was gregarious, well liked, and often the life of the office party. He spoke well of his home life and supported all the office efforts in community outreach. I had heard that his direct reports would cross the globe on foot if he asked them to do so.

In my four years at the company, I had not met a single person who had something negative to say about the man. Although I could not tell anyone else, I did all I could to avoid him.

My aversion to him started when I transferred to the division where he worked. From the first day I saw him, he held me transfixed with a single glance. Within a week, I had followed him to his car, googled him, and collected all the public pictures of him that I could find on social media.

Jerome was not classically handsome. Most people would not even identify him as attractive, but to me, he was gorgeous. His round head, spiky little stray hairs from his otherwise bald scalp, and his big, bushy mustache all kept my rapt attention each time he was anywhere near me. I often left meetings just after he did, so I could watch him walk, and see his meaty buns flex under his khakis.

Of course, he did not know this. I imagine he regarded me as one of the outliers in the office - one that he had not won over with his charm...yet. I did my best to avoid staring at him, even when it would have been permissible, since he often led meetings and team projects. If he asked me a question, I gave him an immediate response, and failing any further inquiry, I would drop my gaze again to my papers and notes.

It was a relief that I was not in his chain of command, as my boss reported directly to the legal department head. We worked in offices at opposite ends of the administration building and we had an entirely separate after-work social calendar. It suited me fine that I could leave my obsession at the office. I even parked far away from his car, just to avoid a possible run-in with him in the afternoons.

The meeting was tedious and long, only because I had to force myself to concentrate on other issues. It could have been a four-hour seminar on any topic, and I would have attended, just to see him up close again. When he adjourned the session, I ran out as if I had been summoned by one of the executives. I could not have stood another second of proximity to him. It only reminded me of my obsession, and my accompanying loneliness.

I maintained my distance and tried my best to focus on my tasks for the workdays. Between vacations, traveling to see clients, and conferences to continue learning about our practices, I was only in the office a few days a week at most. When I had enough paperwork to focus on, I would take that day off and spend it working from home. It was lonelier, but safer for me in the long run.

I simply existed at work for months on end, dodging meetings and being aloof. I had to protect myself, and I had no one that I could confide in for solace. My refuge was compliance and fraud seminars, my specialty in contracts.

Early in the spring, I signed up for an obscure conference in a small, remote town in New England. The conference started

Monday morning and ran for two and a half days, so I took an extra day of vacation at each end of the trip to see the area, hoping for good weather on Sunday. I wanted to use the time before and after to explore the area on my own.

After the flight north from Charlotte, I left the airport in the shuttle, declining to rent a car, as I had heard there were enough local trails and sites within walking distance of the lodge. The ride took an hour and left me drowsy by the end of the journey. I barely had enough energy to check into the hotel when I got to the front desk. Fortunately, I had made all the arrangements in advance, including having the room charges paid up.

I had a salad and some mineral water in the restaurant. There were many couples, and none of them appeared to be in town for the conference. I would have one full day to myself before the classes would start, and I intended to make the most of it. I settled the dinner bill and went back to my room. It was early, perhaps eight o'clock, and I did not want to doze off. I knew it would risk ruining my sleep that night if I turned in too early.

I changed into my Speedo, borrowed the robe from my small hotel room, and slipped on my shower shoes. I was pleased to find that I was alone at the indoor pool.

I walked the perimeter of the area and inspected the water for obstacles. The depth was not sufficient for diving, as the many signs announced. Off to the side, there was a jacuzzi tub with high-powered jets and water warm enough for a bath. It was large enough to seat eight people. I saved that for last, as a reward, depending on how many laps I could do.

I hung my robe on the peg nearest the door and slipped my goggles over my eyes. Once I had lowered myself into the water, I stretched a bit before I began swimming long, slow laps, with the requisite turns at each end. I lost count after ten lengths, but I kept going because it was meditative.

3

On a turn at the far end of the pool, I felt a disturbance in the water and braced myself for an intruder. The pool was wide enough for two of us to swim laps, but I had found that many people seek out the pool as a social area, or worse, as a dating opportunity. I had no interest in either one.

As I continued my free style strokes, I saw ripples and bubbles in the water near me but expected to pass them and keep going. It was only a few seconds later that I felt a hand on my back as I approached the wall.

I stopped, stood up in the water, and looked around for the assailant. There, standing in the shallow end, with a sheepish grin on his face, was Jerome from my office. Standing in the water, it was the closest I had ever been to him. I was only three inches taller.

He was mostly dry, only submerged to his waist, and I could see that the fine black hairs on his chest were not wet, as if he were acclimating himself to the water temperature. I was not even sure if he recognized me, but he was not going to be ignored.

"Oh, hello Jerome," I said flatly.

He looked at me and squinted. His glasses were on the table near where our robes were hanging side by side.

"Larry? From legal? Imagine running into you here. I thought I would be the lone attendee from our office."

"I guess we are in different cost centers, so no one compared the travel requests. It is a great agenda. We should have a good conference, as long as the speakers deliver the information well."

"Oh, sure, I'm looking forward to the sessions on fraud and compliance, but not necessarily in that order," he laughed heartily.

I did not. I just waited for him to explain why he disrupted my laps.

"Hey, I'm sorry, I realize now that I interrupted your workout. I just got in and did not want to startle whomever I found in the pool. I thought it would be better to let them, or you, know that I was here."

"I heard the splash while I was under the water. The sound carries quite well in the water."

"Larry, have I done something to offend you? I know we don't operate in the same social circles at work, but it feels like you have always kept me at arm's distance."

"Well, you did interrupt my laps," I fake laughed. "But I was about to get into the jacuzzi and relax before I went up to bed."

"Mind if I join you? I just came down here to the pool because there was no one to talk to in the bar. Everyone I saw was already paired off, as if it were a couple's weekend."

My face must have registered some level of disappointment because he backpedaled. "Okay, I realize you probably don't want to get into a sexy hot tub with a stocky guy like me. I am sorry if I intruded."

"No, really, it is okay. It's just that...I was going to take my suit off so that I could really enjoy the warm water's effects, with the jets and bubbles."

Jerome raised his eyebrows, looked around for any observers, and then said, in a stage whisper: "Let's do it!" I could smell the remnants of his liquid dinner in the air.

My plan had backfired. I had wanted to scare him out of the tub experience, but it had only enticed him more. "Okay I said, shrugged, and got out of the pool.

I could feel him watching me as I crossed the tile floor confidently. Bending at the waist, I slipped my Speedo down to my ankles, and then stepped out of them. I had spent many hours in the gym, and I knew that other men looked at me because of it, gay, and straight. I adjusted the controls on the tub for maximum jet pressure...and noise.

I sunk one foot, then the other into the water, lowering my body into the warm cauldron of bubbles, rising steam, and pulsing underwater spray. I closed my eyes to settle into the moment, and hopefully miss the entrance of Jerome.

He walked over to the tub, crossed to the side opposite of me, looked around again, and then slipped his trunks down to his ankles. In a move I had not seen since childhood, he backed into the water, bending at the waist, and fishing his left, then right foot down to the bench behind him. I had a full view, in otherwise harsh sodium lighting, of his rounded, hairy, perfect backside. My excitement was more prominent than I could ever recall in my life.

Standing on the seat, he turned around and grinned as if he had just scored the winning touchdown in the playoff games. When I did not grin back, he settled into the seat where he stood. I waited for him to strike up an office conversation but was pleasantly pleased when he closed his eyes and laid his head back on the rim of the tub.

Enjoying the water and wondering how I was going to extract myself from the situation, I allowed myself to drift, mentally. I could not believe my luck.

As I savored the jets pulsing on my back and lower legs, I could feel the water level shift around my chin. I opened my eyes to see Jerome floating on his stomach, holding the edge of the tub in both hands. While I thoroughly enjoyed seeing his slick, wet buns just above the bubbly water, I was grateful that he was not actually kicking with both feet.

When he calmed down and tried to right himself in the tub, he inadvertently touched my erection with his foot. He turned around faster than I thought he could. The expression on his face was priceless.

"Is that what I think it was?"

"Yes, Jerome, I am sorry, but I have that reaction sometimes to warm water and being naked in the bubbles."

He smiled naughtily. "I thought I was the only one!" He allowed his torso to float up in the tub, and his stiffened member pierced the water like a periscope. It was certainly just as hard.

I must have blushed thoroughly because he lowered himself down under the water again. I would not meet his eyes, even though I know he was looking for some level of validation. Everyone at work knew I was gay, and he must have felt rather proud of himself to strip down with the only queer in the office, so far from home. As much as I enjoyed the sight of him, I had never been more uncomfortable.

I closed my eyes and enjoyed the bubbles for the thirty seconds that our silence lasted.

"Larry?" he asked cautiously.

"Yes, Jerome?" I answered politely, not opening my eyes.

"What are you doing tomorrow?"

It took all my energy not to scowl at him.

"I had heard there were some hiking trails nearby and some nature walks that the locals recommend. I would like to get some exercise outside for a change, and the weather looks like it will cooperate, at least through the early afternoon."

"Would you mind if I tagged along? I mean, I may not be the most fit guy in the office, but I can hold my own on a hike."

"I don't see why not." I opened my eyes when I replied. "Perhaps we could set some ground rules first?"

It was his turn to scowl. "What kind of rules? I don't want to play any games, no offense intended."

"What I mean, is that we have to operate on a buddy system. You must watch to see that I am not stepping somewhere I should not, and I will do the same for you. I don't want one of us to be forced into carrying the other back for some dumb injury."

"Sure, that sounds reasonable. What else?"

"We pack what we will eat for the day and consume it as we go. There won't be any walks back just to have a meal in the dining room."

"Oh, okay, but what if we are close enough...that it is not out of the way?"

"Then, of course, we will eat like civilized men."

He smiled broadly. Once his face relaxed, he asked, "Are those all of your 'rules' for the day out?"

"No, there is one more, and it is the most important one that we stick to."

He waited for me to finish.

"We are completely honest with each other. You cannot tell me you are fine if you are in pain, or worse, hurt. I will not ask you to go any further than you feel physically able to do. And I will do the same for you. If I am winded, or tired, or just weary, I will tell you."

He stared at me blankly.

"Is it a deal? I have never been here, and I don't want to become the laughingstock of the office if they must airlift one or both of us out of the woods. It would not be fitting for my image at work."

"Or mine." He forced a grin. "It's a deal. When do we start?"

"I'll want to have a good breakfast, but after that I' m ready to go."

"Not too early, though, right?"

"No, we cannot leave before the sun is fully up. We are in the valley, so I would expect that would be around 8:30. Is that okay?"

"Yes, that' s fine. I just did not want to get up at dawn."

"I may well be up at dawn, doing laps here in the pool. By the way, did you bring any clothes that you can wear for the hike? Shorts and good walking shoes?"

"Actually, I did. I was not sure what I was going to do here, so I packed for a few contingencies."

"Great. I think it will be a fine day," I responded.

"Well, I am getting sleepy in this hot bath, so I am going back up to my room. I won't need a shower to relax me before I lie down tonight. Thanks for suggesting the hot tub!"

He stood up, turned around, and crawled out the way he got in. His beautiful buns, covered in a fine black hair, flexed with his hips, and glistened in the water dripping from his skin.

I closed my eyes and laid my head back just before he turned around. I left him to his privacy when he wriggled back into his cold, wet swim trunks.

"See you in the morning!" he said cheerfully.

"Good night, Jerome. Sleep well, you will need your rest for our hike tomorrow." I could imagine how his face reacted to the idea of a full day's hike.

When I got up to my room, I was disappointed to hear the couple next door. They were obviously enjoying the bed more than I planned to that evening. I toweled off, turned on the television to drown out their noise, and lay down on the bed. After setting the sleep timer on the TV, I pulled the covers over me and drifted off to sleep.

Sunday Outing

I attempted to swim some laps before breakfast, but there were two couples winding down the evening in the jacuzzi. I ignored them at first, but they hopped into the pool to cool down, and quickly got in my way. I was glad to go and save my energy for the hike.

I skipped my usual shower, ran a comb through my wet hair, got dressed and went down to breakfast. I was looking forward to some quiet time before the day with Jerome. When I entered the dining room, he was already at a table for two. He threw up his hand and waved me over.

I got to the table but did not sit down right away. "Okay, Jerome, the honesty has to start now. You really did pack well for this conference. Are those the new Merrell hiking boots I've seen at the REI catalog?"

He chuckled to himself. His wide smile brightened his face as no other I had seen before. "Yes, they are. I have to admit that I have a bit of a shoe fetish." He looked around the room, then continued. "I love to try on shoes and boots. I always buy the ones that fit, no matter the cost. I have shoes for every possible activity in my walk-in closet at home!"

"Well, good for you! I try to stretch my budget on things like shoes, and I always seem to regret it. But I don't skimp on inserts; I always protect my feet." I pointed to my thick, wool hiking socks."

He nodded in approval.

I looked around for the waiter. "Is it a buffet or do we have a menu to order something specific?"

"I don't know," he frowned. "I came in and the lights were on, so I seated myself. After about fifteen minutes of waiting, I got my own coffee. And I have just been sitting here, sipping it, to make the cup last."

I retrieved the pot and poured us each a fresh cup. When I returned to the table, I made myself comfortable, despite the lack of food.

"Did you enjoy your swim?"

"Yes, I did. How did you know I was at the pool?"

"I knocked on your door on my way down this morning. When you didn't answer, I just assumed you went down for some more laps."

It bothered me a little that he knew my room number, but I said nothing about it.

"Yes, I went down and only got about ten laps in before I was interrupted. Again." It was my turn to grin comically.

"What...what happened?"

"Some of the couples you saw last night in the bar were still cavorting this morning. When they moved from the jacuzzi to the pool and started splashing each other, I left."

"Wow, did you hear them 'going at it' last night or what? I thought I was staying at a brothel!"

I must have blushed because his face changed dramatically.

"Yes, I heard them. I had to turn on the television to drown out the couple in the next room so that I could get to sleep."

"I guess there is the allure of hotel sex, for couples that have been together for a while. I know I used to enjoy those parts of the trips."

"I would not know. I am as single as I can be."

It was his turn to blush. I guess he did not want to talk about relationships any longer.

A waitress suddenly appeared at our table. "I am sorry, no one told me you gentlemen were here." She looked at him, and then at me. Her forehead scrunched up as if she were confused.

"Is there something wrong?" I asked.

"Are you two here for the couples-therapy weekend? I thought I saw everyone yesterday, but I would have noticed the two of you." She bit her lip. "You do sort of stand out, if you know what I mean."

"No, we are here for a business conference that starts tomorrow morning," Jerome responded curtly. He offered no further information.

She apologized, but then took our orders for breakfast. When she walked away, he was grinning.

"What is so funny?" I asked.

"She thought the two of us were...a couple."

"Well Jerome, we are. We are eating together this morning, after a night when I saw you in your birthday suit."

He blushed down to his chest hair. "I am sorry, I had consumed a few drinks at the bar. I hope you were not offended, or worse, repulsed."

"Neither could be further from the truth. I thoroughly enjoyed our tub experience last night."

He smiled faintly but asked no further questions.

We finished breakfast with some small talk about the office and our failing cafeteria. We both knew that new contract negotiations were underway, and the management company was doing all they could to keep us signed up.

Hikers, Unite

We went back to our rooms, got our gear, and then met in the lobby. We each had hats, light jackets, small daypacks, hiking boots, and shorts that showed off our knees. While my legs were more muscular from my workout regimen, his meaty thighs were far more attractive than mine would ever be. I made a point of getting each of us a map from the front desk, just so we had a backup. I chose two trails to tackle before lunch, with a possible third one for after, if the rain held off.

We stepped through the door, and were both surprised by the cold, damp fog that blanketed the ground. I followed the signs out of the parking lot, leading us to the first trail. We got to the entrance, and I stopped. Jerome was right behind me and almost ran into me, as he was looking down at his phone.

"I have no bars...none. I was hoping to use this for navigation, but we will have to rely on the maps."

"Jerome, neither of the trails is exceptionally long, nor difficult, according to the guidebook. Would you like me to lead for the first hour?"

"Sure, you go first. I will take the next shift."

When I hesitated, looking around on the ground, he looked confused. "Did you lose something, Larry?"

"No, I was looking for a stick to carry, for the first part of the hike. You will see why shortly," I said coyly.

I picked up a large branch that was too massive for a walking stick and walked past Jerome carefully with it. I started up the trail with the stick held out in front of me, like a lance for a knight on a charging steed.

He followed, cautiously, and kept my pace, but stayed a few feet behind me. We were the only people out that morning, but I was sure there were other critters that could hear us, even if we could not see them.

Not a hundred yards into the trail, I stopped and re-adjusted the branch. Curiosity got the better of Jerome, and he broke the silence with an uncharacteristic burst of irate words.

"What in the hell are you doing with that damned stick? You look like a fool, jousting with the trees!"

I stopped, put the stick down, and walked up to the leading points of the branch. I pointed down.

Jerome walked over, looked down, and then his entire body wriggled with disgust. The five most prominent twigs on the branch were covered in spider webs, and most of the residents were quite angry that they were now part of my defensive strategy.

"I ran cross country through high school and college. The trails we used were always through the woods, much like these. The first runner each day would either get covered in webs or learned to carry a stick like this one. It is only for the few hours in the morning, as they have had all night to build their snares for the next bugs to come along. I just don't want to be covered in sticky filaments, or worse, be on the menu for a spider."

He shook his head, wriggled again, and retreated to where he stopped when I had put the stick down. I picked it back up, and we set off again.

"Do we have to maintain this silence in the woods?" he asked, irritably.

"No, we can talk about anything you like." I smiled to myself. "But remember our agreement on honesty."

He was quiet for a few more steps, then the silence got the best of him, and he started rattling off questions, like a reporter in a briefing room.

"Where did you go to college?"

"I went to Northwestern in Chicago for undergrad, and Loyola for Law School," I replied.

"Have you always wanted to be a lawyer?"

"No, I had my heart set on being a writer. I wanted to change the world with the written word. I double-majored for my BA degree, pre-law, and English literature."

"But you did not pursue the writing?"

"No, I had a few successes before I got into law school. I sold a short story and a novella, but I was not going to make enough money to live on, not even with great critical accolades. There was only the rare cash prize."

"How long have you been with the company?"

"I started four years ago, working through some of the contracts with procurement."

"Has it really been that long? I am sorry, I don't think I even noticed you until last fall."

"I transferred to my current position about two years ago. I keep a low profile, and we have only worked on the one acquisition together, so that is not hard to believe."

We were making good time through the trail and stopped at the first clearing for some water and a breather. I visually scanned my hiking partner for signs of stress. I was pleased to see that he was neither flushed with exertion nor breathing heavily.

"Why are you looking at me like that? Do I have a spider on my hat?"

"Rule number one - we watch out for each other. I wanted to make sure you were not winded, nor red as a beet from the first hike of the day."

"Oh, thanks," was all he said.

Once we were sufficiently hydrated, we holstered our waters and continued the trail. Jerome's questions continued for the remainder of the hour it took to finish the first circuit. We covered my career, childhood, the size of my family, religious preference, and travel experiences.

At the next trail, he offered to go first, and I handed him the branch.

"If you just grip it loosely in your hand, you will feel the resistance when the web catches. It is important to slow down a bit at those passages because there can be a few residual threads of sticky web left behind."

He nodded, concealing his doubt with a brave face, and set off.

He must have been concentrating on the stick because his questions stopped. When he hit the first web, anyone in the county would have thought that he had pulled the biggest fish on record out of the local lake.

"I GOT ONE!" He exclaimed.

I had to grin along with him, because it is a great feeling to dodge such a nasty sensation. We inspected the end tips for our latest victim, then went back to our walking pace.

As he got more comfortable with the process, he walked a bit faster, and we had finished the second trail just past eleven.

We found a clearing with some large, flat boulders that we used as impromptu outdoor furniture. I plopped down and swigged my water bottle in triumph.

"This is the time to have a little snack. Perhaps that piece of fruit we stole from the breakfast bar?"

"I agree - I thought I had eaten enough breakfast, but I am a bit hungry now," he said.

We rested in silence, eating our fruit, and finishing the first water bottle. I made sure we had at least two more bottles each, so we were safe.

"Larry?" Jerome said cautiously.

"Yes?" I responded.

He paused, scrunching his face up as if he were composing his question. I could tell that he was just stalling – which meant he was nervous about asking me. I made a point to drop my gaze to give him the courage to just ask.

"I have always gotten the impression that you don't like me. You are curt with me at work, and rarely speak up in my team meetings. Have I done something that you don't like? I mean, most people like me - and it really bothers me when someone does not."

He left his words hanging in the air, a sad confession from a well-respected professional in our office.

I counted to five before I started to form the words to let him off the hook. "Jerome, I am an introvert. It is problematic for me, in a group, to be an outspoken member in a work situation. I even find it difficult to advocate for me when I find myself in the firing line. It doomed my career as a trial attorney. That is why I went into contract law."

"But...I have seen you interact with other people at work, and you display an entirely different personality. It is almost bubbly at times."

It unnerved me to see him so hurt. I knew I had to be very diplomatic about my response.

"Jerome, once I get to know people, I am incredibly open and friendly. I must keep my guard up at work, simply because I am called upon to deliver bad news about contracts and negotiations. I don't want my colleagues to see me as a friendly push-over, as I often must be the last line of defense for our company's interests."

His face relaxed. "Oh, I did not realize that you were put in that position. I am sorry if I misconstrued the situation."

"Might I say, though, after these next few days, that you and I will be on particularly good terms. We might even be friends outside of work. At least as long as you don't try to lose me in these woods!"

"I would never do that. And thanks, I would like to be friends." His face went back to the sad boy-on-the-playground look.

"Jerome, I get the impression that you are immensely popular at work. Is there something that I have missed?"

He stared at his new boots. Kicking them together to knock the dust off, his face was a mask of anguish as he thought about my question. He cleared his throat. His response, when it started, was far more subdued than our earlier conversations on the trail.

"I don't have many friends." He paused, seemingly on the verge of tears. "In fact, I don't have any friends that I can count on."

"I don't understand. You are very well liked at work. I have never heard anyone say anything bad about you." I swallowed more water. "Never."

He wiped his eyes on his sleeve, dropping his arm in a defeated motion that belied his mature age.

"That is just it, Larry," his voice cracked. "People seem to like me, I am nice to everyone, but whenever I try to get to know someone better, I seem to push them away. I don't know what I am doing wrong."

I wanted to hug him, but it seemed inappropriate for the setting. I smiled wanly. "Jerome, I have the same problem. It seems like I just start getting to know someone, and then they stop responding to my invitations. Maybe I come on too strong. I do tend to spoil people that I like with generous gifts. Perhaps they read the signals wrong."

He steadied himself on the rock. He peered up at me and made eye contact for the first time since we had gotten serious in our conversation.

"Do you find you have the same problem with women? I noticed that you are not wearing a wedding ring, and you came to this wonderful resort alone."

I took a deep breath and let it out slowly.

"Jerome, I am gay."

"Good golly, I had no idea!" he exclaimed.

"I am not surprised. Many people tell me that. Strangely enough everyone knew in high school. So, it still blindsides me when people ask how I am faring with the ladies."

"I am sorry, Larry, I did not mean to pry," Jerome said.

"You are not prying. We must be honest with each other if we will be friends. I would rather not have any acquaintances that I would have to hide details from."

"Was it difficult? Admitting the truth and coming out? I am not sure that I could be as brave."

"I have known it since I was a young man, but I have yet to find the right gentleman to settle down with. Sometimes I wonder if I have just been too much of a workaholic introvert, to protect myself from the endless cycle of dating rejection experiences."

He just stared at me in my gush of information.

"It is okay, really. I am 'out' at work, and will tell people if they ask, but I don't wear a pride flag on my sleeve - or on my suit lapel."

"I guess I was just not 'in the know' or would not have asked. I am sorry."

"Don't be - if you don't ask questions, you never learn about people."

Jerome nodded solemnly. We let the silence play out for a bit.

"Say, Jerome, I will tell you what. Let us do our best these next few days to get to know one another. Who knows, perhaps we could be the friends that we have never had."

Jerome smiled. "That sounds great, Larry." Then he frowned. "Only, I am really embarrassed about my behavior last night. I really was an ass, coming into the pool to interrupt your laps, drunk and all."

"Jerome, it doesn't matter now. I think we were both a bit lonely, and I was relieved when you did not disappear on me. I don't know how long I would have made it out here today, alone in the woods with just my thoughts."

Jerome slid down on the boulder until his feet were touching the ground, and then he lay back flat to stretch out on the rock. I got the impression that he did not want to face me.

"Larry, I have to be honest with you. I was just being agreeable last night when I consented to your rules. I got up this morning, dreading this day. I almost left you a message on your room phone, telling you that I was too hung over to do the hike today, just to avoid this."

"Jerome, you have kept up well this morning, and we have already covered two trails. I can't see why you would think it would be that tough."

"Larry, I had no fear about the exercise. I wrestled in high school and college. I was concerned that I could not be honest with you, because I don't do that very often. I hide what I am feeling and put on the happy face of the office clown, just so people don't pity me."

"Thank you for telling me. I got the feeling that you might back out, but I am so awfully glad that you did not." I was trying my best not to picture him facing me on a mat, dressed in nothing but a wrestling singlet.

Jerome sat up with a startled look. "You are? I thought you were just being nice. I regretted impinging on your plans for the day, but I just could not stand to spend another day alone."

"Can I ask, then, why you came up a day early, with no plans? You must have known how remote this resort was."

He sighed deeply. "I just thought, if I came up early, maybe I could make a few acquaintances before they discovered the real me and disappeared again. Even in our town, I get quite lonely at home since my wife left me."

His eyes were cast to the ground, and I was trying to think of a way to be supportive, without patronizing him.

"I am sorry, Jerome, I had no idea how difficult it was for you. Let me just say, as your friend, that you can share anything with me, and I will never tell it to another living soul. I am a great listener. It's just that...you must tell me if you are just venting, or if you are looking for help. I love to provide solutions, so I don't always know when I should just shut up and listen."

He smiled weakly. "Thank you, Larry. I will keep that in mind."

I stood up and stretched. I looked down at my watch. "It is now just after noon. If you want to eat, we can finish our packed lunches. If you want to continue our hike, there is another short trail. We should try to be back inside by about three, when the rains are supposed to arrive."

"Are there any other options?"

"Sure, there are. We could go back down the hill and have a grand lunch in the dining room. We could go back to the pool - or even the jacuzzi. All the randy couples should be checking out soon. We will have the entire resort to ourselves until the others arrive later in the afternoon."

"You would not object to seeing me in a bathing suit again?" Jerome laughed to himself.

"No, I would not. It was not...half bad." My broad smile betrayed my inner thoughts, and I laughed nervously.

He stood up and stretched. "Let's head down the mountain and get that lunch you offered. I am still a bit hungover from last night, and I think I could use a nap this afternoon."

We got ourselves pointed in the right direction and I smiled broadly. "You know the best part of walking down now?" I asked.

"No, what?" he asked cautiously.

"We don't need the branch to clear the path of spider webs anymore."

"Oh, good! I was tired of carrying that thing. I think I might have hurt my shoulder when I let it hit the ground one time."

"Really? Let me take a look."

I took a step toward him. He tensed up, and pulled back initially, but then he relented. I moved around and I stood behind him. I reached up and kneaded his left shoulder until he cried out.

"Yes, you have strained a muscle. Let's get you back down to the resort and see what they have to offer for massage therapy."

"Wow, that sounds wonderful. I hope it is a gorgeous Scandinavian gal."

"Don't get your hopes up, you might have to settle for me."

"I am not sure I would like that as much – are you qualified?"

"You bet I am – all of my customers tell me so. I just hope you are not a chintzy tipper!"

We both laughed.

Even with the sounds of nature waking up around us, the walk down the mountain was quieter. Our shoes made crunching sounds on the trail, and neither of us felt as if we had to fill the time with small talk. We had reached a peace between us that I did not think possible when we set out that morning.

Afternoon Storm

We dropped our packs next to the table and washed our hands before we started the meal. We waited for the server quietly, sipping water to rehydrate ourselves after the long hike. I got the impression that he was wondering how long we had to keep up the honesty pledge, but I wanted him to ask, so I said nothing to the contrary.

After a few minutes of wondering if there was anyone on duty at all, I recognized the face of the woman moving toward us before she identified us. We got the same surly waitress that we had for our breakfast service.

"Your favorite couple is back. And we want a huge lunch to make up for all the calories we burned on the trail this morning," I exclaimed.

She frowned, furrowed her brow, and said nothing. Her pad was in her hands, and she waited for us to decide on our meals. Jerome ordered sweetened iced tea, and a salad with grilled chicken on it. I made it easy and picked the same items.

After ordering lunch, I went to the front desk to ask about massage therapy. I came back to the table with the information and spread my arms in a flourish of excitement.

"I have good news, better news, and the best news of all."

"Yes?" he responded.

"They have an in-room massage therapy service, but they are off on Sundays."

"Which category of news was that?" he demanded.

"That was the good news. The better news is that they will let us borrow the table."

"And what could be the 'best news' after those two statements?"

"That I work on my friends for free. I don't even accept tips."

He mock-scowled at me.

"What? I am a certified massage therapist. I have my license if you want to inspect it."

"I don't know. It's just that...will that be crossing the line for you?"

"I am a professional, and a friend, I would not work you over too hard, or make any of your muscles worse, if that is what you are worried about."

"What I meant was...wouldn't it be awkward...with you being gay and all?"

"Not for me. I have practiced on many men - strangers, and acquaintances. I have even worked on my brother's shoulders. There is a professional distance in the massage business, if you will."

"But I would have to take my shirt off and-"

"You had more than that off last night," I said, cutting him mid-sentence, defensively.

He blushed deeply and dropped his gaze to his plate.

"Larry, I am sorry, I had forgotten about that already."

"It is fine."

"I hope you were not..."

"If you don't want the massage, I withdraw the offer. I don't want you to be uncomfortable."

Jerome picked at his meal when it came. The silence was punctuated by the waitress clicking the buttons on her phone in the corner. There was no one else in the room, and probably no other guests in the resort.

I cleaned my plate, and he had only eaten a few scant forkfuls. After we charged the bills to our respective rooms, I got up and pushed my chair back under the table. I waited for him to change his mind or say something to break the ice. He got up, tried to push his chair up to the table, and then winced in pain. He really had hurt himself. I waited for him to make eye contact. He never lifted his gaze.

Grabbing my pack, I turned and started walking toward the lobby to take the elevator up to my room. I could hear him rustle in behind me, and then he touched my shoulder.

I turned around to see him with tears in his eyes. I wanted to hug him, but I was angry at being rebuffed. I waited for him to speak.

"Larry, I am sorry. I am just so uncomfortable in my own skin. I cannot believe that anyone would want to touch me. How can I make it up to you?"

"I accept your apology. If you are not willing to let me work on that shoulder for you, at least go sit in the jacuzzi to soothe it for now. Take some Tylenol or Motrin if you have it. And don't drink any alcohol, it could exacerbate the inflammation."

"Okay, thank you. I will try those things."

"We had quite the walk this morning. Almost eleven miles. Perhaps a nap would do us both some good."

28

"And if I change my mind about the free massage?" he asked hopefully.

"Then you just have to knock on my door," I responded. I smiled briefly, got no response, turned, and walked away.

I changed out of my hiking clothes. Putting on some loose-fitting gym shorts and a baggy t-shirt. I unpacked my suitcase, hanging my clothes up for the week's events, and hung up my still-wet swimsuit to dry in the bathroom. Trying to get ahead of the crowds that might be coming in for the conference, I called the front desk, but I got a recording when I asked for more towels. I got comfortable on the bed and was just starting to nod off when there was a knock at my door.

I got up and opened the door, expecting the maid service for my towel request. I was surprised to see Jerome, looking sheepish and defeated. He had changed clothes and looked like my Phys Ed uniform twin, even down to the color scheme.

"Yes m' lord, may I assist you with something?" I said in a terrible fake British accent.

He smiled wanly. "Could I come in...and talk?" He made eye contact, then dropped his gaze, sullenly.

"Of course, please come in. Make yourself comfortable." I swung the door wide and let him find his way.

He walked to the center of the room, and then looked around for a place to sit. My armchair was full of bags and assorted travel stuff. The desk chair was covered with computer bags, a laptop sleeve, and assorted accessories. I suddenly felt like a total slob.

He sat down on the one corner of the bed that I had not covered or rumpled up. His body language reminded me of prisoners I had seen in a documentary: placid, compliant, and completely defeated by their circumstances.

I gave him plenty of space, but I had to sit down on the other side of the bed because there was nowhere else. There was an implied urgency to his request, and I did not want to distract him with any panicky cleaning.

"Can I get you anything? Water? Whisky?"

"Doctor told me not to drink any alcohol, but I would love some, thank you."

I smiled at the rebuke. I took the pint of Crown Royal out of my bag and prepped two glasses with ice. I poured two fingers in each one, being generous, considering the volume of the ice. I handed him the glass and forced a smile.

He sipped it slowly, stalling for time, or perhaps waiting for the buzz to loosen his tongue. In an effort to get him to relax, I piled up the mound of pillows that I had scattered on the bed against the headboard. I propped my back up against the pillows on my side and relaxed with the drink in my hand. He shifted a few times, then stood up, and matched my posture on the other side of the king-sized bed, keeping a safe distance between us.

When he crossed his ankles, I realized that he had come down the hallway from his room in just his socks.

"I just don't know where to start." he said quietly.

"Jerome, you really can tell me anything. Start with what's bothering you the most, and we can work on the rest, if you want to continue."

He stalled a bit more, taking small sips of his whisky. At last, he began to speak. "About two years ago," his voice hitched, "my wife left me. She said I was boring, and old, and too ugly to look at anymore."

Without a word, I placed my handkerchief on the bed between us. He picked it up gingerly. Then he gripped it like a lifeline.

"I cannot stand the loneliness anymore and I don't know what to do."

I waited. Even I knew this was too early to step in with any advice.

"I am always trying to buy friendships from the people around me. I can pay for lunches, or treat everyone for drinks after work, but no one ever wants to be around me when I just need a buddy to hang out with."

He really had me captivated by the depth of his pain.

"I just don't know how to be 'myself' and be a friend that people will want to spend time with."

I waited. I could hear him sniffle, and I suspected he was crying, but I had to give him privacy; I needed him to let go of his fear of me seeing that.

"Now you make this very generous offer, and I send you packing as if you had asked me for some kind of perverted sexual favor. You did not deserve that; I am so deeply sorry. I am just so scared."

"Jerome, what are you afraid of? I am not going to reject you or hurt you. I wanted to help you."

"I realize that now. I just have never come to terms with the whole gay thing. I just don't understand how a man could be attracted to another man - when women are so wonderful."

"I cannot explain it to you, any more than you could tell me why breasts hold so many men captive."

31

He chuckled. "I wish I could explain it away, sometimes they can be so distracting."

We both laughed at that one.

"Jerome, I really believe that our sexual urges, the things that grab our focus when we should really be, as mature adults, paying attention to everything else, are just there to remind us that we are alive. We should be enjoying every second of life, even if we cannot satisfy every need or desire. We know, rationally, that we cannot act on whim, but we can stop and smell the roses, as it were."

I could tell his mood was lightened, and he had put down his drink, but I knew that there was more bothering him.

"I can tell you, if we are being completely honest, that it happens to me, also. I got so fixated on a particularly gorgeous guy that I had seen around. I started to lose the ability to concentrate. It dominated my life for months before I finally got myself back on track. I think it is just mother nature reminding me to live a little and stop taking every day so seriously."

He grunted, and then drained the rest of his drink. The glass clunked on the table, jingling the ice remaining in the bottom.

"As for your wife, I can tell you, categorically, that she was wrong. I find you to be a charming, warm, sensitive guy with a lot of good qualities. If she cannot see that, then perhaps she was not looking awfully hard."

He reached over and took my hand in his. We sat there quietly for a few minutes.

"Thank you. It does help to let it out," he said quietly.

"I have all afternoon, and every night this week. You know where to find me."

"Larry, I have so much more that I want to talk about, but I don't want to chase you away with my sack of sorrows."

"Jerome, I don't know what you want me to do, but as it is, you are in my room, and I am not leaving."

We laughed a bit at that one. The sun was setting behind the mountain range and the room was getting darker, even though it was early afternoon. Then we heard the thunder, and we both realized that the predicted storm had arrived - not sunset.

"It's just that I...I don't know anymore. I can tell you that I don't want someone to solve my problems for me, I just want to be able to tell them to someone else without fear of judgment."

I squeezed his hand once. "What would help you do that, Jerome?" I asked. "Should we get drunk to loosen your tongue a bit? Do you want me to massage your shoulder - that sometimes brings out an unexpected rush of words? We could go back down to the jacuzzi and sit in it until we are prunes. Does any of that sound like it would work?"

"Actually, I want to do all of those. Where do we start?" he laughed nervously.

I picked up the phone and called the front desk. "Could you bring the massage table and some extra towels up to my room, please? Thank you."

Then I hopped up and poured him another drink, bigger than the last one. He looked like a forlorn puppy in a cage, rather than a mature man, reclining on a bed in an exclusive resort.

The knock at the door startled both of us. I got up, let the maid in, and tipped her a fiver on her way out. I moved the two chairs, set up the massage table, draped it with clean towels, and then made eye contact with Jerome. I patted the table and said "Ready?"

He got up, crossed around to the table where I stood. He was still quite apprehensive. I took his empty glass out of his hand and then turned to face him. He was waiting for me to give the commands, as if he had no more say in what was to happen. I stepped forward and embraced him. At first, he stiffened, but then he relaxed and hugged me back. We stood there for a few moments, just holding each other. When I relaxed my grip, he held on a bit longer, and then let his arms fall to his sides.

I put my hands on his shoulders and spoke directly at him, slowly and carefully, "Jerome you are my friend. I love you. I will not do anything to hurt you or make you uncomfortable. Do you believe me?"

He teared up, and then nodded.

"Now I need to work on your shoulder. You will need to take off your shirt and get up on the bench. Try not to strain the muscle any further. Let me know if you need help."

I stepped into the bathroom to wash my hands and fetch the massage oils. When I came out of the bathroom, I could see that he had dropped his shirt and gym shorts on the rug next to the table. I made the circuit around the room, turning down the lights. I dropped my old-school iPod into the clock radio setup and put on some light jazz.

He had haphazardly draped a towel over his back, covering his waist and most of his legs. He tensed up when I straightened the towel, but he relaxed when I let go of the drape. I oiled my hands to begin.

"Now, I am going to take this very slowly, we need to identify where you hurt the most, so I can be gentle on that spot. We only want to loosen the muscle a bit so the healing will be faster."

Using my fingertips, I prodded the large muscles in his shoulder, pushing each one with a different finger and watching him closely for a response. When I found the area, he flinched. I pushed a bit harder, using each finger in the area until I found the perimeter of his pain.

"You have definitely hurt your deltoid on this side. Before I get started, are there any more areas you have not told me about?"

I thought maybe he was drifting off to sleep, but he was just being coy. "Jerome, are you there?"

"Yeah, I am here. There is one other place, but..."

"Are you going to tell me where it is, or will I have to tickle it out of you?" I ran my fingers lightly down his furry flank. He recoiled and laughed, then groaned as the pain quickly reminded him of why he was on the table. He lifted his head up so that he could talk without the table pushing on the side of his face.

"Okay, okay, you win. I hurt my right...um...thigh when I jumped up on that big rock. The pain radiates down my back, and into the top of my leg when I step down."

"Well, Jerome, that sounds like you have the beginning stages of sciatica. The nerve runs along that area and can get inflamed. I am sure we can do something about that. Anywhere else?"

"Yes," and he paused. "My feet hurt. I hope my new boots aren't creating that pain because I really like them."

I laughed out loud. "My sister says the same thing quite often. She loves a pair of shoes so much that she could not believe that they would betray her feet in that way."

He chuckled and put his head back down. "That is it, the sum total of my physical pain, for today anyway." The sound was muffled by the table where he again rested his left cheek.

"Well, just relax and let me get started on this shoulder. Is the lighting okay?"

"Yeah, but I will just close my eyes anyway, if that's okay."

"Are you warm enough? I don't want you to get chilled."

"No, I am extremely warm blooded. I never get cold indoors."

I poured more oil on my hands and got to work on his shoulder. He recoiled a few times, but mostly he just lay there, passively groaning with the deep muscle massage that I did so well.

I worked for thirty minutes on his shoulder before he stopped tensing up. I moved to the other shoulder and loosened the muscles so that he would be completely relaxed in his posture. I think he drifted off to sleep at one point.

"Jerome?" I said quietly.

"Yes?" he replied, more drowsy than tipsy.

"We need to identify the other pain spots. Do you need a break or a trip to the bathroom?"

"No, I am fine. The pain starts in my lower back and runs down through my right leg."

"Jerome, I am going to move the towel so that I can work on that location, is that alright?"

There was silence at first, and then he reached up with his right hand and pulled the towel off himself. It dropped to the floor. He had stripped down before he got on the table. The only thing he had kept on were his socks. I nearly gasped at the sight of his glorious buns, but I bit my tongue, and kept my professionalism.

I got more oil on my hands and spread a little on his lower back. Slowly, moving in tight circles, I ran my tented fingers around the area, watching for reactions from him. He tensed up as I got to the ridge just before the swell of his gluteus maximus.

"Jerome, I am going to move further down your leg so that I can trace this pain. Is that okay?"

"YES!" he cried out. He had lost his inhibitions of me touching him, or the alcohol was helping to loosen him up.

I used the same motion over his right buttock, tracing and identifying the sensitive track of pain that indicated the sciatica nerve. Moving further down into his upper thigh area, I could tell that the pain tapered off about halfway down to his knee.

Starting with his thigh, I worked backwards up the pain channel, releasing the muscle that spasmed when the nerve became irritated. The light hairs on his skin tickled my hands until I could get them covered in oil. From then on, it was like working on a beautifully sculpted piece of marble. His muscles were firm, with extraordinarily little fat. They responded well in my capable hands, and I enjoyed working on him immensely. When I finally reached his lower back, he was dozing.

I stepped back, flexing my hands and wrists. As much as I wanted to enjoy the view, I also felt a need to protect him. I put the towels over him and let him sleep for about thirty minutes.

When he came to, I was snoozing on the bed. "Larry?" he asked, groggy from the nap.

"Yes, I am here." I tried to speak mid-yawn. "I drifted off as well."

"Are you finished? I mean, I feel wonderful, but I don't remember much."

"That is good to hear. I worked on your hip and then stopped. I did not want to start on your feet since you had drifted off."

"Oh, okay. Does that mean you have quit?" he asked sadly.

"No, I want you to be engaged. I could actually do more damage to your feet if you are not with me to identify the painful parts."

"Okay. I understand."

"Do you need a break? A bathroom stop, or some water?"

"Both, please." He moved to sit up, and the towel covering him fell to the floor. It did not seem to bother him.

"Larry?"

"Yes, Jerome?"

"I cannot jump down. My feet hurt too much."

"Hold on, I will help you."

I moved over to the table and shoved the small ottoman up under his feet. I held out my hand for him to grip. He eyed me suspiciously, then broke into a big smile and took my hand. I helped him down. He padded into the bathroom in just his socks - very confidently, I thought. The toilet flushed and then he washed his hands. When he returned, I had set up the chair for him to sit in for the next round of massage.

"Here, Larry, step into your gym shorts and then sit down on this chair. I covered it with towels to absorb some of the oil on your back."

He frowned as if I had asked him to leave. "I am comfortable. This is fine, really." His lack of modesty surprised me.

"Larry, I want to work on your feet while you sit in this chair. I don't want the enormous tent pole that you showed me last night to be staring me in the face while I do this!"

He grinned broadly and then walked over to where he had dropped his shorts. He bent at the waist to pick them up, almost as if he were trying to show off.

"I see your hip is better now, if you can move like that without pain."

He stepped into his shorts and then turned to face me. "I have a friend that is a specialist in making me feel better." He smiled so brightly that I choked up.

"Thank you. Now, move over to the chair, take off your socks and brace yourself."

"Why? Is this gonna hurt?"

"You bet it is! The feet are more cartilage and bone than muscle. The nerves are close to the surface, and there is not much I can do to shield you from the effects of the examination."

He shuffled over to the chair and plopped down. I slowly took off each of his socks and laid them next to him on the floor. Each foot appeared on the ottoman, and I moved in, positioning myself in a chair facing the bottoms of his upturned feet.

I put a bottle of water in his hand. "Do you want more whisky?"

"No, I'd better just have water for this next part. Thanks."

I moved my hands over his feet, palpating for pain points and soreness. He had no blisters or calluses from the morning's walk, but he did have severe tenderness in the center of each foot. His face changed when I moved to stand.

"What' s wrong?" he asked.

"I think I need a different solution. Massage oil is not going to help your feet," I said.

I went back to the bathroom and retrieved my tube of salve.

"What's that?" he asked, nervously.

"It is a cream that I use for soreness. I picked it up at a pharmacy in Germany and it is THE BALM!" I raised my voice, holding the tube up over my head like a trophy for a winner's pose.

"Ha, ha, ha. Very funny."

I squeezed a spot of the thick white cream into my left palm, and then worked it into the soles of his feet with my fingers. He tensed up when I started, as the pain was quite intense, but he relaxed as we progressed through the procedure. The pain was worse in his left foot, or maybe he was just getting comfortable when I surprised him by prodding his sole after he had gotten so relaxed.

I finished with the other foot, moving my hands over his ankles and the dorsal of each foot to use up the rest of the balm. He drained the water bottle and crumpled it noisily. I washed my hands and returned to the room. He had laid his head back in the chair and closed his eyes.

I sat down on the bed and let him relax while the eucalyptus oils were absorbed into his skin. Neither one of us stirred for the next twenty minutes. My eyes opened when I heard his chair squeak.

He got up, slowly, gingerly put pressure on his feet, and then padded around the carpet in a circle.

"You are a miracle worker! It does not hurt at all to walk."

"Why, thank you, kind sir. I aim to please. What about your shoulder?" He moved it about slowly, and then in a wider arc.

"It is as good as new!"

"Jerome, are you right-handed or left?"

"Left-handed, why?"

"Just be careful the next couple of days. You could still injure it. Perhaps you could use your right hand each night before you go to sleep?"

He blushed, then grinned brightly. "How did you know?" he asked.

"I am a single guy, duh. We all have those habits."

"Well, Larry, if I were into guys, I would marry you in a heartbeat. A lawyer, a masseuse, a great listener - what more could a prospective mate want in a partner?"

"Well, thank you, Jerome. So far, I have not been able to find anyone that admires my qualities as much as you do. If you know anyone, maybe you could get me a referral."

We both laughed, but then he stopped.

"You know, I might know someone. Let me do some research."

"Don't tease me, and don't get my hopes up! Now, what about the rest of the evening? Are you hungry? Do you want to shower up before you leave an oily spot on each piece of furniture you touch?"

He reached for his shirt on the floor with his dominant hand but winced in the process. "Wait! I will get it," I said.

I went over to the table and got the shirt for him. "Do you want me to put it on you?"

He stepped over to me, with his hip touching my arm as I straightened up my back. I was surprised how relaxed he was with me standing so close to him.

"Are you kidding? I am going to strut down the hallway in just my shorts. Maybe all the other guests will all see me leaving your room, half-naked, with a big smile on my face," he laughed. The door closed quietly behind him, and I flopped onto the bed. The tent pole in my shorts was beginning to be uncomfortable under the stress of the fabric.

A Revealing Night Out

Dinner was quiet. There had been an influx of businesspeople for the conference. We ate together but did not talk much. At the end, we each paid our own bills by charging the meal to our respective rooms.

We walked over to the elevator and Jerome cleared his throat.

"Larry, what are you gonna do now?"

I turned to face him, smiled, and said, "I thought I would do some laps in the pool. I don't want to lie down with a full stomach, as I might go to sleep too soon, and then spend the rest of the night awake."

"Oh, okay."

"Why, did you have something else in mind?"

"No, it's nothing, really."

"Jerome, please don't shut me out. I am just filling in the time while I am here. I am open to suggestions."

"Yeah, well, I had wanted to talk some more, but I don't want to do it in an echoey indoor pool."

"Okay, then what do you suggest?"

"Oh, I don't know. Is there anywhere quiet that we could sit, maybe have a night cap?"

I thought for a second, and then smiled. "Yes, I think I know just the place." I looked him up and down and then asked, "Did you bring a coat?"

"Yes. Why?"

"Let's go get it." I moved toward the elevators. He followed in behind me, quietly matching my pace, but not my excitement.

We met back in the hallway, halfway between our two rooms. With our coats and hats already in place, I led the way to the stairwell, with a key in my pocket. He followed silently, as excited as a kid on an adventure.

We climbed the stairs to the roof and were delightfully surprised that the clouds had cleared. There was a star-filled sky above us, which we never had the opportunity to experience in our light-polluted city. I produced the key and unlocked the large cabinet on the far corner of the roof. As I swung the doors back, he whistled. We were both stunned by what we had to work with.

The telescope was top-notch, professional quality, and in pristine condition. "Jerome, I had kept this option a secret, in case I needed to escape from the stuffy business folks that I spent all day with."

"Do you know what you are doing?" He asked before he dropped his coat on the nearest chair.

"Of course, I do. I love to look at the constellations, or even the moon. It is all beautiful, even if I don't know the names of what I am seeing."

He stepped back and looked at me strangely. "What?" I asked.

"I just cannot believe that you are still single. You are so full of surprises."

"You keep rubbing it in, and I will really hurt you next time I get you on my massage table."

"Ha! That is just an idle threat. You wouldn't hurt a fly."

We both laughed. I stepped back. Using good body mechanics, I pulled the telescope forward on the rails that brought it out from under the protective cabinet. I took off the caps at each end, and then swung it around to get a good look at the moon. It was only missing a sliver of its bright surface, and there was enough light to see incredible amounts of detail. I stepped back, and let Jerome have a look.

"Wow. Just wow. I have never seen such a beautiful moon." He mused. "Have you?"

"I have seen one more beautiful than that, Jerome, just this afternoon, in my hotel room."

He stepped back and looked at me in the dark. "Are you just saying that to tease me?"

"No sir, I was quite impressed. It was a joy to work on something of such high quality. Quite a privilege, in fact. Maybe I will get to do it again, sometime."

"Thank you. It is good to hear someone say that, for a change, even if you are a guy," he chuckled.

I walked over to where the deck chairs were lined up for sunbathing. I lowered myself down to the first one in the row, and pulled a pint bottle out of my coat pocket. I held it up and shook it a little to get his attention. He shuffled over and took the chair next to me. His feet splayed out to the sides as he lay back and sighed deeply.

"So, what is bothering you, Jerome? Do you just need to vent for a bit?"

It was so quiet we could hear his watch ticking for a few moments. Finally, he sat up, and reached for the bottle. He uncapped it, took a long swig, and offered it to me. I took the bottle and had my own, smaller sip. I placed it on the deck between us.

"I just don't know where to start, so please forgive me if I ramble."

I remained silent, enjoying the stars above me and the warmth of the whisky in my stomach.

"I grew up in a tight-knit family. We moved around quite a bit for my father's job. We never made many friends because we didn't stay long enough to establish connections. I was close to my brother and sister, but I had a falling out with each of them. Now I feel like I am an orphan, with siblings that do not want to talk to me. When my wife left me, I was nearly suicidal. We had no children - I had no one to talk to. I did not want to go on living, especially if it meant that I would be alone for the rest of my life."

He took another sip of whisky and held onto the bottle. "I drank heavily for about a year until I could get it under control. I tried exercise, self-help groups, meditation, yoga, alternate spirituality, and even explored world religions. Nothing seemed to give me the connection that I wanted so badly. I wanted other people in my life to share experiences with."

He set the bottle down on the deck between us. I stared at the skies and listened with all my concentration.

"When the divorce was finalized last summer, I actually felt liberated. I made a bunch of resolutions about changing my life for the better. I stuck with many of them for a time, but I felt myself slipping again, and I didn't want to go on."

He went noticeably quiet, and I wondered if he had fallen asleep. I let the stars keep us company, and I had another sip from the bottle.

"When I booked this trip, I actually thought that I could go through with it. I planned everything out, and even left notes for the people who would have to clean up the mess I left behind at home."

I got a chill that scared me out of my daze.

"Wait, Jerome, what are you saying?"

"Larry, I was going to kill myself this week, after the conference. I wanted one last chance to find some friends, but I was so embedded in my own self-doubt that I knew it was a lost cause." He sobbed and put his hands over his face.

"Jerome, you cannot be serious. You have so much to offer, why would you want to do that?"

"I don't know, now. But I can tell you one thing I did not count on."

"What is that?" I asked cautiously.

"You," he said in a half-sob.

"Me?" I asked.

"Yes. I gave you every chance to push me away, I interrupted your swim, drunk. I insisted on sharing a hot tub with you, when I could tell by the look on your face that you wanted to be alone. I pushed my way into your planned hike, even as I was regretting the rules you had laid out. I questioned every reasonable request you made of me. I cannot believe that you did not desert me, the way I acted."

"Jerome, I am so sad for you, and at the thought of losing you. Please promise me you have put those plans out of your mind."

"Larry, I am sure I have lost my will to go through with it for now. But I don't know what I am going to do when I go back home and try to find a purpose for myself."

I stood up and took his hand in mine as I towered over him. He was sobbing unashamedly in the lounge chair. I pulled on his right hand to get him to stand, and then I embraced him and let him cry on my shoulder. I cried along with him because I knew exactly what he meant about the loneliness.

After our tears tapered off, I had Jerome sit down while I put the telescope away. I dropped the empty pint bottle in the trash, and then went back to where he was sitting. I sat down on the chair next to him and took his hands in mine.

"What do we do now?" he asked.

"Jerome, I know this sounds trite, but now that we have found each other, I am convinced that we will be friends until one of us leaves this planet, at a very advanced age."

He smiled weakly.

"In the meantime, we need to decide what to do about the conference. Do you think you can sit through three days of compliance-legalese?"

He shook his head. "I don't think so. What are our other options?"

"I have plenty of vacation time. We can check out, go somewhere else, and pay the company back for our expenses."

"You would do that for me?" he asked.

"No, I would do that for us. I think we both need to find some excitement in our lives, and this might be the cosmic signal we needed to set us on our path to find it."

I stood up and motioned for him to do the same. I put my arm around his shoulders and led him to the stairs. We went to his room, and we flushed the sleeping pills that he had packed down the toilet.

I pulled him into a bear hug and spoke softly as he cried in my arms. "Jerome, I love you. You are my friend until you can no longer stand to be around me, and I want you to know that you have done more for me already than I ever could have asked from a life-long friend. Do you understand?"

He nodded but did not speak. I was the first to break the embrace, but he was more forlorn than desperate for human contact. As I backed away, I assessed his mental state, but understood that we were now over a rough patch. He unzipped his pants and stepped out of his trousers. His shirt came off with a grunt, and then his boxers hit the tops of his feet. He was finished for the day.

After he undressed, I wondered if he was even completely aware that I was with him in the room, or just so far beyond hope that my presence did not affect him at all. I put him to bed and left him to return to my own room.

We Change Directions

The next morning, as the business folks around us rushed to get their breakfast before the conference, we took our time and lingered over our coffee until the dining room was empty.

Our surly waitress came back over and asked, "Don't you need to join the conference group? I hear they are starting up in the ballroom in the annex!"

"No, we have decided not to go," Jerome replied lazily. "Please put our breakfast on my tab and get me one more cup of coffee. Thanks, hon."

She marched away in a huff. I smiled at him and waited for him to make eye contact.

"You are a changed man today. If I didn't know better, I would suspect that you had gotten laid last night."

"Right hand was the charm, first thing this morning," he responded with a wide smile that lit up his face and made my heart flutter.

We got a shuttle to the airport with no solid plans. Given that we only had a week, I did not want to go too far off the map, but I did want to do something impulsive and different. We had a choice of three destinations with flights that were not completely full yet.

"Well, Jerome, what is it going to be?"

"Larry, I sometimes have trouble deciding which movie to pay for at the cineplex. How am I supposed to choose a city for an impulsive adventure?"

"Jerome, this is easy. Neither of us wants to go to Charlotte. That is just too close to where we work, right?"

"Yes," he replied.

"So that leaves two choices: Boston, where we can connect to a dozen other cities, or Chicago."

"Which one do you want, Larry?"

"You want me to choose?"

"Larry, you are my best friend. I trust your instinct."

"You say that because I am your only friend, and you are a coward."

He laughed.

"Okay, I have chosen. We have twenty minutes to get to the gate."

We bought the tickets and got our boarding passes. I had to rush him through the security line, just to make it to the gate.

While we waited in line to board our first plane, I did a quick search on my phone for available hotel rooms. When I found nothing suitable available, I pulled out my ace card. After I sent a couple of texts, a room in one of the most exclusive hotels in the world was booked in my name.

Four hours later we touched down at Louis Armstrong Airport. The plane taxied into the gate, and we got off with the rush of people, anxious to start their own adventures in New Orleans.

"Do we need to rent a car?"

"No way," I said. "If we get our own vehicle, we are more likely to isolate ourselves, and not mix with the people we came to meet."

"Oh, okay he said glumly.

I led him out to the taxi stand and we got in line. We got into our cab, and I told the driver where we wanted to go in the French Quarter. He did a double take over his shoulder at the two of us in the back, and then sped off into crazy traffic.

The door for the hotel was in the alley behind one of the small side streets in the periphery of the French Quarter. The Cat's Paw was a famous boutique hotel in the area, usually patronized by women, with women. I led the way in, watching a curious look on Jerome's face. We got some scandalous looks on the walk to the front desk, at least until I spoke up.

"I am looking for Sarah Brooks. I am her brother, Larry."

"Ms. Brooks is out running errands, but she told me to expect you. We have a room for you - is it just the one room?" She peered around behind me to inspect Jerome. Her business demeanor changed to a devious smile when she saw him, fidgeting behind me.

"Yes, we will share the room. Thank you."

When we got up to the suite, it was as luxurious and plush as I had ever seen in a Hollywood movie. The bed was enormous, but we would have to share it, after all. There was a small dining area, a lounge with two chairs and a settee, and a small kitchen with a microwave and a coffee maker. The bathroom was as big as the last room I had checked out of, and even Jerome was impressed.

Jerome shuffled over to the bed and collapsed, face down. "I did not think we were ever going to make it here. I am exhausted, in every way possible." His voice was muffled by the blanket under his cheek.

"Why don't you take a quick nap? We gained an hour on the flight from Boston. It is only one o'clock."

He did not argue. He pushed himself up. Once he was standing, he slipped off his shoes, stepped out of his pants, pulled his button-down shirt off over his head, and then dropped his boxers where he stood. He crawled into bed and pulled the top sheet over his lower half. Only his sock feet stuck out of the covers, which was a familiar sight to me after only two days with him. I read quietly while I waited for the text that would summon me down to the front desk.

My phone buzzed. Sarah was back in the lobby by two o'clock. Jerome was still snoring, and he had kicked the sheet off. His naked body was sprawled on top of the covers. It was all I could do not to stare at the hunk of the man I had sleeping in my bed, even if he were not mine to keep. I did not even want to sully the memory by filling my smart phone with pictures of his beautiful figure, but I did consider it, if only briefly. I let myself quietly out of the room and took the stairs down the three flights to the lobby.

Sarah was waiting in her office. As the manager, and part owner, she had a lot of influence. I admired her entrepreneurial spirit but could not imagine working for such a demanding perfectionist. She rushed to embrace me, and then began her interrogation of my impromptu visit to her adopted home.

"What are you doing in town? I thought you were up in New Hampshire, at that compliance conference in the woods!"

"We checked in on Saturday, spent the day together on Sunday, and then decided Monday morning that neither of us wanted to be there, or listen to what the speakers had to yab about."

"So, who is the new boyfriend? Did you just pick him up at the hotel on a whim? That is not like you at all."

"Jerome is a colleague from my office. He is affirmed as a heterosexual, and he is only along for the most fun week that I can guide us through."

"You really do play it safe, brother. I was hoping you were having a torrid affair, and the office was unaware."

"No, I just want to show the man that there is more to life than work, conferences, and routines. I figured Nawlins was the very place to do that."

"Will I get to see you while you are in town?"

"Absolutely. Just tell me when and where you can fit me in. We have no set plans. I think we will fly back to North Carolina on Friday, so that we can have the weekend at home to recuperate. Are we clear to keep the room until checkout time Friday morning?"

"Sure, but you are paying the going rate, at the family discount, of course."

I went back up to the suite where Jerome was just starting to stir. He stretched, and then sat up, hanging his legs over the side of the bed. When he stood, he made no pretense of covering himself up. He just walked into the bathroom in his socks. Washed up and refreshed, he stood, naked, apparently waiting on instructions from me.

"Perhaps we could get dressed and go out for a walk? It is not too hot, so shorts and walking shoes should be fine."

"Okay," he said sullenly.

"Jerome, is there something wrong? You only have to tell me what you want to do, and I will probably agree."

"Oh, I'm sorry. I was just a bit groggy from my nap. I will be ready to go in a jiffy."

He suited up and was prepared to hike the streets of the French Quarter in ten minutes. We went out the door like adventurers - with touristy t-shirts, brightly colored baseball hats, and sunglasses. I was relieved that we had enough sense not to dress like a couple, in matching outfits.

As we window shopped and watched people, our conversation lagged. Given my own state of fatigue, I knew exactly what we needed to get us going again. I led the way as if I were a local.

There was one table left - right on the corner where we could each ogle our respective lusts as they passed by - and we snagged it. Cafe du Monde, famous for French Donuts and strong coffee, is one of the places I love to show new people. We gorged ourselves on Beignets, nearly covering ourselves in powdered sugar. Once the caffeine kicked in, we were raring to go.

I paid the bill and got us out of there. To draw him out of his shell, we walked along the river front until we found a bench to sit on. I settled in and exhaled noisily.

"Well, Jerome, what do you think of New Orleans so far?"

"This is one crazy town. Did you see the people with...?"

"Yes," I cut him off. "There are not many rules in this town."

"What are your plans for us?"

"I have no plans, per se, Jerome. My goal is to show you the time of your life. It might be just the two of us, touring around and eating ourselves sick. We could get snockered and stagger around like the other tourists. Maybe we will meet some people that we want to spend more time with, and that would be great, too."

"Larry, I don't want to upset you, or spoil the mood, but I have to ask - why are you doing all of this for me?"

I hesitated, and he tried to backpedal.

"It is not that I don't appreciate it; I just feel a little weird about taking all of this...attention from you. What are you getting out of it?"

"I need this too, Jerome. And...I really like you. I think you have a lot of great qualities."

"I just get the impression that you are...patronizing me, because you feel sorry for me."

"Nothing could be further from the truth. I think we are far more alike than you realize."

He smiled and nodded. He did not look convinced.

"Much as you have already stated, I don't have many friends at all. I have really enjoyed getting to know you and helping you these last two days - especially since I know it is not a pretense to romance. I can let my guard down, and be my honest self with you, without trying to impress you for the big conquest later."

"That is comforting, because I have really come to admire you over these last two days," he said.

"Thank you! Now what do you fancy tonight, a snazzy Jazz club, a topless bar, far too many drinks and dancing with strangers, or a quiet meal on the roof of our hotel?"

"Honestly?"

"I would prefer it. There is no reason to try to manage my feelings or not say what you think – we are friends."

"Thank you. I was just..." He trailed off, leaving the sentence hanging.

"Yes, Jerome? Tell me what you want, and I will make it happen."

"Then, I choose you. A quiet dinner anywhere would be fine."

"Okay," I responded.

"I still feel...a bit...fragile. Is that okay?"

"Of course, it is. I will make the arrangements. Anything else?"

"Could I get another massage?"

"Do you want me to find you a buxom blonde from Scandinavia to rough you up?"

"No," he laughed. "I trust you to do it right." He blushed. "Is that okay?"

"More than okay, it would be my pleasure," I beamed.

He smiled and patted my hand. "You really are a friend."

I sent the front desk of the Cat's Paw a few texts for our requests. I roused Jerome off the bench and gave him a choice of a walk back, or a rickshaw ride at high speed. He chose the rickshaw, which surprised me.

The driver did not even struggle with the weight of two grown men, nor did she question where we wanted to go. Within minutes, she had us standing in front of the hotel door, with her hand out for cash. I tipped her well and got her card for any future rides we might need.

The elevator deposited us on the top floor, and Jerome just shuffled along. I wondered if I had already worn him out with our flights, sightseeing, and the sugar rush that afternoon. The massage table was set up in the room. The menu of services available was placed prominently with a phone number to call for their in-house masseuse.

He went to the bathroom for about twenty minutes, and then emerged wearing nothing but a towel, which was draped over his shoulder. The towel fell off as he crossed the room, and he did not even notice. He climbed up on the table, lay down on his stomach, and sighed like a tire losing all its air.

My street clothes were soaked from the humidity, and too snug for me to have the range of motion I needed for a massage. I changed to some dry, loose-fitting gym clothes. I got my massage oils and approached him from the side, so he could see me. I put my hand on his right shoulder to get his attention.

"Are you comfortable? Do you need a towel or sheet to stop the chill?"

"No. I really never get cold, especially indoors."

"Are you ready to start?"

"Yes."

I oiled my hands and spread a little between his shoulder blades. Once I had smoothed it all out, flattening the hairs down, I started with my usual routine. I worked his neck, shoulders, lower back, and then legs, from his feet up to his thighs. I worked his buttocks over, kneading them like bread dough and producing some delightful groans from the man on the table. I finished and asked if he needed a break. When he did not respond, I thought he had fallen asleep. When I looked into his face, I could see that he was weeping.

"Jerome, what is wrong? Have I hurt you? Was I too rough?"

"No, I just feel a bit down. I don't know what I have done to deserve you, and all of this wonderful attention."

"Now you are just brooding. I am sure, given different circumstances, you would help me if I needed it."

Jerome was silent.

"Jerome, am I wrong?"

"No, Larry, I just cannot imagine what I would be able to do for you..."

"I am sure we will get to a point in our friendship where you will be the dry shoulder for me to cry on, okay?"

"Okay he sniffled.

"Now, are you relaxed enough, or do you want to turn over and let me continue?"

At first there was no response, and then he leveraged himself up spryly and turned over with a thud against the sturdy table.

Starting at his feet, I worked on his ankles, calves, and knees. I really kneaded his thighs deeply, as they have more bulk of muscle than anywhere else. I was duly surprised that he maintained a flaccid penis throughout, as I was sporting a boner since I had started working on him that afternoon.

I gently worked his hips and flanks over, remembering that he was quite ticklish. His pecs were in great shape. With the feather hairs sleeked down in the oil, I thought I was working on a Greek sculpture by one of the great, ancient masters. Finally, I massaged his shoulders, neck, and scalp. He lay there, passively, and groaned occasionally.

I moved to the side of the table to talk to him again, and the prominence in my shorts brushed his hand.

"Wow!" He said.

"I'm sorry, I cannot help it."

"No, really, I am impressed. Do you always have that reaction when you do massage?"

I was silent.

He lifted his head and opened his eyes. "Larry?"

I picked up a towel and wiped the oil from my hands, then I slumped into the armchair.

"Jerome, I have a confession to make."

"Uh-hunh, what would that be?"

I cleared my throat. "Remember on our hike when you asked if I did not like you? When you felt I was avoiding you at work?"

"Yes, why?"

"I had been avoiding you. You are that man that I have been obsessed with for the last two years. I have focused all my energy, and efforts on you. I even stalked you for a time, on social media."

He sat up on the table and stared at me, incredulous at my disclosure.

"Maybe it is a defensive tactic I have, to keep me safe from real relationships. I have done this before, electronically stalking a man that I was infatuated with at my last job. He had a wife and children, and no interest in even being friends."

He stared at me, mouth hanging open.

"To me, you are simply the most gorgeous man I have ever encountered. If we weren't such good friends now, I would kidnap you and hold you hostage in my basement, just so I could look at you."

He laughed.

"Does this bother you? I mean, maybe, creep you out a bit?"

"Well, a little," he laughed again, self-consciously. "If you had told me this after work one night, having drinks, I would have avoided you like the plague, perhaps even filed a restraining order." He saw my face fall. "I am only kidding about the restraining order."

"But now?"

"Now, I can honestly say that it is thrilling to have someone, anyone, feel that way about me. It really does change my world perspective, especially since I can say, without reservation, that I genuinely love you."

"Really, Jerome?"

"Of course, I do! Just not as a boyfriend, though. I am sorry, but I have to see some breasts to get my blood pumping."

We both laughed.

"So, now what do we do?" I asked. "Do I need to back off and stop staring at your beautiful, Greek god body?"

"No, I kind of like being idolized. I will let you know if I want you to stop it – but it will be sometime in the distant future."

"Good, because I am not sure I could stop looking. I won't touch you without your permission, I promise. Now, what would you like to do this evening?"

"Anything...well, almost anything you want," he chuckled.

"Are you hungry? This is a great town for food."

"You promised me dinner on the roof. I know it sounds sedate, but I need one more day of downtime before I try to put myself out there for some wild fun. Is that okay?"

"It sure is. I will arrange for dinner. Are you going to shower up?"

"Yes, I should get this oil off my skin. But don't lose that table, I may need some more man-handling by my best friend."

I beamed with pride. "I may have to let them take it, but we can certainly get it back. I have connections here."

Jerome showered and dressed in his khakis for dinner. I changed into my business casual clothes that I planned to wear at the conference. Because access was restricted, the porter came and took us up to the rooftop garden. There were already two other couples there, but neither of the pairs of women had any interest in seeing us, so we were put off into the corner. There was a slight breeze, and the humidity that so defined the region was softened by the moving air.

We started our evening out with cocktails, which is probably mandated by law in New Orleans culture. As we sipped our drinks, Jerome was smiling so much that I became suspicious.

"Have you finally eaten the canary, Mr. Tomcat?" I asked.

"No, I have just had an extraordinary few days, the likes of which I could not have imagined a week ago."

"I, too, have been pleasantly surprised about the recent turn of events."

"But there is more to it, and I think you can help me."

"Most certainly! I will do anything for my friends. That is easy to say, because I only have the one."

"Ha, ha. I really doubt that I am the only person you would call a friend. But I am serious, I need your help." His smile faded.

"Okay, tell me what I need to do. Is it dangerous?"

"No," he laughed. "Well, maybe."

"Now you have piqued my interest. Please go on."

The waitress, a stunningly beautiful woman with dark eyes and a fluidity of motion that reminded me of a ballerina, interrupted our chat with the first course. She placed two small plates, one before each of us on the table. She walked away just as quickly.

"Wait, what is this?" Jerome asked.

"I don't know, actually. I told them we wanted the four-course meal - chef's choice. It looks like a pâté."

"It looks strange, should I be worried?"

"Jerome, other than Paris, there is no other place in the world that knows food as the people here do. While Paris is consistently good, I think New Orleans food gets better each time I visit."

Using his salad fork, Jerome cut a small piece of the dark square on his plate and brought it up to his nose. He sniffed it, and then made a face.

"Watch what I do, please." With my knife, I cut a corner of the pâté off the small block on my plate and smeared it on a toast point. Adding a tiny leaf of basil, I popped it into my mouth. He watched my face for a bad reaction, but of course there was none.

"Okay, I'll try it, but I don't expect to like it," he said quietly.

He repeated my actions and chewed for a long time. He said nothing, but then quickly reached for another toast point.

When he finally made eye contact, it was a guilty smile that spread on his face. I grinned back, and we continued to eat the savory mushroom compote that tasted like heaven to me.

The waitress brought out our wine. "I am sorry, sirs, but we had trouble locating this bottle. May I open it for you?"

"Of course, please," I replied.

She expertly leveraged the cork out of the very dusty bottle and then poured a small amount in my glass. I swirled it around, sniffed it and closed my eyes.

"I can feel myself transported back to Provence, with the breeze blowing softly over the fields of lavender and -"

"Just drink it already!" he croaked.

The waitress smiled, and I swallowed the small amount in the glass. "Is that acceptable?" she asked.

I nodded, unable to find the words at first.

"Do you like wine? Are you allowed to try it while you work?" I asked.

She tilted her head down, looking over her vintage granny glasses. "This is New Orleans, not Kansas."

"Touché!" I said. "If you will get a glass, I would like you to try this wine - it is beyond incredible."

She retrieved a glass, poured a full glass for Jerome, and another for me. She watched me while she poured her own, apparently waiting for me to stop her. I did not, so she filled her glass as well.

We clinked our glasses together lightly, and then all drank our first mouthful together. The reviews were unanimous.

"Wow!" she said. "I have never had any wine like it in my life!"

"Me, neither," Jerome said.

"Is this your last bottle of it?" I asked, cautiously.

She nodded.

"Then we must savor this one, as if there were no tomorrow."

She left and took her glass with her. The liquid never moved in the glass despite her brisk walking speed.

We ate a few more bites of the pâté, but then I put my knife down. When he made eye contact, I spoke.

"Can you tell me what this problem is that I can help you with? Or will you have to kill me if I learn the sordid details of this secret?"

He laughed heartily. "Larry, this is intensely personal, and a bit delicate, but I am absolutely convinced that you are the only person that can help me solve this."

"I am all ears, tell me ALL the sleazy details, while I nosh on this wonderful food, and get tipsy on hundred-year-old wine."

"Larry, this is hard for me. I appreciate your willingness, but I may need more of this wine before I relay anymore."

"Sure, take all the time you need. I am here. You could even get undressed, if that would make you more comfortable, although I don't think the ladies dining nearby would find it as appealing as I do."

He blushed deeply. "Have I made you uncomfortable with that? I am sorry."

"No, no, NO! Of course not. I cannot stress that enough. I have longed for two years to see you undressed, and to have that, in my hotel room, with you relaxed and nonchalant, has been one of the absolute highlights of my year! Please don't ever stop - even if I start to drool."

He laughed again. "Usually, I am not so comfortable with other people, but there is just something about you that puts me at ease."

"Well, how about this? We finish our meal, have a bit more wine, and then go back to the room to talk. If you are ready."

"That sounds great. We really must pace ourselves, though. If all the food is this good, we could be miserable by the end of the meal."

"I assure you, it will be this good, and perhaps better."

The courses continued, with a crescendo of dessert that left us both in a stupor of epicurean happiness. We finished with coffee and brandies as the temperature started to fall. I settled the bill and left our waitress a generous tip.

Back down in the room, we were both stuffed and too miserable to sleep. I brushed my teeth and changed to my gym clothes with a loose elastic waistband. I sat down in the lounge chair, stretching my legs out onto the ottoman and groaned audibly.

Jerome was cagey. He paced at first, then brushed his teeth, but paced slowly around the room after, as if he were working up the courage to say something difficult. I let him have his space, and the freedom to decide how to proceed. Closing my eyes, I laid my head back on the chair.

"Hey, the massage table is gone!" He exclaimed.

"There are other guests that the hotel must serve. Do we need it tonight?"

"No, I guess not," he replied.

I opened my eyes. He was standing in the center of the room, hands on his hips. One thumb was hooked behind his belt. He had perspiration on his forehead.

"Jerome, have I put you on the spot? Do you need some space? I could go for a walk if you need to be alone."

"No, I am just trying to get up the courage to tell you some things...stuff that I am not very proud of, actually."

"I understand. Take your time. It could even wait. No reason to hurry."

He was quiet for a while. I did not hear him move around, but I might have dozed off for a bit. When he finally spoke, it sounded like a completely different person.

"Larry, could you sit down with me? I need to see your eyes when I tell you this."

I got up, cautiously. He had taken his pants and shirt off but had kept his socks and boxers on. He was sitting at the dinette table, with his hands clasped before him on the table.

I sat down and said nothing. I made tentative eye contact, in the most non-confrontational show of acceptance I could muster.

He sighed.

"A few years ago, I had a falling out with my brother. We had loud, angry, vicious words, and I said many things that I was ashamed of - even then - as they came out of my mouth. We have not spoken since that night."

I blinked but maintained my silence. I moved my hands to the table to rest my arms.

"When my sister found out, she sided with him, as I would have expected. She will not speak to me, either."

He took my hands in his, clasping his strong, muscular hands around my clamped palms. When he looked up, there were tears in his eyes that bespoke a deep pain. I felt myself tearing up, just seeing him like that.

"I said terrible, terrible things to my only brother," his voice hitched, "and I cannot get him to even listen to me now to apologize." He cried freely, holding my hands while the tears flowed down his face.

I cried for him as much as with him. "Jerome, what do you need me to do?"

"I would like you to talk to him if you can get through. He has blocked me on all of his social media accounts."

"And what would you like me to say? I am acting as a...lawyer...to set up mediation?" I said, trying to lighten the mood.

"I want the chance to apologize to him and make it up to him any way that I can."

"Sure. We can look at some options together."

"I have not told you the worst part."

"And what would that be, Jerome?"

"While I will not repeat what evil things that I shouted at him, I have to tell you that I initially pushed him away because he came out as gay."

"But...you seem to be so...at ease with me..."

"I have nothing to say in my defense. He caught me on a low point in my marriage, and my life. While you and I were wandering in the woods, I may have been surprised, but I was not feeling mean enough to push you away. We are also not related. It hurt me more that I did not know about him by that point. And my views have softened on the issue, over time. I certainly will do anything in my power to get my brother back."

"Golly, this might be a tough one."

"Larry, as my friend, I am confident that you can make this happen. While it may take some time, I will pay any expenses you incur and make it up to you in any way that you would request."

"Jerome, it hurts me to my core to see you in such pain. I will do everything I can to make this right for you."

"Thank you, Larry. You don't know how much that helps, just hearing that you are willing to try."

"Could I ask one favor, though?"

He looked up, a bit wary, and then spoke, "Yes, of course. Anything."

"Could I have a hug? I feel so bad for you, that I just want to hold you until you stop crying."

He burst into another flood of tears but nodded and stood up. I stood too, took two steps toward him, and then engulfed him in my arms. We cried together for several minutes, for the second time in two days.

A New Day

I gently pulled myself out of sleep. While I recall staying up rather late to talk, I hardly remembered getting into bed the few hours before. I was hungover from the late-night meal and uncharacteristically not hungry for breakfast. I did not recognize where I was at first. The filtered light streaming through the curtains told me that it was well past sunrise.

The massive figure of flesh next to me reminded me of the last two days. I smiled when I saw the fine black hairs that covered my friend, sleeping on top of the covers in the full glory of his birthday suit. The sight of him excited me beyond all reason. It almost felt like the honeymoon I had never gotten, with a friend I cherished so deeply that it no longer mattered that we would not get to express our love physically. I turned on my side and watched him sleep, stifling fantasies as they formulated in my head.

I must have nodded off again, because I woke up with him staring at me across the bed, with a wistful smile on his face. He had showered and shaved, but had not dressed, and I was more than pleased to see him that way again.

"Good morning, sleepyhead," he said. His smile was genuine.

"Good morning, friend. What do we have on our agenda for today?"

"You had promised me a wild good time. But I fear the day is slipping away from us."

"What time is it?"

"Just after twelve."

"What?" I sat up in bed and looked around. He had straightened up the room and had hot coffee in the pot, ready to drink.

He got up, and I admired his skin in motion as he moved across the floor and poured me a cup of joe. He unabashedly brought it back over to me, watching my face for any reaction to his domestic task, and his chosen uniform for service. I smiled brighter than the sun coming through the windows.

"Shall we get dressed and get out of here?"

"For the record, if I ran the world, there would be a law that you would never wear clothes again. But if we must leave the room, I suppose I could allow you to wear something suitable for the climate."

He smiled brightly. I could not imagine him reacting badly to anyone being gay, but we all have our moments of shame.

After a quick coffee and pastry on the street, we took some time to explore the local amusements. Neither of us wanted to gamble. He was too distracted to enjoy any female performers, as he called them, and neither one of us wanted any more to eat for the time being. We spent more time strolling and talking than actually pursuing anything useful or entertaining.

I tried to remember the last time I had felt so comfortable in someone's company, and I came up short. I felt closer to him than I felt with my family members. That was when my phone buzzed.

In a short exchange of texts, I set up dinner plans with my sister for the following evening. I was relieved that we would not be returning to the rooftop of the hotel, as I had eaten way too much food in that setting. It would not be my last time doing so, and it was not the restaurant's fault.

I broke the news to Jerome. I briefly considered taking him along, but Sarah had made reservations for two, not three. He said he could entertain himself for the evening.

Back at Cafe du Monde, we plotted our surveillance of his brother, brainstorming for the right moment and method for me to contact him. I longed for my legal pad to scribble on, but I had to make do with napkins and a cheap pen from the hotel. I covered myself in powdered sugar, laughing in the absurdity of the working conditions. We had reached a stage where we were wonderfully comfortable with each other.

"Okay, so let me start building a dossier on this brother of yours. I will need his full name, last known address, and any nicknames he might use on social media."

"Sure, I have all that in my phone. I will send you a screen shot."

"Do you have a recent picture, or will his accounts have one that we can pull down? I am thinking I want to do some research, but ultimately, my best chances are to meet him in person if I am going to convince him to listen to you."

Jerome went silent and stared off across the street. His sudden mood shift left me uneasy. When he did not answer the next few questions, I sensed something was wrong.

"Hey, are you having doubts that I can pull this off? I don't know that it will be quick, but I will do my level best to make this reunion happen, okay?"

He did not respond.

"Jerome, what is wrong?"

"I am having second thoughts about this. I'm sorry. It was impulsive of me to even bring it up. And it is really not fair of me to ask you to do this. You have already done so much for me. I feel like I am intruding on your life, and your vacation."

He got up and walked away. Fueled with caffeine, carbs, and sugar, I settled the bill by dropping a twenty on the table, and then ran to catch up with him.

"Jerome? What happened? Did I do something wrong?"

"No, but let's just forget about finding Sherman, okay? It suddenly seems like an unbelievably bad idea."

He continued walking. I was really torn. I wanted to help, but I knew there was something he was not telling me. I caught up to him and matched his stride in silence.

We made the entire circuit of the tourist highlights in the immediate area, and I could see that he was searching for our hotel street.

"Are you getting weary? Do we need to go back to the room?"

"It's okay, just point me in the right direction, and I will find it. I think I have the key with me."

I was stymied. But I did not give up.

"Can I plan something for dinner? Maybe a little lighter fare, and certainly a bit earlier in the evening?"

"Why don't you go and have some fun? I am just going to go back to the room and rest."

"Okay, the hotel is four blocks that way. Don't miss the turn at the alley, and you will be at the front door. I will be up soon."

We parted ways and I did not even watch him walk down the street, which I always thoroughly enjoyed. I kept turning the conversation over in my head, wondering what had triggered the moody responses that had plagued our afternoon. I asked about names, nicknames, addresses – most of that would have a public presence, anyway. Then I asked about his brother's...picture.

I stumbled off the curb and almost went flailing in the gutter. "He doesn't want me to see what his brother looks like!" I said to no one. I stopped and scanned my phone for messages, clues, anything. When there was nothing else for me to do on my own, I went back to the hotel.

Jerome was leaving with his bag as I got to the lobby. I was crushed. I just stopped and waited for him to see me.

When he finally looked up, I thought he was going to collapse. He looked so frightened and shaken that I was worried for his health.

"Jerome?" I said softly.

He looked up, startled that anyone knew his name in the lobby. I could tell that he had been crying.

"Please talk to me," I pleaded.

He sighed and leaned against the wall. "I really should go; this is not going to work. I am sorry."

We were suddenly the feuding couple in the lobby for everyone to observe. I just wanted to get back to the room so we could sort out the issue.

"Please, Jerome, even if you feel you need to leave, could you give me five minutes to explain what changed? I am worried about you."

"I just don't think that would be a good idea. I need to go."
He started walking toward the door.

"You really are my only friend, you know," I stated, on the
verge of tears myself.

He made it to the door but stopped. His shoulders heaved,
and he lost his composure. I slowly walked over to him and then put
my hand on his shoulder.

"Please talk to me. I am lost in confusion without you."

He turned to face me, his face a mask of anguish. I waited
for him to signal what he wanted to do.

He walked past me, pulling his rolling bag back over to the
elevator. He pushed the button and just stood there. I followed
before he changed his mind.

His tears had stopped but the elevator ride was painfully
quiet. He stood over to the side, leaning on the wall as if his strength
were gone.

The doors opened, and we walked over to the room. I keyed
the electronic door lock and swung the door wide. He followed me
in, and then collapsed in the chair closest to the door.

"Larry, I am sorry, but I cannot talk about this right now. Let
me compose myself and figure out what I am going to do." He never
lifted his head to meet my eyes.

"Sure, relax. Can I get you anything? A water?"

"Nothing, thank you." He said, rather curtly.

I sat down at the dinette table and put my head on my arms.
I had learned in law school that a witness will often go silent when
they get to details that they just cannot imagine sharing. They lose

their resolve to cooperate, and will often take whatever consequences are dealt, even if it means jail time for contempt.

That was where Jerome was. He had been accommodating, upbeat, and excited about the process until I asked about a picture. As a legal clerk, I had seen many terrible things, but I could not conceive of why he would want to hide this from me, now. I just had to wait for him to change his mind, if he ever did.

I woke up with Jerome's hand on mine. Despite the copious amounts of coffee, my body had given up and slept while I waited him out. I was still not sure if it would pay off, but at least he was still there.

"Larry, I owe you an explanation. I am not sure I want you to go forward with the search, but I do not want to treat you badly after all you have done for me."

He was fully dressed and sweating profusely. My clothes were damp from the humidity and our walk through the heat. With the air conditioning on full blast, I was nearly shivering with the cold.

I sat up straight, leaving his hand on mine. I shook my head to wake myself up, and then made eye contact. He had washed his face, and his mustache was still a little wet. The pain in his face was more than I could stand.

"Thank you for staying to talk to me. Would you mind if I got some water? I must have gotten dehydrated while I was out in the city."

"I will get it." He got up, walked over to the refrigerator, and got two waters. When he brought them back to the table, he stumbled. I jumped up, and was able to catch the waters, but not him. He went down on the carpet and grunted in pain.

I quickly put the waters down on the table and went over to him. He had pushed himself up to a sitting position. I simply sat down on the rug with him.

"I am sorry. I am just so muddled over this predicament. Please forgive me for waffling and dragging you into my personal life."

"Jerome, I really do want to help you. I will do whatever you ask me to do, as long as we are still friends afterward. Nothing is more important to me than that, right now."

He started crying again. I reached out and touched his hand, which he quickly pulled away. I was at a loss for what I could do.

He leaned over on his hands and pushed himself up. I did the same but kept my distance. When he moved over to the large sofa, I grabbed the two waters and followed him. He gave me no indication where he wanted me to be, so I sat next to him on the couch, with a full cushion's width between us. I set the waters down, one in front of each of us.

"Larry, I know I am being a jerk. And I don't want you to...stop being my friend, but I am really torn on what I should do here, and I cannot think of the words to tell you what is going on."

"Jerome, I am here. Take your time and tell me whatever you can."

He breathed deeply a few times and steadied himself. Both of his hands moved to his knees, but I don't think he was trying to stand up. Finally, he grabbed the water bottle and struggled to open it. I glanced up to see him sweating profusely despite the cool temperatures.

We sat in silence for another ten minutes. He fidgeted for a while, then leaned forward and took off his shirt. "I am burning up!"

He dropped the wet polo shirt on the floor next to him. He had saturated his t-shirt with perspiration.

I said nothing.

He pried his shoes off with his feet, leaving them lying on the floor next to his feet. Still, he said nothing. I waited. He lifted his t-shirt over his head and dropped it on the floor on top of his other shirt. The hair on his chest was speckled with moisture. It glistened in the soft light of the afternoon. My heart quickened just looking at him, enjoying the close-up view of a fine male specimen.

When he stood up, I thought I had lost him, but he just unbuckled his belt and pushed his pants down to his ankles. His boxers were askew, but he sat down again without bothering to fix them. He pulled each leg out of the pants, and then propped his stocking feet up on the table. He sighed deeply.

"Larry?" He asked.

"Yes, Jerome?" I responded, just turning my head slightly to see if I needed to be aware of any gestures.

"I am terrified of losing you. I know it sounds crazy, but I have never felt so good about another person. I was not even this relaxed with my wife."

"Jerome, I will be a part of your life for as long as you want me in it. I am sorry if I ever gave you the…"

He cut me off. "What I have been trying to tell you, unsuccessfully, is that I'm scared I will lose you when you find Sherman."

I said nothing. I realized that he had finally given his brother a name, but I was beyond confused about the situation.

"I can tell you, that the last two days have felt like I was high on drugs." He said, matter-of-factly.

I turned in my seat to look at him, bringing my left knee up onto the empty cushion so that I did not have to be twisted at the waist.

"I have never felt better about myself, nor have I ever felt so worthy of another person, as I do, when you are with me."

I maintained my silence, willing him to continue.

He was looking off at the far wall, as witnesses do when they must deliver contrary evidence in a courtroom. "I even feel a level of attraction to you that I have never felt before, with a man."

He sipped his water, and then placed it on the table.

"I don't know what to do. If I leave, I am sure that I will lose you. If I stay, the same may happen. And I don't want to live through either one of those scenarios."

I leaned forward and took his right hand in both of mine. He was trembling.

"Jerome, what is wrong? Please tell me – I cannot help if I don't know what the issue is."

"Okay. Larry, I...am terrified of losing you. I love the attention you give me, the compliments, the companionship. I just...think, if you...find my brother, I will lose you, and all of that attention."

"Why, Jerome? I just don't understand how he could possibly come between the two of us."

He turned to face me. He put his hand over mine. I looked at his tear-stained face and willed him to tell me what I could not understand.

"Larry, Sherman and I are...twins. He looks just like me. And he is gay. If you really feel the way you say about me, and the way I look, I have no chance of ever keeping you as my friend, if you could have him as a boyfriend."

I gasped.

He nodded, sullenly.

"I'll have to admit, I never thought of that as a possibility. But really, do you think that he could come between us? Maybe he has a boyfriend – or even a husband." I asked hopefully.

"Except for a few miscellaneous scars, he looks exactly like me. The last time I was able to check his profiles online, he was still single."

"And what makes you think he would even like me? You and I have been through a lot in two days. We bonded under extraordinary circumstances."

"And how could he not like you? I have only known you for a few days, and I love you. Truly I do."

It was my turn to cry. I laid myself down onto the cushion between us, with my head at his flank. He put his hand on my shoulder and held it there. I finally got myself under control and sniffled a few times.

"So, Jerome, what do you want to do?"

"I don't know, what are my options?"

"We can call off the search and let the relationship with your brother stay like it is. Perhaps he will want to reconcile on his own."

"Or?" he asked.

"You can reach out to him, or your sister, and see if you can persuade him that you really want to make it up to him."

"Or?"

"We can take a chance, and hope that, when I do eventually find him, I really hate this...Sherman...and how he has distanced himself from you, no matter what he looks like."

"Ha, ha! Or?"

"We start your gay indoctrination tonight. I will teach you everything I know. It won't take longer than about ten minutes, I promise."

"Well, that seems the most promising. Will I need new shoes for this training?"

"Absolutely. I could lose my membership card if you had the wrong shoes for the ceremony."

"What does it entail?" he asked.

"You have to take your clothes off, which you are already extremely comfortable doing, apparently. But I get to take mine off, too, and at the same time."

"Nah, you lost me on that one. I just don't like hairy, muscular legs, even if they do belong to my best friend."

"Okay, but can I see you naked again, and soon? I am already starting to forget some of the details. I guess I have short-term memory loss."

He laughed, stood up and dropped his boxers. He stepped out of them, and paraded around the room, giving me the show of a lifetime.

"Wait, let me get my camera!"

"Nope, you cannot afford my rates as a model. If you cannot remember from day to day, I will just have to show you again and again and again."

"Jerome?" I asked, grinning wildly.

"Yes?"

"Not that I am complaining, but that could get really awkward when we get back to the office."

He ran around the coffee table and jumped on top of me. It was the closest that we could be, and we were not going to let his lack of clothing bother us. It only made me more excited.

We settled down, and I kept my clothes on, unfortunately. The mood was lightened, and we decided to go out for dinner, even if it meant that he had to put clothes back on.

On the way to the restaurant, I cautiously asked him a question.

"Jerome, I have a question, but I want you to wait to answer until you have thought about it. What about your brother? If you still want me to seek him out, can it wait until this week is over? I don't want us to be consumed with that when we should be getting down in a town known for so few rules."

"Yes, I want you to look for him. I might even let you out of my sight to do it, but I feel safe that you will come back."

"Thank you, I appreciate your trust."

"It is not so much trust, as Sherman's modesty. He did not like to get undressed for anything when we were at home together as kids – you would be starving for a sight of skin in his company."

"Point well taken. I am not sure I could go for exceptionally long without a chance to worship my Greek god." I bumped his elbow with mine and we both laughed.

Back in the hotel after dinner, we collapsed on the sofa. I could not believe that we had almost parted, over such a simple problem.

"So, Jerome, do you think you are going to need a massage soon?"

"I don't know. I am concerned that you are just using me for future jack-off material."

"And that would be bad because...?"

"I don't know yet, but I think I need to play hard to get, especially if I am going to be naked every time we are indoors together."

"You will have no complaints from me on that."

We both laughed, and I left the room to take a cold shower.

Dinner Plans

I was awake first and spent some quiet time reading on the sofa. It was long before dawn, and I did not want the day to start any faster. I could wait for him to shuffle off to breakfast when we both were ready.

Jerome stretched, yawned, and then padded into the bathroom. We still maintained our distance for our respective morning routines. We had achieved a comfortable solution for two men living in the same hotel room with no romantic entanglements. It felt good to have a friend that was neither pushing me to change, nor adapt my style to theirs.

He emerged from the bathroom about thirty minutes later, just as naked as when he went in. I could tell that he had showered and shaved, but there was not enough hair on his head to suggest that he had washed any of it. His mustache glistened in the morning light, and my heart stirred.

I really wondered how long I could go on like this. We had no plans to live together once we returned home. I was determined to make the most of this arrangement while we resided in the southern city of sin.

"Okay, Larry, what is on our agenda?"

"Well, I have dinner plans with my sister tonight. I am sure she is going to grill me about this...setup...as well as why I am still single. I guess we will be about two hours."

"Okay, so I could go next door and enjoy the professional dancers for a while."

"You mean at the 'Twirling Baton' club in the alley?"

"Yeah, that is the one. The posters outside are great."

"You do know that those are men, dressed as women, right? It' s a drag show."

"Is that why they are all so tall?" He exclaimed.

"Yes," was all I could think to say.

"I just thought...oh, I don't know how I rationalized what I saw on the marquee signs. Perhaps Mother Nature is starting to confuse me?"

"We need to get you to a real titty bar, or you just may lose your membership in the macho he-man club."

We both laughed.

Jerome assured me that he was fine entertaining himself. I gave him the card from the rickshaw driver. I told him locals could get him into places that he would not know about, and they can also keep him out of harm's way if he treats them well. I stressed that generous tips were part of the treatment.

I went down to the lobby and met Sarah in her office. She smiled impishly, and then took my arm as we left the hotel. I was relieved that we would not be on the roof. I had a good chance of not gorging myself in a new place.

Just a few blocks later, we entered a small storefront that I would not have braved alone. We passed through a darkened storage room and then through a busy kitchen. Finally, at the back of the building, we got our table for two. It was one of ten tables, all of them for couples.

Sarah knew the owner, so we had a great seat for privacy. She glared at me across the table, and I suspected I was in the firing line for my impulsive visit. I knew, as she did, that I would tell her anything she wanted to know. I only keep secrets when they belong to others. My work was always off limits for disclosures. Now my close friend Jerome was one of those for whom I kept confidences.

We settled into our chairs, and I glanced at the menu. I had already decided that I was not going to get four courses of food, despite my urge to splurge. Sarah, dressed in a slinky dress and looking like a model, never seemed to eat anything but salads. I envied her self-discipline.

"So, brother dear, what is up with you? And who is this new boyfriend?"

I scowled at her, but she broke my will with her gaze, and her winning smile. I sighed and then started filling her in.

"I have seen this guy around the office for the last two years. He is a bit of a dreamboat, I will admit, but I never expected to be sharing a hotel room with him, nor be this...close to him, emotionally."

"I will never understand your taste in men! When there are so many hunks to choose from, you go for the bald, stocky ones. So how did you get here, with him, under these circumstances?"

"I can only tell you so much, as some of it is private, but I assure you that we are just friends, and that he is having difficulty after his divorce. I don't think he would mind me telling you, as he is quite open about his experience."

"It sounds like she left him. Was there someone else?"

"You know, he did not say. I gather, from what he has told me, that they grew apart, and that she blamed him for her boredom. Of course, as a lawyer, I know I have only heard one side of the story. Her report may be far more devastating to his case."

Sarah laughed. "You do like to play both sides of the coin!"

"I think you are mixing your metaphors, but I know what you mean. After years in contract law, I have come to recognize that each party is not just fighting for the best deal, they are often jockeying for position, and for validation of their arguments."

"Remind me never to come to you after a breakup. It sounds like you would blame me, and then ask me why I was so difficult."

"That is not true at all. What I am trying to say is that everyone has their story, and their perception of what 'happened' at any given point. We try to reconcile events with the details that we have taken in, sometimes forgetting important clues that might have led us to a different conclusion."

"Gosh, you have been single too long. You are now starting to rationalize Bernard's critique of your failed relationship."

"Hey, that is not fair! I accepted responsibility for my part in that breakup, but I don't accept that he concealed so much from me."

The server approached the table with caution. She did not know if she was intruding on a lover's quarrel, and I did not even see her expression until Sarah looked up.

"Good evening. Have you had a chance to look over the menus? And would you like to start with a cocktail tonight?"

"Yes, I would like a cosmopolitan and the California Salad with smoked salmon," Sarah replied.

I had not decided on a meal, and I was embarrassed to admit to it. "I will have the same, thank you."

I glared at Sarah when the waitress walked away. "Did we have to get so heavy into this in the first five minutes? How about some pleasantries and good news?"

"Fine. Julie and I are still an item. We moved to a larger house and have begun our work as foster parents - for dogs, of course. The hotel is paying off, after years of struggle. I have not heard from our older brother for about three months, and I no longer want to pursue my PhD, in anything."

"That was fast. Okay, well, I am still single - which you knew. I have not really dated anyone since Bernard left. I miss his dog more than I will ever miss him. Work is work, and I am thinking about spending some time traveling. I just did not want to go alone. Would you fancy a trip to Europe soon?"

"I would love to go, but it would be dependent on timing. We have busy stretches where I would hesitate to even go home for all the chaos the patrons of our establishment can create."

"We can compare calendars and see if something fits. I could not go for more than two weeks or so at a time. I wouldn't mind doing one of those river cruises, I just don't want to be the only one on board without a walker and a steady supply of incontinence pads in my suitcase."

Sarah cackled loudly enough for the other patrons to look over at us.

"You are awful! Why don't you go alone - but pick one of those gay cruises? You might find someone to fill up your calendar with something more fun than sightseeing."

"I don't know. Those things always look good in the brochures, but I suspect it would not be much different than the seniors cruise, but with fewer clothes, and far more drama."

"Eww. Yeah, not good."

"So, do you think that this Julie is going to make an honest gal of you? Perhaps some wedding bells in the future?"

"We have talked about it, but it just does not seem like a good idea right now, financially. We would take a big hit on taxes, and I am not sure her university benefits are enough of a back-fill benefit in the long run."

The waitress brought our drinks. We clinked glasses together and sipped the mixture with gusto.

"I guess I had never thought about the practical side of the marriage certificate. I just wanted someone to pledge their love to me, in a display of affection that might mean a real commitment."

"And how would you expect to achieve that with a straight man in your bed?"

"Jeez, you are crass. I'll have to admit, I never thought it would go this far, but it has been quite rewarding."

"You mean he has begun the process of converting over to your team?"

"NO!" I laughed. "I wish, but no. Jerome is simply one of the kindest, warmest men I have ever met. He does not have pretenses of machismo, nor does he play any of the he-man psychological games that I have experienced with other men. I don't know if women even this do, but sometimes I get around a straight guy, and he starts to amplify his own heterosexual traits to distance himself from any suspicion of being gay."

"Yeah, women do that. I get irritated with them, but most straight women irritate me, anyway."

The waitress smiled awkwardly as she arrived with our salads. "Will there be anything else?"

"Um, yes, could we get a bottle of white wine? Perhaps a vintage Sauvignon Blanc?" Sarah asked.

"Would you like to see a wine list? We have several to choose from."

"No, please, just bring us your favorite."

I saw the waitress roll her eyes when she recognized the patronizing tone, but I said nothing.

"I think she liked you, before you started hating on the straight gals," I laughed.

"The statement, if she heard me at all, was out of context. What I meant was that so many people are just so uncomfortable with themselves that they try to project a suit of armor as a defense against any impunity. I find it more refreshing if people are just honest about what scares them."

"And that is exactly where I am with Jerome. After an initial awkward evening and a hike through the woods, we achieved a stasis that has kept us on solid ground ever since. He told me several things that I would have trouble confiding to another person, especially so early in the friendship. But it brought us closer together and I feel...protective of him now."

"Can you honestly say that you have not conspired to get him out of his clothes?"

"I did not need to. He stripped down the first night and hopped into a jacuzzi with me."

"Well, that was probably just the alcohol."

"Maybe, but the next day, he exposed himself again, for a massage." I smiled. "And he is nearly an exhibitionist in our hotel room. There are not many straight men I have met that would be so...bold and fearless."

"I think he is just teasing you, testing how far he can push your buttons before you...cross the line."

"He is not that deliberate. He cannot be. The room is absolutely chilly, yet he says he is too warm. He even sleeps on top of the covers, while I am wrapped up like a babushka."

"Just be careful, okay?"

"What do you mean? We are friends, and we are amazingly comfortable around each other. I was even quite honest with him about my prior crush on him."

"You told him about your last job? That you had to leave?"

"No, I did not. When I transferred to the new office, I fell for Jerome, as I have been known to do. He thought I did not like him because I worked so hard to avoid him. Now he knows that I found him attractive, and he seems to be okay with it."

"But you still find him attractive, yes? Will that not create some resentment down the road when you don't get anywhere with him?"

"I may have a solution for that."

"Yes? I am intrigued," she replied.

The waitress returned with a dusty bottle of wine. I sampled the vintage, nodded vigorously with approval, and she left us to carry on with our salads and gossip.

"He has a twin brother, who is gay. He wants me to find him and...start the process of reconciliation."

"Did they quarrel?"

"Epically. When Sherman, the brother, came out to him, Jerome went off on a tirade, and pushed his brother away."

"How did you get in the middle of this?"

"He asked for my help. I was hesitant, at first, but I don't see why I could not try."

"I cannot believe that there are two men that look like that." She said, rolling her eyes.

"I know, nor can I believe my luck!"

"Does this Jerome know that he is going to be replaced with the twin?"

"I don't know that it will actually happen that way, but I have a good feeling about this."

"Why is it all of your crushes look like the spitting image of our father?"

"Have you actually seen Jerome?"

"Of course, I have seen him, we have cameras covering all of the public areas in the hotel."

"I had not thought of that. That IS what gay men do, we look for a father-figure replacement. Didn't you know that?"

"I don't know. It just gives me an uneasy feeling, like a Greek tragedy, waiting to happen."

"Har, har, har. Very funny. I don't choose the men that I am attracted to, it just happens."

"I just don't get that, but I am viewing this from the female perspective."

"Men respond to the visual first. I can tell you my crushes are far more realistic than the guys who only want the perfect-body twenty-something twinks. Those guys only exist in movies and catalogs, and their looks are the sum-total of their value to the planet. There is not enough substance in a pretty boy to base a relationship on. My interests are real. I like down-to-earth, beefy men with dad bods, and some gray hair. Actually, the less hair on their head, the better."

"I know, you have told me this before."

"What about you? What first drew you into Julie's orbit?"

"She spelled my name correctly on my coffee cup. Most people forget the silent 'H' at the end."

"That was what, five years ago?"

"Yes. She finished her PhD, got a tenure-track position, and I have been doing my best with my own spelling ever since."

"And her looks never played a part in your romance or attraction?"

"Of course, it did! I am not blind, but I like to think that I am not so shallow that I would follow around a beautiful woman with the hopes she might get tired of being stalked and just commit to me on the spot."

"That hurts."

"I am sorry, but that was kind of 'Fatal Attraction' scary with you in that last job."

"I hope I have put that behind me now. I never expected to like Jerome so much, but we have come to an agreement on our friendship."

She put down her fork and stared at me intently.

"Does he understand all of the implications of your friendship?"

"You probably see more problems than solutions, but perfectionists often do."

"Thank you. I pride myself on being able to dissect a gift horse, all the while making it leaner and faster to ride when I am finished."

"IF the horse doesn't die in the process!"

"Now you are being crass. What is the long-term plan for this relationship with Jerome?"

"We have not discussed it. I think we are both just living in the moment, for a short spell. We will have to navigate being friends at work, as I may be the naysayer on contracts that he wants to push forward."

"Yeah, there won't be any conflict of interest there!"

"Thanks for your vote of support in my professionalism."

"Hey - I worry about you. I think you are still pretty fragile after the last breakup."

"I have put that behind me. I don't think that either one of us was mature enough for the relationship we tried to create."

"At your age? When will you be ready for a solid commitment, if not now, in your thirties?"

"Men mature a bit more slowly than women do. That is why men used to marry young girls after they were established in their careers."

"They also died shortly after, leaving a rich widow with children. I was hoping that finding a father figure would mature you a little faster."

"Now I feel like you are just shooting arrows at me. Why did I ever agree to have dinner with you?"

"Because we are related, and you have no choice. It is legal for me to stalk you. Shared blood gives me that right."

"I gotta remember to change my phone number when I get home." I said sarcastically with a weak smile.

We finished our salads, and the bottle of wine, which I knew was going to break the bank. It was almost as good as the one I had with Jerome on the roof of the hotel.

The waitress appeared at our table, on cue. "Would you like dessert or coffee this evening?"

"Yes, I would like an espresso. And could I see the dessert menu?" I asked.

"There is no menu, we have two options. Would you like to hear them?"

"Yes, of course," I replied.

"There is an apple dumpling with a cider caramel sauce. And we have a white chocolate cheesecake with a mixed berry puree."

I looked at Sarah. She did not want to meet my eyes, so I cleared my throat.

"Would you like to split one of those?"

"No, I want my own, silly," she said to me. "I will have the dumpling, please," she said to our server.

"Just the espresso for me, thank you," I said.

The waitress turned and left us alone.

"Walk me through these scenarios, Larry."

I looked at her suspiciously, but I knew what she meant. It was a game we played often.

I scrunched up my face to show her I was thinking, as if I had not previously considered the pathways this thing could play out.

"I fail to contact his brother, or at least fail to convince him to hear me out, if not Jerome."

"Or?" She asked.

"I do contact Sherman, we reach some level of agreement, and I make the meeting happen."

"That is the one that concerns me."

I scowled at her, wondering what she had foreseen that I had not. "Why?"

"We will get to that. Are there any other scenarios that could play out?"

"The other option, which I had not mentioned, because I am an optimist, was that Jerome also has a sister. I may be able to get through to her and have her act on my behalf to broker a meeting with her brother for either me, or better, Jerome."

"And that is all you can think of?"

"Yes. Why?"

"Let's start with the last scenario. If the sister must step in, I am guessing it is because the brother did not want to talk. That makes your task more difficult, but could create an unrealistic hero's image of you, in Jerome's eyes."

"Thanks, sis. Just what I wanted for my life's goal."

"I am just being practical. Managing Jerome's expectations is your most important task in this project."

"Yeah, I guess you are right. We will have to continue working together."

"Working backward through these scenarios. You could win over the sister, and the brother, and then reunite the family. I am not sure where that leaves you. It might foster some resentment for one of the three parties. You were an outsider that inserted yourself into the family's business."

"I was asked to do it," I replied, raising my voice.

The waitress arrived with my espresso and Sarah's apple dumpling. She disappeared quickly, with the empty wine bottle and our glasses.

"We both know that, but it may escape them at the time. Sometimes people do blame the messenger, even if it is good news."

"Okay, what else?"

"You win over the sister, but not the brother. That would leave her as an ally, and perhaps put her into a more active role. You would still be an outsider, but less culpable if there were any...unpleasantries."

"You are exhausting me, you...you...perfectionist!"

She smiled at a triumphant win but continued.

"Now, the other scenario that worries me is the happy reunion with the original contact to the brother."

"Why?"

"If they are identical twins, and you have already shown a predilection for swooning over this type of man, you may find yourself at odds. It may be difficult to remain on good terms with either one."

"Why?"

"If you stick with Jerome, and just become acquaintances with the brother, it may always be a shred of worry for Jerome that you are using him. Either for his looks, egad, or just to get in with Sherman, as a long-range plan."

"Gosh, this is making my head hurt."

"No, that was the wine, and that espresso is not helping."

"Great, now I have to guzzle water the rest of the night."

"You should, anyway. But even if you repair the broken brotherhood, as it were, if the twin is still single, what would keep you from pursuing him? He is bound to have a similar personality to Jerome. And you already have quite an infatuation with your current bedmate."

"Hey - we are friends."

"Which is just another euphemism for not having consummated yet, in male terms."

"I would think that those PhD programs would be afraid of you, and your cutting analysis."

"I only do this for friends, and beloved family," she replied, smirking.

"Are those all the pathways for this request to play out?"

"No, but you already know the other one."

"I don't think I do," I replied, cautiously.

"You charm this Jerome to the point that he wants to at least try some heavy petting with you. Then you have your friend, an occasional sex buddy, and there are only complications for him, if he really does like it both ways."

"Wouldn't that just stir up jealousy on Jerome's part if Sherman entered the picture as a friendly contact?"

"Absolutely."

"So, what are you telling me to do? I don't feel like I can just back out of this search. I made a commitment."

"You have not considered the one thing that will insulate you, protect you, from all of the bad outcomes."

"And that would be what?"

"You find someone that is receptive to you and provides you with solid ground from which to operate. You need a new man in your life, and he cannot be chosen from this pool of family discontentment."

I slumped in the chair like a rag doll. "I feel as if I have just endured a year of therapy in ninety minutes!"

"You have. And I do not charge for my services. But I will let you pay for dinner."

"I just knew I would be paying for that bottle of wine!"

"And it was worth it, to have your life dissected, rearranged, and presented back to you as an opportunity by someone who loves you."

"I thought the waitress was just tolerating us."

"I meant me, your only sister."

"Oh. Thanks. What about our brother?"

"He will not respond to my requests. Maybe you can have better luck."

"I will try. Will I see you again before Friday?"

"No, I am going to a business conference tomorrow in Atlanta. We are courting the upper echelon of women at a vacation seminar. Our hotel can provide them a safe space where they can congregate without being preyed upon by the lecherous straight guys."

"Good luck with that. I know I am certainly impressed with the place, and the service."

I paid the bill, and we walked back to the hotel. She got in her car and sped off. I had to find my way up to the room, with a few more doubts in my head about the relationship I was pursuing with Jerome.

I kicked off my shoes and stepped out of my good slacks. Jerome, already there and pacing the room, was too excited about his evening to do much else, so I let him fill me in on all the details he could remember.

"Angie took me to a bar that only the locals know about!"

"Did she ask why you were alone?"

"Yes, I told her the truth. You had a family event. I let her think I am the paramour that they don't know about. Yet."

"You are devious! I like that in a man."

"Thanks. I had dinner at the bar while a local band played some bluesy songs. They were quite good." His face changed. "And then, Abigail sat down. Next to me." He almost looked frightened.

"Yes? YES? What happened?" I almost shouted.

"We hit it off. She is in marketing and lives in Charlotte." He stopped and raised his eyebrows. "I got her phone number, and she insisted on taking mine."

"What? No dirty details from this evening?"

"No!" He laughed. "I think she was suggesting it, but it did not feel right."

"Okay. That is a mature attitude."

"Larry, something has changed for me. I now know that there are people, at least one man and one woman, that are attracted to me. It gave me a confidence that I never had before."

100

He looked up with moist eyes. "You did that for me, and I am ever so grateful."

"Jerome, that is wonderful. Will you see her again tomorrow?"

"No, she flies back to Charlotte in the morning."

"Jerome, I am really proud of you! Most men would have pounced if they had the chance, yet you chose to play the long game."

"You know, we could have had a great time tonight, but there was just something about her that told me to wait. Let this feeling grow. See where the relationship leads. I may have stirred more interest from her because of it."

"Great! Simply great! But don't think I will put up with you playing hard to get," I laughed heartily.

"I am not worried about keeping your interest, for now. Besides, she is beautiful, and I would bet she does not have hairy legs."

"Why is that?"

"She was Miss North Carolina. It was a few years back, but her poise is admirable."

"So, she ticked all of the boxes for the Jerome checklist?" I asked.

"Almost. She is not a masseuse."

"At least I still have that going for me."

"How did your evening with Sarah go?" he asked, then added, "Larry, was I one of the topics of conversation at dinner tonight?"

"No, Jerome, you were THE topic tonight."

He showed his hurt so quickly on his face, that I had to rescue him.

"While my sister was rather inquisitive, especially because of...this situation, I told her that we were here to celebrate your divorce. I said you felt a little down, and I volunteered to show you a good time."

He smiled. "I knew I could count on you, Larry."

"I do have to explain that my sister and I are close. She knows the type of man that I am attracted to, and you certainly fit the bill. Initially, she thought we were here for a tawdry affair. I had to let her down easily, as she has been pushing me to find someone."

He blinked a few times, as if I were going to ask him to be a pretend date.

"While I would like to kindle a romance sometime in the future with a new man, I could not be happier with our friendship. I fear going back to work and having to be all business-like around the office with you."

"Larry, I don't understand. You mean we won't be friends at work?"

"Of course, we will be, but this trip is different. When we are here, on our time, no one can hear what we say, nor see how we behave around each other. When we get to work, everyone will know we are friends, but I want to protect you from any rumors or suspected conflicts of interest."

"Oh, okay. I think."

"Jerome, I work for the company on legal matters. If our friendship could be perceived as a liability or risk for the company, because we must confer and work together, then I will have to step aside and let someone else handle those matters."

His face fell, and I was backpedaling fast.

"Jerome, I cannot tell you how much this friendship means to me. How much YOU mean to me, and I do not want anything to come between us, ever. But we do need to protect the company's interests at work."

"Of course, I am sorry – I must still be on edge."

"Good. If I have my way, we will eat together quite often, and not because you are shackled to the pipes in my basement."

"You are a hoot, Larry." He stopped moving about, and the perspiration was evident on his forehead. As if on cue, he started taking his clothes off. Shoes, pants, shirt, t-shirt fell to the floor. His boxers dropped to his ankles, and he instantly looked more comfortable.

"Does this mean we are not going back out tonight?" I asked.

"Um, yes, I guess it does."

"Good, I would like to get back on a regular schedule, and this town is just not the kind of place that knows what a reasonable bedtime is."

"So, what do we do now?"

"Well, it is ten o'clock. We could watch TV, play a game – there are a bunch in the closet near the kitchen area, or..."

"We could get the massage table back up here?" He finished.

I could not contain my smile. I made the call to the front desk and changed into my gym clothes. He had no preparation, short of removing his socks.

The table arrived, and I tipped the porter while Jerome waited in the bathroom. I am sure we were already the talk of the town, and we did not want to give them any more fuel.

I closed the door and put the chain guard on the lock. He slowly emerged from the bathroom, like a child about to be punished.

"Now don't keep me waiting, or I will be rough with you!" I said sternly.

"I doubt that, seriously!"

I took a step toward him, and he moved around the other side of the chair to avoid me. He stayed ahead of me for less than a minute until I finally caught him. I grabbed his arm to stop him. He was a bit winded from the excitement and laughter. I immediately squatted down, and then put my right shoulder into his left hip, effectively lifting his entire body up on my shoulder when I stood. He struggled playfully, laughing like a toddler being tickled.

"Now you know that I can catch you, perhaps you should know there are penalties if you try to run from me."

"Like what?"

I ran my open hand over his furry buns, and he struggled more.

"I could spank you right here, and you are powerless to stop me." I slapped him twice quite firmly on his left cheek.

His squirming reached an unmanageable level and I put him down to stop the silliness. He was red in the face from the inversion, but his penis was erect, as well. I had not seen that since the first night in the jacuzzi.

"I am sorry, Jerome, did I take it too far?"

"No, it's just that, I get excited from that kind of...treatment."

"I see, well perhaps you should let your new girlfriend know that, but not on the first date," I said, laughing.

He was looking sheepish, as if there were more to tell.

"Jerome, I cannot explain sexual responses in myself, much less others. I know I like a bit of slap and tickle myself; it is nothing to be embarrassed about."

"Oh, okay. I was just concerned..." He stopped, chewing his lip.

"About what?" I asked.

"While I find it thrilling that you are attracted to me, and that you get a boner each time you work me over on the massage table, I never thought I could get an erection with a man. It was just a surprise, that's all."

"I am sorry, I did not know it would happen. Do you want to call off the massage?"

"Hell no! I have earned it now."

"You sure have. Make yourself comfortable on the table, and I will reserve my hands for kneading, not slapping. Until you tell me otherwise. Okay?"

"Okay" he said with a big grin and climbed up on the table. There was a noticeably light pink handprint on his left cheek.

He groaned in all the usual places as I worked him over in my standard massage routine. Without prompting, he flipped over, and I finished the massage. I stepped back to stretch my arms, wrists, and fingers. He sat up and smiled with a brilliant flash of teeth.

"If I did not know better, Jerome, I would think that you are high on something," I said.

"I am, and it is you," he sighed. "Or maybe it is New Orleans!" He finished.

"Well, I am thrilled to hear it, but I am not sure I am going to let you follow me home Friday. You might never leave."

"And that would be bad, because...?"

"I would, eventually, like to get laid again, and it would be awkward if I brought a man home, and he found you there, naked, and waiting for a massage."

We both laughed. He was looking to see if I had the same response, I always got from massaging him. It was there, and exceedingly difficult to hide.

"I think I will shower up and get ready for bed, if you are through with me, that is." I said quietly.

He blushed deep red and nodded.

I exited quickly and left him to relax in the afterglow of the massage while I showered up and took care of business. He was dozing on the bed when I emerged from the bathroom.

Last Vacation Day

Our last full day in New Orleans dawned hazy and overcast, with humidity that rivaled many of the greenhouse gardens I had been to over the years. Neither of us felt like doing anything touristy, and I could not risk another massage, or Jerome might be so relaxed that he would be immobilized.

We had a late brunch, getting quite drunk on mimosas, wine, and Irish coffees, along with our huge plates of food. Neither one of us wanted to stumble around the crowded streets, so I called for the rickshaw back to the hotel.

When I got in, I barely got myself seated when Jerome fell backward onto me, covering me, more than the small bench. It rocked the rickshaw and got the driver's attention.

"Hey, boys, don't wreck my ride. Wait until you get back to the hotel to jump on each other, okay?"

We started giggling and remained useless for the rest of the trip. We were fortunate that she remembered us, and the tips, to get us back to the Cat's Paw in record time. "You two are certainly the happiest honeymoon couple that I can remember."

"Thank you." I nearly slurred my words. Jerome stared straight ahead, struggling to stop the giggles. It only worked for a few seconds, and we lost it again.

Stumbling as quietly as we could through the lobby, I got into the elevator and held onto Jerome to keep us both upright. The ride to the penthouse was quick, and I had the key in my hand to open the door. When it flew open, we both sighed. It was cool, and dark. We would have to sleep off our late breakfast to even pack our bags.

I hit the bathroom and was not surprised to find Jerome already stepping out of his boxers when I returned. He had a strange look on his face.

"Jerome? Is something wrong?"

"Kind of. Can we talk for a bit?"

"Do you want to sober up first, perhaps take a nap?"

"No, this would be more difficult for me to say when I am no longer feeling this...loose."

I got two waters out of the refrigerator, slipped out of my shoes, and dropped my pants on the bed. He stood waiting, watching my movements. When I sat down on the sofa, pushing myself into one corner so that I could put my legs up on the ottoman, he crossed the room to the couch. He turned his back to me and sat down in the crook of my arm. His naked, furry body pushed up against mine, and I started to feel a bit worried.

"Larry, I need to say this to you, and I have to admit, I planned it. I did not turn down any alcohol today, and I have purposefully put myself in the one place where I feel the most comfortable, but not have to face you."

My heart was hammering in my chest. My mind was racing, and I was losing my buzz.

"Jerome, I am all ears. You have my attention."

"Larry, I think you know this, but I love you. I really, really do."

"Okay, Jerome. I had suspected as much." I laughed, but he did not.

"What I simply cannot understand is how I will cope with those feelings on Friday, when we go our separate ways at the airport."

I said nothing, hoping he would explain further.

"I don't want to lead you on - this is not a romantic love, as I am not attracted to you. I am sorry, but I cannot change that. What I do know is that I feel closer to you, more comfortable with you than I have ever felt with anyone in my life. I fear - and I am serious when I say this - that I will have withdrawal over the weekend. I will want to call you or hang out at one of our houses for the duration, and I just don't think that will be fair to you, in the long run."

I took a deep breath and let it out. I was on the verge of tears.

"You have provided me with a spiritual awakening that I tried for years to achieve with programs, people, and organized groups. I am so torn about how to manage this going forward."

I moved my hand from the back of the sofa and pulled my arm up under his chin. I leaned my head over to the back of his neck and cried softly. His voice hitched, but he continued.

"I hope that means you feel the same way. Where does this leave us on Saturday morning when I don't have you around?"

"I don't know, Jerome. I ache at the thought of us parting. But as you said, this will not work, long term, and I don't want to resent you in the future for not giving me something that you are not capable of delivering."

"So, what do we do? Cold turkey? Part at the airport and have no contact until work Monday?"

"I think that would be worse. Maybe we should plan to wean ourselves off. You come over to my place on Saturday for a few hours, and I will visit you on Sunday for a few more. Unless you have plans?"

"Ha, ha, ha," he stated flatly.

"Okay, do we need to establish any ground rules?"

"What, like we are on a hike?"

"No, I just want to manage expectations, for each of us."

"Oh, okay. What do you suggest?"

"Jerome, we live about two miles from each other. I could walk it in thirty minutes if I wanted to."

"What? How did you know..."

"I stalked you, remember? On social media. I have your address. I was thankful that I did not live on your street or would have used my telescope."

He started to laugh.

"You think I am kidding?"

"No, I have seen you in action with one of those things. You are quite the seeker when you want to be."

I remembered the night on the roof, and our praise of two beautiful moons.

"Jerome, I welcome you into my home any time you want to be there. You can even have a key. I fear that you may suffocate because I do not keep it this cold inside. But you would be an ideal fixture in my bungalow, especially in this beautiful suit of yours."

I ran my hand down to his belly, ruffling the furry hairs from his chest to his navel. I stopped when I felt the stirring in my boxers.

"But my ground rule, if we have any at all, is complete honesty. I need you to tell me when you are down. I would like to hear when you are happy, also, but I don't want to lose you in any sense of the word, because you did not tell me you were struggling with something."

"I promise. If you agree to one rule of mine," he said through his tears.

"Of course, anything."

"You have to tell me when I am getting too clingy, or in the way. I don't want you to start dreading my arrival, or my phone calls. Okay?"

"It's a deal. I promise."

We sat that way, with my arm around his neck and hand on his belly, on the sofa, until we were both asleep. We must have slept for a few hours because I was chilled to the bone when I finally started to stir. He had moved his hand to my left thigh, and that was the only warmth I felt. My calves were freezing. I did not want to stir and wake him, but my yearning for water and the bathroom were beyond urgent.

I uncrossed my ankles, and he ran his hand up and down my leg affectionately. With a single pat from his warm hand, he pulled it back to his lap and leaned forward. We got up and practically raced each other for the bathroom. I got there first, and he let me have a bit of privacy. Once I moved over to the sink, he stepped in and relieved himself.

Back out in the room, I paced around, thinking of what we could do that would top off our week. I crossed to the coffee table and retrieved my water. When I turned around, there he was. He put his arms out and embraced me. I wrapped my arms around him, trying to keep the water bottle upright. I gave up and dropped the water, hoping the cap was tightly attached. It took all my willpower not to run my hands down his back and over his beautiful buns. His skin was warm, while mine was cool to the touch.

"Jerome?" I asked.

"You do know that I have a private office at work, right?"

"No, do you really? I have a desk in the middle of an open floor plan. It sucks."

"I only bring it up because you can visit me anytime you need a hug, and no one will be the wiser. Okay?"

He squeezed me harder, then he let me go, and stepped back. "Okay. Thank you. I may have to take you up on that."

"I hope so," I smiled. "Often."

We spent the rest of the afternoon packing and sobering up. We were both so dehydrated that we finished all the bottled waters in the refrigerator. I am sure they would charge us for all of it, but I was not worried about expenses.

When dinner time arrived, neither one of us wanted to go out. There was just too much pageantry of dining in the food capital of the south.

"Would you mind if we got takeout and hung out here for our last night together?" he asked.

"You make it sound like we are flying to different parts of the world tomorrow, but no, I don't mind. We could even watch a movie if we can agree on a film."

"Okay, but I am picky about my movies. I don't want to watch something I have seen before, and I despise violence."

"Comedy or drama?"

"A bit of both. I love it when I get engrossed in a story that I don't even realize that I am attached to the characters until it is over. It takes a drama to do that."

"Let me try to understand this. You are a project manager, and as techy as they come, you are built like a linebacker, a gorgeous one, but still, and you want me to pick a film that might make us both cry?"

"Yes, absolutely. I am not afraid to cry in front of you!"

"Can I pick a classic film that I have seen?" I asked, laughing as I did.

"Sure. My wife, I mean my ex-wife, did not like movies very much, so I have about a decade or so of lost culture in my life."

"Okay. If I get to choose the movie, you get to choose the food. What did you have in mind?"

"BBQ! Ribs, with lots of messy sauce, and all the fixin's. And beer."

"Consider it done, sir!" I stated emphatically.

I made all the arrangements, and then added the leaf to the table so that we could spread out the volume of food we had ordered. The beer was locally brewed, and a bit stronger than we were used to, but we resolved to eat enough to counteract it.

We dove into the food like wild animals after a long hunt. Other than lip smacking and guzzling the brews, I don't think we made any other sounds. We certainly did not slow down long enough to talk. The food was better than any we had consumed all week.

When we pushed back from the table, he was nearly burgundy in color, covered from chin to navel with sauce. I almost offered to help him clean up, but I wanted to maintain our boundary, for both of us. He had a quick shower while I cleaned up the remnants of our feast.

I wiped the table down and put the rest of the trash in a large bag for the maid. When I finished, I was just as messy as he had been – but it was my shirt and boxers that were now soaked with sauce, not my skin.

All week, I had kept myself hidden from him to make him more comfortable. I also expected that having my clothes off anywhere near him would just embarrass me more, as I often got a quick physical reaction. I suppose I was too tired to even think about it, and I stripped off my underclothes for a shower.

When he exited the bathroom, glistening in moisture from the humidity, I might as well have been a randy teenager. I did not realize how quickly I had reacted, until he spoke.

"Are you going to faint with that much blood rushing to one area?"

I blushed deeply and looked down. "No, this is quite normal for me, especially in the presence of such exquisite scenery."

"I am sorry if I am teasing you. I really don't mean to."

"I know, and it is all of my own doing. I fantasized about you for so long that I will probably never get over seeing you. But that is one of the benefits of such an arrangement. I can take care of this in the bathroom, and be back to my usual, placid self by the time you have the movie queued up."

"Now I feel bad, Larry. Here you are, walking around like a saint, and I am teasing you to the point of blue balls."

"I never thought you were doing it on purpose. Please let me into the bathroom and we can watch the movie once I get my shower." He cast his eyes down and stepped aside to let me pass.

Neither of us spoke for the first thirty minutes of my favorite movie. I stretched out my arms to get more comfortable on the sofa, and he took the opportunity to put his hand over mine. I turned my hand palm up and clasped his. It was a difficult peace, but unavoidable in the circumstances.

Goodbye, New Orleans

I woke up early on Friday, anxious to get moving. I let Jerome sleep for a bit, wondering how I had managed to end up in a hotel room with my dream man, naked next to me, but having no chance of anything more than a hug. But I would not change it, nor risk losing my new friend, for anything more.

When he finally stirred, I was on my second cup of coffee. He lifted his head, then laid it back down.

"Are you not ready to face the day?" I asked.

Something unintelligible came out of his face, pressed against the mattress. I smiled, and poured him a cup of coffee, with his one sugar and one creamer. I set it on the table next to him, just within his reach. Then I went and stood at the foot of the bed.

He must have sensed that I was there. "What are you doing?"

"I am trying to decide."

"On what?" he asked as he turned over on his back.

"There, that helps. I have chosen. Thank you."

"What are you talking about?" he demanded. Reaching behind him for the hot coffee, I rushed to save him from spilling it. I put it in his hand.

"I needed to compare. It matters to me, now, which way I will chain you up in my basement. I love your back, and your beautiful buns the most." I reached down and encircled his ankle with my thumb and forefinger.

He pulled his leg, but I held on.

"I even think the shackles I have ready for you will fit. I was concerned that I should have gotten a larger size."

He heaved himself up to a sitting position, sloshing some of his coffee on the side of the bed, but not burning himself.

"I thought queers were all about the dick. You said I had a tent pole!"

"No, for me, it is your backside. I love the swell of your cheeks, and the way the hairs feather out over the muscle. I think I am getting myself excited, just talking about it. And it is not like I will ever have the tent pole to work on, so I will settle for your best asset, which is a joy to behold, or massage, as I am allowed."

"Ha. I think the joke is on you, Larry. I would bet that, inside a month's time, you will want to take a restraining order out on me to keep me away. I will be stalking you, Mr. Lawyer."

It was my turn to grin like a fool. "Okay, but I am hard to convince. It may take a lot longer than a month."

"Challenge accepted!" he almost shouted.

We cleaned up, dressed for the travel day, and checked the room one last time before we left. Despite the hangover, and the impending loss of my naked muse, I was glad to be going home. We did not linger, desperately wanting to keep our emotions in check.

Homeward Bound

We took a cab to the airport. "Domestic flight to Charlotte," I told the driver. We were quiet in the back. I suspect that the driver had experienced many quiet rides, either from hangovers and regrets, or just plain exhaustion.

Standing on the curb at the airport, Jerome hesitated before going into the terminal. I had to pull on his elbow to get him to move. He stepped in behind me and followed my lead all the way to the counter. We got in line to check our bags and as s we inched forward in the mass of people, I noticed Jerome was almost sullen.

"Jerome, you don't have to be so down-in-the-mouth. Those women promised they were not going to press charges... this time," I said with a wicked smile on my face.

He looked around, expecting the people around us to stare. None of them even looked up.

"Ha, ha, Larry."

"Just trying to get you to perk up. Should I ask them to separate us so that you can brood for the two hours on the flight home? I would hate to interrupt a good pout."

He finally smiled. "No, I think I can tolerate sitting next to you for a bit longer."

We got to the counter, and I flashed my airline credit card. The incredibly attractive woman made eye contact with me, but I was uncomfortable with her stare.

"I can upgrade the two of you to first class, based on your status with the airline, would that be acceptable?"

"Um, sure. Thank you." I sputtered.

"And just so you know, I will be serving that section on the flight. I look forward to seeing you again," she winked.

I turned and left, hoping Jerome was behind me. We went through security and continued to our gate. He tried to sit down, but I took his arm and pulled him over to the first-class lounge.

"I take it you don't fly first-class very often?" I asked.

"No, never, actually."

"Well, I can tell you that we do not sit with the 'riff-raff' in these plastic chairs. Please follow me." I led him over to the imposing frosted glass doors.

We flashed our boarding passes and entered a sanctuary within the cold, sterile environment of modern air travel. The carpets were thick. We left our bags in a reserved area, and the chairs were so plush that we could get lost in the comfort.

I sat down at a pair of leather chairs with a small table between them. A server came over with a menu and Jerome struggled to understand the process.

"My friend is new to the first-class lounge experience. Could you give him a brief overview?"

"Sure. My name is Agnes, and I will cater to your needs while you wait for your flight. Anything on the menu is available at no charge, and there are service counters around the perimeter of our lounge for any business needs you may have."

"I am Larry, and this is Jerome." I motioned toward my companion. "Our flight leaves in about two hours. I am not sure we will be able to concentrate with such a lovely lady attending to us, but we will try to maintain our manners."

She smiled brightly but could not overcome her natural plainness.

"Are you hungry, Jerome? Perhaps a cocktail?" She asked.

"I will have a mineral water with a twist of lime, please." He responded.

"Could I have the same, please? And we would like to share this cheese plate. It looks heavenly," I added.

She nodded, took the menus, and disappeared.

"Jerome? Are you okay?"

"Just a little hungover. The water will help. Not sure I want any cheese, though."

"It is a good source of protein and will help stabilize your blood sugar. But it is up to you."

"Okay he mumbled. He closed his eyes and laid his head back on the chair.

Once we had finished two waters each and had picked over the best parts of the cheese plate, he was feeling better.

"Jerome, I am going to need a favor."

"Sure, Larry, what can I do for you?"

"I want you to hold my hand."

"Here? In this frou-frou place?"

"NO," I laughed. "On the flight. Just once or twice."

"I never thought you, of all people, would be afraid to fly."

"It is not that." I paused to think. "Remember how the attendant kept staring at me? When we checked in? She gave me the creeps. But if she thinks we are a couple, then she will leave me alone, I hope."

"Larry, she was gorgeous! And that is called flirting. It is what people do. You should be used to it by now."

"Why would you say that?"

"You are quite handsome. Has no one ever told you that?"

"Just my ex. He was a jerk. I knew he wanted something, or more money, when he started in with the compliments."

'You are what, 6-2? You have all your hair, and an awesome body. It is not like you are a stout guy like me, with no hair on my head, and a developing potbelly."

"I have told you before that I think you are gorgeous. My sister says you look just like my father." I regretted saying it as soon as it came out of my mouth.

"What? Really?" He asked.

"Yes, she looked at you on the security cameras in the lobby. I cannot defend her sneakiness, but I like to think that she was worried about me. Or at least curious."

"How old do you think I am?"

"I don't know, maybe 45?" I hedged my bet with an intended compliment.

"I just hit 38. Do you want to see my driver's license?"

"No, I believe you. But that means my crush is gone. I was looking for a father figure, and you are barely as old as my brother."

"How old are you?"

"I just turned 34 in March."

"You have two university degrees and three decades on the planet, yet you don't realize that you turn heads when you are in the room? The attendant didn't even look at me. I could have used someone else's identification to check in and she would not have noticed."

"Oh, okay. I had not experienced that level of attention before. Perhaps I am just in a fog."

"I guess I will let that slide for now. And if you really need a father figure, I am happy to roll up my sleeves, and take you down a few notches."

"Now you are just teasing me." I adjusted the fly on my slacks as I felt some stirring.

He smiled broadly. "I may be short and stout, like a teapot, but am quite strong, and I can catch you, if I have to. Just remember that."

I laughed nervously. "Perhaps once we get home. It might be a bit awkward here in the lounge, okay?"

"Sure. It' s a deal." He replied with a wild grin on his face.

We boarded the flight and settled into our first-class seats. Once we were under the watchful eye of Jacqueline, I made a point of holding Jerome's hand on the arm rest. She must have noticed because she did not flirt for the remainder of the flight. Jerome, however, pretended to have trouble with his seatbelt. When she helped him adjust it, he got a good look at her ample cleavage, so I knew he was still playing for the other team.

Meeting Resistance

We landed and got our bags off of the carrier belt. I could feel that he was getting antsy, as he would not make eye contact with me. I turned and began strolling for the door, waiting for some indication that he was going to get honest with me. I had not gone three steps when I heard him.

"Hey! How are you getting home?" he asked.

I stopped and turned around to face him.

"I parked in the deck. My car will get me there, if I remembered to fill up with gas before I parked it."

"Oh. I took a cab over here."

"Jerome, would you like to ride with me? I won't charge but half the going rate for a cab."

"Sure! That would be great," he replied, smiling for the first time since we got off the plane.

"You have cash, right? I don't want any of that foreign currency."

"Will you take a postdated check?"

"From you? I don't know." I turned and started walking again. He caught up to me.

"Perhaps we could take it out in trade, then?" He said with a devilish smile.

Traffic was light. In just under thirty minutes, I drove directly to his house with no input from my passenger. I pulled into the driveway and stopped. Jerome did not move. I waited for a moment, but he was frozen in his seat. I reached over and put my hand on his knee.

"Were you going to invite me in, or do I have to kiss myself goodbye?"

"Larry, that is not funny. Please be patient. I cannot go in there right now."

"I don't understand – don't you feel well?"

"No, I feel a bit queasy. I am not prepared to deal with what I left behind."

"What do you mean?" I asked, understanding his dilemma as soon as I finished my question.

"Could you come inside, just for a few minutes?" he asked, timidly.

"Jerome, look at me." I squeezed his knee.

He turned his head. His eyes were moist, but he was still in control of his emotions.

"I will come in and stay as long as you need me to. I am sorry, I had forgotten all about...how you had left things."

"Thank you, Larry."

We got out of the car, and I grabbed his bag from the trunk while he shuffled his feet up to the front door. His keys were in his left hand, and he had his briefcase in his right.

The door swung open, and all the mail was on the floor. He stepped around it and walked into the main room. I looked around, not knowing what he was surveying. I put his bag down, took a few steps forward and stopped next to him, meeting his shoulder with my upper arm. I reached down and took his left hand.

"Talk to me, Jerome."

"It's just that...I did not expect to be back here. I had said goodbye and left for good. There are some letters on the dining room table that I cannot bear to think about. Would you shred them for me, please?"

I listened for more, but he sniffled. I pulled his hand, turning him toward me. I wrapped my arms around him, and he cried for quite a long time.

The light was fading, and my knees were locked from standing in one place. I pulled him over to the sofa, and we sat down, side by side. He took my hand.

I now understood why he had been so hesitant to come home. My ego took a small blow, but I also understood that he had a lot of issues, and many of them were tied up in this house. It was the home where he had lived with his wife.

"Larry?"

"Yes, Jerome?"

"I don't know what to do."

"I am not sure I understand, but we can take it one step at a time."

"Okay he said quietly. He squeezed my hand. "Thank you."

I waited for a few minutes. He had stopped sniffling. The afternoon was becoming evening.

"So, Jerome, what would you like to do now? Are you hungry? Thirsty? Need a bathroom break?"

"No, I am okay for now. How about you?"

"I am good. Did you want to slip out of your clothes, or are you just a tease when we are in a hotel room?"

He finally smiled.

"Would you mind if I got a glass of water and turned some lights on?"

"No, go ahead. I guess we have to get back into a home routine," he said.

I got up and turned two table lamps on. Then I went in search of the kitchen. I returned shortly thereafter with two glasses of water. I was pleased that he had at least gotten up. He was sorting the mail into two piles, just as I do when I have a week's worth to review. There was one pile for catalogs and junk. The other was bills and notices.

Suddenly, he gasped and sat down on the floor where he had been standing. I put the water glasses on coasters and went over to him. Standing next to him so that my foot almost touched his thigh, he reached out and put his hand around my calf. It was then I realized what he had found.

The postcard from the hotel we had stayed in was in his hand. It was a night shot, and there was a lovely crescent moon over the roof. I had written on the back, in my best handwriting, "I did not have to go up to the roof to view the most beautiful moon that I have ever seen."

"Larry?" He croaked.

"Yes, Jerome?"

"When did you send this postcard?"

"The morning we checked out of the conference hotel."

"I simply cannot believe it. Nor can I believe that you are single!"

127

"You say that again, and you are going to regret it, buster."

We eased into the evening. I had already decided that I would have to stay over. When he went upstairs to unpack, I went back out to my car and got my bag. I left my suitcase in the foyer until he was ready to tell me more. I could hear water running and guessed that he was taking a shower.

There were three letters on the table. One for Mandy, who I assumed was his sister. Another had 'Sherman' written in neat script in the center and the third was blank. All three were sealed.

As a lawyer, I had handled documents that were extremely sensitive for the parties involved. This was a different level of intensity, and intimacy. As much as I wanted to save them for him, or even read them myself, I did exactly what he had asked. I found the shredder in his home office and fed each one through the crosscut blades.

I got some dry goods out of the pantry and whipped up a quick dinner of spaghetti with marinara sauce. I pulled the only bottle of red wine out of the rack and popped the cork. By the time he showed up in the doorway, dinner was on the table, the glasses were full, and I had some music playing for the meal.

I thought he had put on a nightshirt. It turned out to be a very baggy, extremely long t-shirt. It was a sexy look for him. But then again, I could not think of one that would not be appealing, in my biased viewpoint.

"You did not have to dress up for me, I have gotten accustomed to seeing your furry skin, at all times of the day."

He forced a smile. "I did not want to send the wrong message."

"I will still be a gentleman – even in the presence of an irresistible sculpture."

"Thank you for doing all of this."

"I was getting hungry. The last thing I ate was that cheese plate in the airport."

"How long do you think you can stay?"

I put my hand on my chin and looked up at the ceiling. "I will have to leave here no later than 8:45."

He glanced over my head at the clock on the wall. It was half past seven. He frowned, with his forehead furrowing worriedly.

"I meant Monday morning, silly. I have a meeting in my office at nine."

His smile returned. We sat down to eat, sipping the wine like adults, and slurping the spaghetti like kids. We finished the bottle of wine but not the pasta. I put the dishes on the counter and followed him into the living room. He sat down on the sofa and pulled his legs up beside himself.

I took the recliner across from him and met his eyes.

"Are you going to be okay?" I asked.

"Sure. It may take some time, but I am definitely on the path back to where I need to be."

"Good. You know, you can talk to me about anything. We don't have to have secrets if you need help...with anything. And I really mean anything."

"I know. I cannot express how grateful I am to you...for everything you have done. I just feel a little guilty, sometimes, taking so much from you with being able to give anything back."

"Well, maybe we can level the playing field, and you will not feel so beholden."

"Just how would we do that?" He asked.

"I need some more truth serum, first. I will be right back."

I got up, went back to the kitchen, and pulled a bottle of scotch out of the cupboard. I returned with two glasses and the bottle. I plopped down on the sofa right next to him. I certainly had his curiosity peaked, so I did not leave him hanging for long.

"Jerome, I was very nearly in the same position as you about six months ago."

"Really? That is hard to believe. You have everything so...together."

"I am going to share the details. Stop me when you have heard enough."

I poured us each a tall drink, replaced the cap, and put the bottle on the floor at our feet. I sipped a lot more than I normally would, but I needed to overcome the sudden nervousness that I felt. I took a deep breath and started.

"I was in a relationship. It was one that I had convinced myself would be the love of my life. We lasted for about eighteen months, and then one night he left. When I finally tracked him down, I discovered that he was living with someone else."

I drank more scotch.

"I had met the other guy around town a few times, and never thought twice about their friendship. Suddenly all the pieces fell into place, and I realized that I had been bankrolling their affair, while I was waiting at home for Bernard to make it big on the art circuit.

"It is not just that he cheated. It was the layers upon layers of dishonesty that kept me invested in 'us' when he had never been serious about anything but the paycheck that I brought home. I was devastated. I hated myself, I despised him, and I contemplated revenge on his new love interest.

"I called Sarah. She came up and helped me straighten it all out. I did not seek vengeance, as much as justice. I called a few friends in the business and had his next few art shows canceled. I had paid the deposits and arranged for the sponsorship underwriting, so it was within my right to do so.

"He threatened to sue, and I urged him to do so. He had no resources, and I have a few contacts from law school that would have provided me with all the ammunition I needed to defend myself. It was not until he threatened to blackmail me that I caved.

"He knew that I could lose my job, and it would be very difficult to find another in this state, considering how the bar works."

I stopped to drink some more of the scotch and grimaced when it burned my throat.

He took a polite sip but was not drinking as much as I was trying to guzzle.

"We settled out of court, to keep the matter private. I spent most of my savings, but I walked away with my dignity, my job, and my reputation as a lawyer."

"Larry, what in the world could he blackmail you with? Certainly, everyone at work knows you are gay. And would anyone care if they didn't?"

"It was much more than that. I was asked to leave my last job. I was incredibly lucky to find the one I have now. To get it, I exhausted all the favors I had banked over the years. I took this job at far less money than I had made before, but it was my last chance to find work in this state."

"Gosh, it sounds serious." He gulped a large swig from his glass.

"Yeah, I can definitely say that it was one of my darkest hours."

I finished the scotch in my glass. He did the same and held it up for a refill. I poured more for each of us but did not match the previous volume. I was already feeling it.

"I had a job as a corporate lawyer for a large conglomerate. As I moved up in the hierarchy, I was increasingly distracted by a particular man. I really thought he was interested in me at one point, so I put out signals to let him know I was interested in him. When he did not respond, I got remarkably close to breaking the law. I followed him, watched him from a distance, and made a nuisance of myself when I felt that I could justify talking to him."

I had another swig of the whisky, finishing my last swallow. I put the glass on the floor next to my foot.

"At the very least, I was guilty of criminal trespass. In the worst-case scenario, I could have been arrested and charged with stalking, which is a felony. I was lucky to escape with my freedom, much less with my license to practice law."

"Golly, Larry. I certainly did not..."

"Nor did I, Jerome."

"I guess we all have our weaknesses."

"You know the funny thing about it? He was not half the man that you are, nor as attractive. He had some good qualities, but nothing compared to the man I have gotten to know this week." My breath hitched as the tears came.

"Larry?" he asked.

I began to sob, letting the alcohol take away my shame, and my dignity. He moved over and put shoulder up against mine. He took my hand and held it in both of his.

New Routine

I awoke early the next morning with a pounding headache, in a room and a bed that I did not recognize. Once I could blink enough to get my eyes clear, I could see the familiar shape next to me on the bed. I slowly got out of bed, trying to let him sleep. As I pushed myself up to a standing position, I heard his muffled voice, talking into the pillow.

"The bathroom is the first door on the left," was all he mumbled.

I was still a bit drunk and stumbled into the dark hallway before I made the turn. It was not until I was finished that I realized that I was naked. While I often slept that way at home, I had no recollection of how I had gotten that way, or when. I found a plastic cup in the bathroom and drank about a pint of water from the tap.

I went back to bed and lay down on top of the covers. I had no nausea, but I knew the headache would be with me for a while. I closed my eyes. The bed moved slightly and then I felt Jerome's hand in mine. I could not help but smile.

We stayed in bed well past sunrise. He curled up behind me at one point, laying his arm across my midsection. His furry belly tickled my back, and I could feel the heat rolling off him. I was too hungover to get excited, but it did help to know that I had not alienated him with my drunkalogue.

I was the first one to sit up, but not by much. Jerome heaved himself up and got to the bathroom before I did, laughing a bit at his speed and knowledge of the obstacles in the room. He left me in the bathroom alone and went back to the bedroom. When I passed through the threshold, he stepped up and embraced me.

"Now, I think I have returned the favor. I listened to your drunken, tearful rambling last night. I am still your friend, and I do still love you. Okay?"

"I am scared to ask what I said last night. But thank you, and I love you, too," I responded.

He released his grip and broke away from me by one step, keeping his hands on my elbows and looking into my eyes. "Now, I would like to get you some breakfast, and we can talk about where we are heading with the research for my brother. Lastly, I think you should do something about your unhealthy, but completely understandable, OCD streak over these stocky bald men."

He stepped into a pair of boxer shorts and pulled a pair of mismatched socks on his feet. "There, I am dressed for Saturday, in my typical three-piece suit!" He stated.

"While I admire your attention to detail, for me, you are overdressed." I smiled as I replied.

I looked around until I found my boxers. I stepped into them and added a t-shirt for the chilly air on my shoulders. I followed him down the stairs, holding the handrail so I would not tumble down. I was still not very steady on my feet after all the alcohol.

He started the coffee, and I rummaged through the pantry. All I could find was some instant oatmeal. I pulled out two packets and heated the water in the tea kettle. He got out some cereal bowls, added spoons, and put them next to the stove.

"I have a lot of questions...about last night," I stated cautiously.

"Let me see... you told me about how you lost your last job and how you secured the current one. You went into graphic detail about your last boyfriend, and the messy breakup after. You got kind of irritated with me and tried to leave. I calmed you down, and assured you that I still cared about you, despite the ugly tears, drunk ramblings, and defeatist attitude."

"Wow. I am so embarrassed."

"Then I turned off the lights, led you upstairs and convinced you to stay with me. You let me undress you, which was a first for me, at least with a grown man. I allowed you to spoon with me after we got in bed, initially. I had no worries that it would go any further because you were snoring before I could even get comfortable."

"I am humbled by your honesty, and the lack of shame I displayed when I drank too much." I told him.

"I can say, if it had been our first date, I might have been calling for a restraining order today. But you are safe for now, as long as we keep you sober during the daylight hours."

We both laughed, even if it made me uncomfortable to look him in the eye.

"Well, I won't make any empty promises about 'never again' but at least I have no fear now that you know some of my darkest secrets, and yet you have let me stay in your home."

"I have also learned not to threaten to take you over my knee. I have never seen such an instantaneous physical response. Talk about a tent pole!"

I could feel my face redden as he talked. "I am sorry, I cannot help it."

"It is fine, really. You already knew that I have the same reaction, so let's keep that as our little secret, okay?"

"I am willing to put it behind us." I grinned with the pun.

We dug into our oatmeal. It was easily the most comfortable, if not the tastiest meal I had ever consumed. We sat quietly, sipping coffee, and waiting for our hot cereal to settle our stomachs.

"So, tell me, Jerome, what are your plans for the next two days?"

"I have some laundry to do, and I want to put my bags away from the trip. I suppose I need to go to the grocery store. You have seen that I have no fresh food in the fridge. I hesitate to stop at the liquor store, as you might stay over again. Especially if I must undress you each time. I am not quite ready to give up my status as a heterosexual he-man."

"Just how long do you plan to use last night's behavior as a weapon?" I asked, with a smirk.

"At least until the next time, or I when finally have to take you over my knee to subdue you."

I blushed and he laughed. I joined him in the laughter after I saw that it was easier to go along than to protest, especially with the residual headache.

"Okay, I guess I need to do the same tasks. Should I go home and take care of my chores?"

He looked hurt, but only for an instant. "Can't we do them together?"

I paused to take in what he was suggesting.

"Of course, we can. Let's make a list!" I retorted.

Our near-constant companionship began with an extended trip to the grocery store, my house, and the locksmith shop to get extra keys made. I made dinner again that night, but with far more ingredients, and in the comfort of my own kitchen. We cut back on the alcohol intake, but we continued to share stories and spoke in a candor that I never expected to find with a man that I was not dating.

Work, Life Balanced

The return to work that Monday was a shock for both of us. We agreed not to have lunch together our first day back, but we sent text messages to each other all day like teenagers. It was almost a given that we would have dinner that night, at one of our respective houses.

From my last meeting of the day, at five o'clock, I sent him a text: *Dinner out tonight - my treat?*

He replied from the parking lot: *Pick you up at six.*

I went home, sorted the mail, and changed from a suit to jeans and a rugby shirt. He pulled into the driveway on time. I hopped in and smiled. It felt good to have a pal.

"What a great day!" He said as he backed out into the residential street.

"That was easy for you to say, I was in meetings from nine until five. I almost ate a blank page from my notebook at lunchtime."

"Sorry to hear that. I had a team meeting with my project group. They finished an extraordinary number of tasks last week, and we are on track to finish early. That means bonuses all around."

"Perhaps that means you should be buying dinner, then, Jerome."

"No way, I was invited here."

He had driven to his favorite chain steak house and parked. The hostess seated us at a high-top near the bar. There were several ladies at a nearby table, and a couple at one table further along. Jerome picked the seat with the best view of all of them.

"Have you not learned anything from my bad example? You can get yourself in a lot of trouble by staring too long at the wrong person."

"The key, Larry, is to look away just as they catch you, but close your eyelids to hide the motion. I have years of practice, and I have not gotten into trouble yet."

"Those are famous last words, my friend. Your time will come!" I warned.

The server took our drink orders while we looked over the menus.

"My taste buds are saying 'big steak, baked potato, and apple pie' but my conscience, and recent splurges last week, are leaning toward a salad without dressing," Jerome confessed.

"I find I burn enough calories in the gym to eat what I want, most of the time. I just cannot do it every meal."

"How does that affect your waistline?"

"You tell me, Jerome. You are the first man to see it in months," I laughed.

He grimaced. "Let's change the subject, at least while we are here, please."

The waitress came back with our drinks. We both ordered the smallest steaks on the menu but went all-in with the loaded baked potatoes. After she left, we agreed not to have pie.

Jerome started looking around as I was trying to have a conversation with him, over the music. I gave up and just hummed along with the pop tune while he surfed the crowd for eye candy.

There was no one in the restaurant I would look at twice, except for the guy I was with.

He, on the other hand, fixated on one woman. His eyes were locked in place, and I could not get his attention. Fortunately, the steaks came out and broke the spell. Happy hour ended and the manager turned the music volume down as more families came in for the dinner rush.

"Are you enjoying the steak or the scenery more?" I asked.

"What? Oh, that. I had spotted a great gal with commendable assets."

"I think you are skating on the edge of disaster when you do that. Is she in the group of women or the one with the gangster-looking man?"

"I had not even noticed him, but now that you say it, yeah he is kind of scary."

I turned around to look at the two of them. I locked eyes with the man as he caught me staring at her, and Jerome's fixation. I spun around and went back to my steak. Jerome laughed at first, but then his face froze.

"They are coming over here!" He hissed urgently.

"Oh, shit. Now what do we do?" I whispered at him.

Thirty seconds later, the gangster and his girl were standing next to our table. My hands were shaking. I could barely hold my silverware, so I put my hands flat on the table.

"You boys enjoying the show with my girl? Maybe you should have better manners in public." He said with a gruff attitude and a heavy New York accent.

"I am not sure what you mean, sir," Jerome attempted. He had put his utensils down, as well.

141

"You two low-lifes been staring at my gal's chest since you got here. I don't appreciate it, and I am asking you to stop... now."

Jerome reached over the table and put his hand over mine. The couple scrutinizing us could plainly see the gesture.

"I am sorry if that was what you thought, but we are here, together. I don't have much interest in your lovely lady, but I admired the color of her top. That is currently the hottest color in fashion."

"I think that is the newest Versace, isn't it, dear?" I added.

The man made a face that would scare most hard-boiled police officers, but the lady laughed. We both kept our smiles, hiding the urge to run like kids from a monster.

"Keep your eyes to yourself, and just maybe you won't have any more trouble, got it?"

"Certainly, sir," I said. "I am sorry there was a misunderstanding. Perhaps we could pay for your meal as our apology?"

"You can do that. And I just might forget about this insult." He turned and walked away. The lady winked at me and then followed him.

We finished our steaks quietly and then got the check. Jerome went to the bathroom, and I waited for the waitress. They both arrived together.

"I think we have a problem. The man in the corner," I turned, pointed, and then waved with the check. The mobster waved back. "Has offered to pay for our meals. While we accept that, I don't want him to think we skimped on dessert just to make it a cheap meal, so I'm going to give you the tip, and what we would have spent on dessert, okay? Just please, don't tell him, because I think it would hurt his feelings."

"Sure, hon," she said, taking the twenty.

Jerome and I got out of there and nearly burned rubber leaving the parking lot. When we were sure that we had gotten far enough away, he pulled over and we had a howling good laugh.

"Did you see the makeup smeared on her face? I know teenage girls that could do a better job with cosmetics," I stated.

"I never looked at her face," he admitted, and we started roaring with laughter again.

"Please, stop. I would hate to throw up my free steak with all of this fun."

"Yeah, my stomach hurts. I feel like I have been doing sit-ups," he said.

Once we got ourselves under control, he drove me home. There was no need for me to invite him in. He got out of the car when I did.

"Now we can't go back there for months!" He said when we got inside.

"Nah, that guy doesn't live around here. He might have given Lana a hard time about the bill, but he would not stick around a little town like this for long. There are too many police officers around."

"Lana?" He asked.

"Our waitress. Her name tag was on her visor."

"I never looked at her hat," he said, and we collapsed on the sofa in hysterics again.

We calmed down and composed ourselves.

"Jerome?"

"Yep?"

"Was that the first time you have ever been busted for looking?"

"As an adult, yes. Most women won't complain, and I try not to focus on the gals with a date. But sometimes, I just cannot help it."

"I think we need to get you into rehab for that."

"There is no cure. I would have to go blind or die before I could quit."

"We could have died tonight," I said. "But really, I worry about you. I also want things to go well for you when you call the woman you met in New Orleans."

"How so?"

"Even if you are polite with her, you cannot look around like that at other women. It will hurt her feelings or turn her off completely. She will see you as a letch."

"How would you know?" he challenged.

"I was the letch, remember? It could end badly."

"Oh, right. I guess I need to do something."

"We could still try the conversion thing. Get you a spot to play on my team."

"Ha, ha. No chance. We would have eloped already if I thought I could make you my one and only."

I reached over and squeezed his hand. "Thanks."

"My stomach aches from the laughter. I regret the steak, but the punchline made the calories worth it." He said.

We sat in silence for a few minutes.

"Well, I got some stuff to do. You wanna just hang out here?" I asked.

"Nah, I should go home. I have not looked at any of the mail that came in last week."

"Okay. Do you want to have dinner tomorrow? We could talk about our strategy for Sherman."

"Sure, but we should lay low. I will fix dinner for you at my place, okay?"

He got up to go. I stood, took him in my arms and gave him a gentle hug. Neither one of our stomachs could handle a full press after the heavy food and the Olympic level rounds of laughter.

New Ventures

While I developed strategies for approaching Sherman, Jerome had started an online text conversation with his love interest from New Orleans. Abigail was quite the typist, and I sometimes looked over his shoulder and gave him some pointers. I became his relationship advisor, even though I was not in one.

About a month after we had returned from New Orleans, we had settled into a quiet, but predictable routine. Three or four nights a week we had dinner together. We spent all day on Saturday or Sunday parked on the couch at one of our houses, and the other day we did personal errands and chores, on our own.

I got Jerome into a daily gym routine, with rotations through the large muscle groups and cardio three times a week. He transformed his body from a cuddly, squeezable bear to a rock-hard slab of muscle that got more attractive each time I massaged him. I had to cut him back to one shiatsu session a work week, and one on the weekend, or we would have spent all of our free time together with him on the professional table I kept in the trunk of my car.

I presented my plans for contacting Sherman one Sunday afternoon. I wanted to be more circumspect and do my best not to alienate either of them or make him angrier with my chosen approach. Although he said he could be patient, I could tell that he wanted results, and speed.

"Okay, Jerome. Here are the scenarios I have put together. Ready?"

"Yes, fire away," he said, settling in next to me on his couch.

"One. I reach out through social media and try to be friends."

"No, that would be kind of creepy, given the distance from here to Chapel Hill."

"Okay, Two. I reach out through professional networking. Maybe I can find a common link or contact."

"And if he sees your profile? You might spook him with the law degree and experience. I would never call a lawyer back that reached out to me. You can't trust those snakes."

I glared at him sideways. He refused to wither under my stare. "Remember who is on your side at this point, you snake in the grass."

"What are you going to do? Rough me up on the massage table, tough guy?"

"I could just withhold my services. Let you pay for the massage from a professional."

"That might hurt you more than me, but okay, I apologize," he smiled broadly.

I had to smirk. He was right, of course. "Accepted." I took a sip of water. "Ready for three?"

"Sure. Let it fly."

"I stalk him, but not in a creepy way. More like a private investigator would go about it. I trace his routine and try to make a chance meeting pay off as the first contact."

"How would you even do that? Wouldn't that take weeks of following him around?"

"No, not really. But if he looks just like you, I cannot say that I would mind following him around, if you get my meaning," I snickered.

"You are just a perv. I know hard-up old men that are not as lecherous!"

"We all have our talents. There are methods to track what people do, especially if they broadcast their activities online. I know one website that aggregates all social media feeds for a person. The pattern shows itself within a week or two of postings, and I never had to leave my sofa."

"That reminds me, I need to close all of my accounts," he said sarcastically.

"I already know your patterns. I can even predict when you will ogle a woman in public."

"Let's change the subject. I am still afraid to go back to that steak place."

"Okay, number four. I can reach out through the normal dating sites. There are apps, want ads, in-search-of postings, and the like. I could narrow down his characteristics to the point that he would be one of few men that would fit the profile."

"How long would that take?"

"Forever, if he is not looking."

Jerome sighed. "Is there a number five?"

"There sure is. Five. I reach out as a new business proposition. Perhaps go through his subordinates and keep the story going until I reach him in the chain. That is the riskiest, because people get angry if they are being fished. The lost time chasing my new account could cost them profits."

"Yeah, I don't like that one at all," he stated.

"Ready for six?"

"This is getting complicated."

"Not really, we just have to pick the best one and pursue it until we are sure the scenario is played out, or he says no."

"What is six, then?"

"Six. I go to Chapel Hill for a few weekends. Hang out in his neighborhood. Check out the local shops, stay on the lookout for someone almost as gorgeous as you."

"Almost? Why would you even say that? We are identical."

"The scars you mentioned. And I doubt his trainer is as hard on him as yours has been these last few weeks."

We both laughed.

"How long would that take?"

"It would not matter. You promised to pay all of my expenses." I cackled as I finished the statement.

"Jerk!"

"Yeah, I don't think so. I am helping you, remember?"

"Big help you are, spending my money in frou-frou coffee shops."

"Jerome, if he is anything like you in personality, he will have a pattern that I would catch in a day, two at the most."

"Am I that predictable?"

"Yes, in the best possible way. I am the same way - I love my routine. I only break it when I am on vacation. Or sleeping in the same bed as a naked straight guy in New Orleans."

He shoved my shoulder with his hand. We both laughed.

"Is there a seven?"

"Of course. Seven. I will contact your sister. Work through similar scenarios as in one or two. Social Media friending, or 'chance' encounter in her town."

"Mandy is on the road a lot, and she does not respond to many requests. I think it's because of her career. She is also incredibly careful about social media."

"Okay. Eight."

"More? You are exhausting me!" He exclaimed.

"Yes, eight. We craft a very personal, poignant letter, explaining your heartfelt sadness at the situation, taking full responsibility, and offering to make amends in any way he would like." I looked sideways for his reaction. "We mail it to his home address."

"Why would that work at all? He may just throw the envelope away."

"It would be my handwriting on the envelope, my return address, and nothing more in clues until he opened it."

"Then what? He would see who it was and toss it."

"Not necessarily. In the letter you explain that you have a new friend, ME, and we include a picture of the two of us. Arm-in-arm, big smiles, with a pride flag somewhere in the shot."

"I don't know about that one."

"If we can capture his interest with the picture, perhaps he will read enough to see that you have changed."

"That is my least favorite. Is that all of them?"

"Yeah, that is all I have for now. Want to see my spreadsheet?"

"No, that would be too much like work. Can we rank them first before you start?"

"Sure. Good idea."

"I forget the numbers. I like the dating one the best."

"If I approach this as a potential date, he may shut me down after the bait-and-switch. I would eventually have to pivot from romance to contacting you," I announced.

"I don't see how he could be angry. He is single, and you are quite handsome. He would never turn you down."

"Thank you, but suppose he is angry at either, or both of us? We could push him further away, and that would not bring Mandy into our side of the argument."

"Okay. Then I would vote for the private eye tactic. Figure out his movements in a pattern, then swoop in and make the connection."

"That was my favorite as well. He won't know who I am. If I maintain a low profile and not see him too often, it could be the best way to surprise him in a crowded venue."

"When will you start?"

"I could start if I had some food on my stomach. Feel like going out for a steak?" I asked, coyly.

He made a face and growled at me. "Perhaps it is time I take you down a few notches!"

"I am ready, any time," I stated, and then smiled impishly.

"Never mind! It would not be as effective if you are looking forward to it."

We went out to brunch and mapped out the strategy. I had flashbacks to Café du Monde and the powdered sugar snowstorm we created with our laughter as we initially plotted the attack in New Orleans.

The days and weeks flew by in our bromance. I secretly dreaded that it all would end when I finally got through to Sherman. Jerome had other plans in mind.

The Date

Jerome endured three first dates with me before his actual first date with Abigail. I coached, corrected, and coaxed him into being the ideal gentleman for the lady who had been a reigning beauty queen.

We started with clothing and accessories. He had to look the part of a confident, successful businessman, without displaying brand labels. For the season, which was still quite warm for the fall, I picked a light-colored silk tweed sport coat, dark, short sleeve polo shirt, and tan gabardine slacks that contoured well to his rounded backside. The colors all worked well together, and he took an oath not to remove the coat. That was our compromise for the long-sleeve shirt that I had originally chosen for him.

We dressed him up several evenings in a row to get him accustomed to wearing the heavier layers. I even made him do it at my house, where it was not chilled to arctic temperatures. It was important that he looked at ease and comfortable in the clothes, so she did not notice them. I also reminded him that the clothes could not look brand-new pressed, or it would appear as if he had only bought them for the date.

Next, we covered etiquette and manners. He was always to open the car door for her and wait until she was completely settled in before closing it gently, but firmly, enough to catch on the first try. I had him practice with his car, but without me in the passenger seat. I knew I could only push him so far.

He was ready with a golf umbrella that would protect her from any errant drops if there was rain. He planned and memorized the trip from her home to the restaurant, mapping several routes for contingencies. The establishment was chosen for its renowned gourmet, but modestly sized, meals.

I pulled a few strings, through my sister Sarah, and got him a reservation for the perfect table. They would have a table for two with gentle lighting, reduced ambient noise, and out of the main pathways for restaurant foot traffic. Sarah made suggestions for wines, courses, and conversation for the lulls between them. I coached him how to navigate multiple pieces of cutlery, and how to manage the various stemware used for water or wine.

He got tired of holding the door, my chair, and even my purse, to the point of tantrums, but I endured, and he eventually made it all part of his muscle memory repertoire. I think he carried a grudge for a week, even if it achieved his goal of the perfect date.

When the night finally arrived, he showed no signs of anxiety. I offered to keep my distance as he primped for the big event, but he wanted me there to check him over and give him the pep talk that I had perfected. It was not difficult for me, as he looked scrumptious. Gerald McRaney himself would have paled by comparison, Major Dad marine uniform or not.

For me, the worst part of the entire evening started when he pulled out of the driveway at six. As a surprise, I had placed a small bouquet of flowers on the seat for him to deliver to Abigail. Then I paced frantically for the three hours he was gone. I could not decide whether I should meet him at his house afterward or wait for him to call me. I was hysterical with worry and angst. He was as cool as the proverbial cucumber.

I rushed home and took care of some chores, and then debated with myself on where I should be for the remainder of the evening. I finally decided to give him his space, and stayed at home while he wined and dined his dream gal. It was the longest night of my life, but in a happy, nervously hopeful way that bolstered me.

My phone beeped at 10:05. I read the screen without touching it, not wanting him to know that I had seen the message the instant it had come in. The phone had been clutched in my hand for the last hour.

He had sent a one-line command: *Wake up. Will be at your house at 10:30.*

I laughed out loud. I could not have slept at all, waiting for the report on this date. I went downstairs, turned on lights, got two tumblers of ice water, and tried not to stare out the front window in anticipation. As I heard his car pull into my driveway, I suppressed the urge to bolt for the threshold.

When he opened the door, it was a stage entrance that would have earned an Oscar. He closed the door behind him, slunk in, and then pulled me into a bear hug. There were no words, just his breathing. My heart fell to the floor.

"I am in love. And I am terrified," he stated in a stage whisper.

"What?" I shouted. "You had me believing there had been a dating disaster!"

He stepped back, putting his hands on my elbows. His eyes were moist. "No, I was just so overwhelmed with emotion that I had to share it with you."

"Well, thanks for letting me down easy, pal. Now, tell me all about it."

"Okay, give me some room," he said.

"You got it."

"I arrived at her house two minutes before the appointed time. I pulled into her driveway and then walked confidently up to the front door. The flowers you left in my car were behind my back just in case she had peeked out the window."

"Good move!" I said.

"Her next-door neighbor let me in. Abigail was still getting ready. Her friend took the flowers and put them in a vase while we waited. She was a full ten minutes late, just as you predicted."

"She was building suspense. I would not be surprised to learn the friend had texted the details of your outfit while she got the vase."

He smiled. "She did. Now let me finish, please!" he snapped.

"Okay."

"Abigail came down the stairs like a bride in a Hollywood movie making an entrance. We both gasped at her beauty and poise. I did not notice at first, but she wore exceptionally low heels. When I kissed her cheek to greet her, she did not have to tilt her head. We were the same height!"

He started pacing around the living room. I sat down on the sofa and pointed to the waters. He nodded, but then continued.

"Her neighbor offered to lock up, so Abigail took my arm, and we walked out to the car. I opened her door and did all the right things to make her comfortable. When we tried to get to the restaurant, an accident forced me into the alternate route. I cannot even remember what we chatted about on the way. I think she was letting me concentrate on the road. I drove as if I were taking my first driving test. It paid off, and she complimented me on my caution."

He took a sip from the tumbler, and then furrowed his brow. "She started to get suspicious when we got to the restaurant."

"'The waiting list for this place is months long! How in the world did you get us a table here?' she asked me."

"'I had a friend make some calls. I must admit I had never heard of the place. I guess I owe him now!' I responded."

"We used the valet service, and I opened her door, again, before I would even hand the keys over. The maître d' showed us to our table, and I got her chair for her. She definitely noticed the prime location of our seats but said nothing."

He paced some more as I fidgeted, waiting for more of the story.

"The meal went like clockwork. I made some recommendations for courses, we eventually chose the same specials, and I picked a wine that complimented it all. I insisted the sommelier and waiter try the wine with us, which carried the good will throughout the meal, and reduced the amount that we had to drink to finish the bottle. They poured me a second glass, but I never finished it, just to be safe."

He stopped pacing, smiled, and then wiped his eyes with his handkerchief.

"What, Jerome? Tell me!"

"She is an absolute delight to converse with. I heard about her pageant career, her difficult marriage, and subsequent divorce from a man she now calls her friend. She was never coy, or shy, about telling me things that many other people would have withheld, especially on a first date. When she excused herself to powder her nose, she was flabbergasted that I stood up with her."

He took a sip of water, drawing out the story and keeping me on edge.

"I suspected that she was calling her neighbor to report in, but I did not mind. I was smitten and having a great time. When she returned, we had a sumptuous meal, with witty conversation and relaxed demeanors. I really thought we were both having a good time. She disappeared again just before we left, and I kept to all of my assignments, standing, holding her chair, and waiting for her to speak."

He took a reckless swig of water, splashing some down his placket.

"When we got in the car, I offered to take her directly home, or on a slightly-longer, but scenic drive. She giggled at the invitation but accepted the latter without hesitating. As I drove along, I told her about my failed marriage, and hesitancy to get back into the dating world. I confessed that I was not looking when I found the most beautiful woman in the world. It was at a dive bar in New Orleans. I could tell that she was smiling, but I also felt her suspicion. The drive ended at her house, and I walked her to the door."

He cleared his throat. "She invited me in. I accepted but remained standing. I declined the nightcap but asked if I could kiss her before I headed home. There was a look on her face that I could not interpret."

He took a deep breath and then let it out slowly.

"She asked me if I had been coached. She had exchanged texts with her friends, and they had determined that I was too unsophisticated to accomplish all of this on my own. At first, I was hurt. But then, I was emboldened. I told her the truth. My friend, the best friend I could ever have, had put me through a boot camp of sorts. I told her that our date was so important to me because she was special. I did not want to step once out of place and risk losing her attention."

He stopped again, wiping his eyes.

"She said that for years, she had been waiting for a gentleman to come along that could sweep her off to happiness. But that a handsome prince had arrived and had stolen her heart before she could think clearly enough to put up any defenses."

He wiped his eyes again. I had to wipe mine.

"She kissed me full on the lips and I felt like a schoolboy, with a rush of warmth and emotion as I have never felt before. I said goodnight and waved as I got into my car. I drove two blocks up the road and then sent two text messages. One to you, and one to the florist, confirming the flower delivery for tomorrow."

He collapsed in the armchair.

"Wait, what? More flowers?" I asked.

"Yes. One dozen red roses, with a card: Thank you for the best night of my life, so far."

"You wolf, you! Way to go, Casanova!"

He beamed with pride.

"Now what?" I asked.

"I don't know, I am too excited to sleep."

"That is what cold showers are for, buddy."

"No, not that kind of excitement! I feel like I have been given a new purpose in life. I have a friend that I adore, even if he is fairly difficult at times, and I have found a woman that could be my second, and final wife."

"Jerome, have I met this friend of yours?"

He just glared at me.

"Jerome, I am so happy for you. What do we need to do now – so you are ready for the next steps?"

159

"What do you mean? I AM ready. I will see her every minute of the day if I can. Which does not mean that I will stalk her, okay?"

"Ha, ha. Okay. You win. You just have to ask if you want some input."

"Okay, I am sorry, but I am walking on air at this point. I should go home and get ready for work tomorrow."

"Hey, buddy. It is Friday night."

"Okay," he said, looking down. "What are WE doing tomorrow?"

We both laughed.

Man Hunt

As Abigail became more of a fixture in Jerome's schedule, I had to finally stop procrastinating and find Sherman. I started with some exhaustive research.

I learned that he worked at a software company that made focused, industry-specific control modules for factory hardware. Enormous machines could be re-programmed to complete vastly different tasks. His name came up as the brains-behind-the-outfit, but I never could establish if he weas one of the investors or just a hired hand that had found his niche.

Living and working in Chapel Hill, North Carolina, just a few hours from our little town, I thought he would be easy to locate. But I could find no listing for his residence or office. Both came up as post office boxes.

Only after hours of searching and clicking links did I discover an article about his support of a local independent bookstore. It was an alumni newsletter and listed truly little information about him. There was a tiny picture that was just a blur when I tried to enlarge it. I put the bookstore and the surrounding neighborhood on my watch list.

Next, I created a few fictional emails and established techy personas on social media. He ignored all my requests for connections. He successfully hid most of his life from the internet.

He had never been a public servant, had never run for office, and he had no police record or arrests. He had filed a civil lawsuit against an out-of-state college sophomore for hitting his parked car. It was a 1989 Honda, and I was convinced at that point that he was not the owner of the software firm where he worked. He did win the suit, and the settlement was for the bluebook value of the car. A lawyer from Raleigh handled the case. Sherman pocketed less than two thousand dollars from the loss, before the lawyer took his cut.

Mandy, their sister, was even harder to find. I could confirm that she graduated from college and had gotten her CPA. She had no online profiles anywhere and did not appear to own a home. I did not know if she was married, which could have changed everything, not just her name. Jerome said she was not seriously dating anyone when they had fallen out, so he was sure she was still single.

She had no complaints against her accounting license. In a stroke of luck, I found a short blurb about her receiving a certification as a Fraud Examiner and Bank Examiner. I asked Jerome if she had ever worked for law enforcement, but he did not know.

After a week of failed explorations, I gave up on Mandy and just concentrated on Sherman. It seemed like a needle-in-a-haystack search, considering what little I could base on fact.

My profile of him was that of a loner. Sherman lived and worked in a college town. He did software development and drove an old, used car before it was totaled by a drunken frat boy. He liked books, but I could not gauge how deep his affection was for them, or even what topics he preferred.

He was not dating, nor seeking to date via the new online frontiers. He came out at 35, but I could not find a picture, link, or support statement for any of the local pride groups that were so active in his region.

My instincts told me that he would probably be the opposite in disposition from his brother. Where Jerome was a gregarious extrovert, Sherman would probably be a quiet introvert. While Jerome could be oblivious to the men around him, Sherman was probably painfully aware of them.

The only tangible fact that I could rely on was the reaction I had every time I saw his brother. The hairs on the back of my neck stood up, and I would undoubtedly stare at him like Jerome does with the buxom weather gal, every time she is on the television.

Finally, when I felt I was ready, I scheduled a few days of vacation in the early fall and booked myself into a chain hotel near UNC Chapel Hill. I would just have to keep myself focused on the one man, and not allow myself to follow the other gray-haired professors around the quaint college town instead.

Jerome insisted that I keep strict receipts, but I only agreed in principle. I did not want to divert any money that he could use to entertain his new gal.

My friend wanted up-to-the-minute progress reports, and presented himself to be a bundle of nerves, but we agreed in advance that I would have to work on this alone, without hourly updates. I asked him to focus on Abigail, and I promised to call him when there was news to share.

Insanity Check

I checked in with Sarah and had a conversation that felt like a bloodletting at the time. I had adjusted the lights, gotten a glass of water, and found a comfortable chair. When I dialed the phone, I was shocked that she answered on the second ring.

"Brother, dear, how are things up north?"

"Quite well, actually. I have settled back into a routine at work."

"And what about Jerome? Are you still stalking him?"

"We have developed a really deep friendship. He makes a great companion when he is not out on dates with his new lady."

"That kind of leaves you out in the cold now, doesn't it?"

"Not really. I am quite busy with work, and I see Jerome a few nights a week."

"But he is not satisfying all of your needs, is he?"

"I never knew how much I needed a friend. It has been an awakening for me, having someone that I am close to, without all of the posturing for the conquest later."

"You are just rationalizing. I think you need to find someone that can provide you more than Jerome will."

"Maybe I don't want to find someone right now. What is the hurry, sister-dear?"

"You are rapidly approaching forty. You are cranky. Which means you aren't gettin' any. And your best friend is about to disappear into the sunset with his lady. Perhaps you should be thinking about how to fill the empty hours when he marries this gal."

"And why is it so important that I find someone to fill that...space?"

"Because romantic love, and having that love returned, is the purest validation of one's being. It is the only thing that will make us whole."

"Gee, sis, when did you become such a romantic?"

"When Julie proposed. We're getting married!"

"Con...gratulations. I am so happy for you two!" I said, trying to sound sincere, and not jealous.

"You almost sound convincing. It's okay, it shocked me, too. I never thought we would be tying the knot, but we are."

"Do you have a date in mind?" I asked my perfectionist sibling.

"Of course, I will just send you an email with all of the details. You could even bring Jerome as your date!"

"Now that is just being mean."

"I am sorry. Could you do me a favor?"

"You need my help now, after eviscerating me for being single?"

"Yes. Can you talk to our brother? I want him to come. He can even bring his stodgy wife."

"I will reach out to him. I doubt I will use the term 'stodgy' though."

She laughed. "Good night! I am back on shift in an hour."

"Okay, good night, sis. Talk at you soon."

Brotherly Love

I sent my older brother an email that was never read. I left a few voicemails on his service and even called him once at work. I simply could not tell if he was busy, or that he was, in fact, avoiding me.

Finally, I went around him and called his home directly. His wife answered on the second ring.

"Joanie? This is Larry. How are you?"

There was a long pause. "Sure, Michelle, could you call me on my cell? I was just going to step outside for a cigarette." She practically hung up on me.

The phone clicked and I looked down at my hand, as if I had done something to disconnect the call. I waited ten minutes, and then rang her cell phone. She answered right away, pausing to inhale on her cigarette.

"Hello?"

"Hey, this is Larry. How are y'all doin'?" I tried to be chipper.

"Okay, I guess. More of the same, you know." Her voice trailed off with uncertainty.

"Joanie, what is going on? I have been trying to catch Paul for weeks."

"In my opinion? He is having a midlife crisis. He has been withdrawn from life for the last few months. I can barely get him to speak to me. I thought at first that he was having an affair, but I am fairly sure that is just not the case."

"How can you be sure?" I asked, tentatively.

"He has kept his normal routine. There isn't a minute that I could not account for his time away from home. He drives the ten minutes to work, stays there all day, and he is always home on time. When he is not in the main office, he is in the construction site trailer two blocks from work. I just don't believe there are many opportunities for him to see anyone but a burly construction worker. And that is your MO, not his." She laughed a little at her joke.

I ignored the attempt at humor.

"Do you think it would upset him if I came for a visit? I don't want to make things more stressful."

"He might put on a mask of happiness because you are here. Which would not be bad to see for a change. Things cannot get any worse. I practically live alone. He is here, but says so little, I might as well be in a cloister."

"Okay, could we schedule something, how about for his birthday?"

"I guess we could. What do you need me to do?"

"I will just come up for the weekend. We could take him out for a steak on Sunday afternoon. If I can stay with you, perhaps I can get through to him. I can be quite persuasive."

"Um, sure, we could do that."

"Don't go to any extra effort, I will just crash where I can." I suspected they were sleeping in separate rooms.

"Sure, Larry. Can you bring me some of that local cider we got down your way last time? He really liked it, so maybe it would cheer him up."

"Will do. I will ring you back with the details."

I waited for her to say goodbye, but the phone went quiet.

I texted Sarah with the plan: *Making personal appearance for our reclusive brother's birthday. Will hand-carry wedding invite if you get it to me.*

Her response was simple: *Will do. Invite and birthday card for the old grouch, on the way.*

Birthday Weekend

I pulled into the circular driveway at six o'clock after an easy two-hour drive to Greensboro. I had not even gotten out of the car when my brother's Lincoln pickup truck pulled in behind me. We both paced off the distance to meet each other between the bumpers.

"Paul! Happy Birthday!" I tried to be upbeat.

"Larry! Don't remind me," he retorted. He made the last two steps and reached out his hand.

I shook his hand and clapped him lightly on the shoulder with my left hand. "I checked with the lady of the house before I crashed your party."

"There is no party that I am aware of."

"It is a figure of speech. I wanted to be here for your big day."

"You drove two hours in traffic to watch me blow out a couple candles on a cake?"

"I have some things to discuss with you as well. And I have brought some exciting news from Sarah."

He looked at me with a worried face. I could see the pallor that Joanie had told me about.

"Let's go inside. I need to yell at my wife about encouraging uninvited guests." He tried to joke, but it fell flat.

I grabbed my knapsack and followed him to the door. Joanie was waiting for the two of us to climb the three steps to the stoop.

"Hello, Larry! It is good of you to come for Paul's birthday." She stepped forward and hugged me awkwardly. I could smell the smoke in her long, blonde hair. She was dressed quite well for a Friday afternoon, but she was expecting me, even if he was not.

Paul and I stepped over the threshold. Joanie closed the door behind us. He led the way to the living room, with the two of us in tow.

"How bad was traffic?" He asked.

"Charlotte is always a bottleneck, but I took the bypass and missed most of it."

"I don't envy anyone that has to make that trip." He loosened his tie and kicked off his shoes. "Make yourself comfortable."

His khakis were worn but pressed. Dust from the construction site had collected on his steel-toed shoes and down his shins. The blue shirt with the company logo was faded, but I doubt he ever noticed. He was two days shy of forty, and he was in better shape than me.

I took off my sport coat and loosened my tie. I sat down in the chair opposite him and did my best not to grunt.

"Can I get either of you a drink before we get comfortable?"

"No, we should hit the road if we are going to that Italian place that you love so much. Do you think we can get in on a Friday night?"

"Yes, if we leave soon. It fills up quickly. How soon can you two be ready?"

"I am ready now," I offered, standing to demonstrate my readiness.

"Ten minutes. Just need to wash up," he responded. He stood quickly and charged up the stairs, as if he were a far younger man than I.

"Listen, before he gets back, tell me what I can do for you tomorrow. If you would like me to cook, so you can have some time to enjoy the meal, I would be happy to – as fancy or plain as you would like. Or we could go out, anywhere you wish."

"Let me think about it. If you could just talk to him a bit tomorrow, over your male-bonding rituals, perhaps you can get to the bottom of what is bothering him." She turned to look at me. "Please, Larry, I need to understand if I am losing him, or if he is just at a rocky patch with his routine."

I stepped forward and put my arm around her shoulders. "Of course, I will do whatever I have to. Perhaps a good deep-tissue massage will loosen his tongue a bit. If not, we will just have to try some alcohol, and take our chances with his mood in the morning."

She smiled faintly, then pulled away. It was not personal. She was habituated to be ready when he was, and I was not going to be the obstacle that might make him angry about his schedule.

We shuffled out the door a few minutes later. Paul had changed to clean clothes, and some casual shoes.

He opened the truck door for Joanie and helped her get into the cab. I grabbed the backdoor and climbed in while he made the circuit around the vehicle. He had been conditioned to walk around the vehicle before pulling away. There had been too many mishaps on construction sites before the practice was drilled into them.

"Do you have any plans for your birthday? Something I could help facilitate?" I asked, helpfully.

"I had not planned to do anything. I was hoping to escape without a big shindig," he griped.

"Paul, I have nothing in the works. Larry offered to come up, and I agreed it would be nice to see him. If you two want to go off tomorrow, and do some of your guy stuff, that would be fine by me. There will be no party, or cake, or any other guests, unless you tell me otherwise. I would like to take you out for a steak on Sunday. Maybe we could do that before Larry has to drive back?"

"Yeah, I guess that would be okay," he grumbled.

"Was there something you would like to do tomorrow? Wood shop, driving range, target practice? The weather is supposed to be quite pleasant," I asked, hopefully. I felt like a small dog, jumping for attention.

"I am sure we can find something to fill a Saturday. Just don't expect me up before eight."

"Sounds reasonable...for a weekend," Joanie added, cautiously.

He pulled into the parking lot of a very crowded shopping center. With a stroke of luck, we got the last table in the restaurant, way over in the corner away from the door.

"I want the lasagna. No other place even compares to the taste. And the portion will keep you full for days!" He stated.

The waitress came over and stood by our table. "My name is Trish, what can I get y'all to drink tonight?"

"I will have a Peroni, but cut me off at one, please darling. And some water," Paul stated.

"I will have the same, please. Same rule, too." I smiled big for the gal.

"Please get me a glass of the chianti, and some water, too please," Joanie said.

While we looked over the menus and waited for our drinks, I looked around the eatery. There were families, and couples, eating happily despite the line at the door.

Trish brought our drinks to the table and took our orders for dinner. I followed Paul's lead but added a small salad to start. Joanie ordered manicotti and a salad. When she picked up her glass, I took the chance to ask the question I had been thinking about.

"What should I plan for Sunday morning? Was I supposed to pack clothes for a church service?"

"Larry, we have not been to church in years. In fact, I have not prayed since high school. It was a long weekend for me, after Mary Lou told me she was late. As it turned out, prayer worked, and we were spared a wedding at sixteen."

Joanie slapped his hand and frowned at him. "I thought I was your first?"

"You were the first woman I ever loved. And, I hope, the last." He smiled sheepishly. "Mary Lou was just a fling, for my wild youth."

"I hate to break it to you, but you were middle-aged at twenty, Paul," she stated emphatically.

I smiled at the thought. "I have to agree with her. You were always so responsible. I cannot imagine you placing a foot in the wrong direction."

"I had some wild times in college." He said, defensively. "State schools are supposed to provide a place for that. I just never got caught. I graduated, and never looked back."

Our food arrived and all conversation stopped. The cook must have come directly from Italy because the quality of the food rivaled what I had experienced on my trips there.

Trish returned once to check on us, and then again to refill our waters. "I am sorry, y'all, but these new water glasses are only three sips deep." She scampered away when none of us spoke up in her defense.

There were grunts of pleasure all around, and none of us wanted dessert. I paid the bill, over Paul's objections. I doubted he was serious about the implied insult.

When we pulled out of the parking lot, I thought he was headed home. But he had a surprise for us. We got to the construction site and climbed out of his truck to see the progress of the new office building. He kept us on the pavement, so we did not break any rules and Joanie did not risk breaking a heel.

Even in the falling darkness, I could see the pride in him, swelling to fill his already puffed-up chest. He took a deep breath and let it out slowly.

"When this building is finished, my days of kicking dirt will be over," he said, with a finality that scared us both.

"Paul, whatsoever do you mean?" Joanie asked.

"They have asked me to step into the role of vice president. When Charlie retired last year, I never expected that I might be in line for the promotion. They called me into a meeting last month, and I almost thought I was going to be fired. HR and the board know, but no one else in the company does. None of my higher-up friends ever let on that I was in the running."

His voice hitched. Joanie put her arm around his waist. I waited for him to finish his announcement.

"From the moment this building is in use, I will have the corner office, on the top floor," he sighed. "I will spend the rest of my career in a suit, instead of wearing dusty work boots. I will only get to wear a hard hat for pictures."

To me, he sounded maudlin. I realized later that he was on the edge of a huge life change. I stepped up beside him and put my hand on his shoulder.

Joanie turned to embrace him, and I dropped my hand. As they convened, I walked back to the truck to give them some space. They made their way back over to the truck, and we all got in quietly. It was a mile down the road before he spoke again.

"Tell me, Larry, did you happen to bring your table with you?" he asked.

"Yes, I did. Just tell me when and where to set it up." It was difficult not to smile. My massage skills were always in demand.

He pulled into the driveway and stopped behind my car. Popping the trunk, I grabbed my massage table, and then followed them inside.

I put the table down carefully, then we draped ourselves over the furniture. None of us wanted to move after all that food. Against all my instincts, I allowed Joanie to pour us each a small glass of grappa. The digestif worked its magic, and we all felt better when the liquor relaxed us and our stomachs. Joanie got up a few minutes after we finished our drinks and took the empty glasses back into the kitchen. She stopped in the living room on her way through.

"I am going to read for a bit before I turn in. Larry, you can take the room at the end of the hallway on this floor. Everything you need should be there."

"Thank you, Joanie. I am sure I will be wonderfully comfortable."

She climbed the steps agilely. The noise of her footsteps diminished as she reached the top step, and the carpet in the hallway softened the sounds.

We sat in silence for a few minutes, letting the liqueur relax us. I was just starting to doze off when Paul spoke.

"Are you tired, or would you have the energy to work on my shoulders a bit?" He asked.

"Never too tired to help my brother," I smiled weakly. "Can you assist me with the table? And we will need some towels."

He hopped up and single-handedly put the table into its snapped, upright position. Once he was back with some towels, he stripped off his shirt and then his t-shirt. When he climbed up on the table, I thought I heard a grunt, but he did not hesitate.

He put his face in the central hole and relaxed his shoulders for me to work on them. I spread some oil between his shoulder blades, then worked it out in a fan shape to keep my hands moisturized for the efforts.

His deltoids were pure muscle. I could find no traces of fat or loose skin, laying testament to his physical labors. Thoroughly enjoying the process, I was startled when he spoke up.

"Not so hard on the trapezius, please."

"Sure. It feels like you have been carrying some stress around with your toolbox," I joked.

"There are times that I have to step in and show the new hires how to do something. Most of my authority over them stems from my ability to do everything that I ask them to perform. These younger ones - teenagers really - don't have much respect for the title, but I can persuade them through action that my way is better in the long run, just by showing them once or twice."

"Are you going to miss that when you take the desk job?"

"Not the soreness, or the churn of new hires that always need more supervision, but sure, I'll miss being on the ground with my folks."

"Do you have anyone in mind for your current job?"

"Absolutely. Without a doubt. It might be a hard sell for the corporate folks, but I am sure I can make them see why it is a good idea."

"And that is why they tapped you for the new role. Being able to make a sound decision based on facts is a difficult task for many of the folks I work with. Sometimes I wonder how they ever got their jobs."

As I continued to work his neck muscles, he let out a series of groans that signaled the release of some lactic acid buildup. "Yeah, that was what I wanted to hear. Even if you ate too much at dinner, you should get a better night's rest after the muscle manipulation."

"Thanks," was all he said.

I went to wash my hands. When I returned, he had put his shirt back on, and was folding up the table. He disappeared for a second, and then returned with two more glasses of grappa for us.

"If I didn't already know that this stuff worked, I would refuse it, but I am in no position to argue. Thank you."

He settled back into his chair, while I stretched out on the sofa. We sighed, almost in unison.

"Did I hear that you changed jobs recently?" he asked.

'Uhh, yeah, a few years ago. Four. I wanted to get into contract law and found a manufacturing company that needed my particular skills."

"Are you in Charlotte, with all of that congestion?"

"No, Gastonia. Just a few miles out, and far enough away that we don't get much of the Charlotte traffic. Best of both worlds, really."

"If you say so. And Sarah is still in New Orleans?"

"Yes, her hotel business is doing quite well. They have leased out the roof for a local chef to run as a garden restaurant. The food is quite good."

"You have been there? To stay?"

"Paul, it is run by our sister. Where else would I ever want to stay if I am in town?" I laughed a little. "Besides, the patrons are not interested in you, or me. I kept a low profile and enjoyed the few nights she could squeeze me into her burgeoning empire."

"I cannot say that I would want to stay there, with Joanie or not."

"Yeah, I can see how that would be awkward. But I doubt there will be any pressure, should you choose to visit the Big Easy."

"Good." He finished his drink. "I need to take Joanie on a vacation of some sort, but I was hoping for something a little more relaxed, like the Gulf Shore beaches."

"Well, let me know if you need help spec'ing out a plan. I have had rather good luck scheduling getaways."

"Thanks, I'll let you know. I am going to head upstairs. Make yourself at home. There is more of that tonic on the kitchen counter if you want it," he said with a laugh. He knew better.

He went up to bed just before nine o'clock and I stayed in the living room. Given the sounds echoing down the stairwell, I was better to let them finish prior to my attempt at sleep, directly below them.

I pulled my phone out and saw two missed text messages.

I answered Jerome's *Did you make it?* inquiry first: *I made it safely and have communed with my brother over a bottle of grappa. He took advantage of my generosity and got a shoulder massage. I still prefer to fondle my best friend, just in case you were wondering.*

He replied with three words: *"Good, softy, and PSYCHO.*

Julie's question was more involved: *Will you update me for RSVP? I need to ask Paul a favor, please call me when he is within reach.*

I responded: *Have not told them yet. Still breaking the ice. Will have more time tomorrow, after we have bonded. LOL*

I dialed Jerome and went into the kitchen. He didn't answer, which meant he was on another date with Abigail. I was beginning to wonder if I was going to be alone again soon. Turning off all the downstairs lights, I found my way down the hallway using my phone as a flashlight. The room was adequate and was directly below their bedroom.

When I heard the bed still squeaking above me, I turned on the television to drown it out. I did not know if our talk, the alcohol, or their routine, had led to the romantic interlude, but I knew I did not want to hear any more of it.

I dozed for a while, then turned off the television, rolled over on my side, and passed out in a pasta coma. My sleep was fitful until I could finally digest the rest of the meal that had I stuffed in me like a starving man.

Saturday Bonding

I was up early, and I tiptoed around the kitchen to find some coffee. Fortunately, I was fully dressed, as Joanie walked in as I was snooping.

"Good morning!" She stated rather cheerfully. "The coffee pot is set up to start in a few minutes. Mugs are in the cabinet directly above the machine. We have sugar, and cream, but no artificial sweetener."

"Thank you. And good morning to you," I stammered.

She was suddenly in my personal space. As she leaned in to kiss my cheek, I was beginning to think that their mattress exercise was a new development. "You keep up the good work, and I may insist that you visit every month!"

"You are welcome. He is a great guy, even if he can be a typical man at times."

"You don't have to tell me; I have lived with that part of his personality for years. It is just recently that he has been more...introspective. Perhaps it is the milestone of forty that scares him."

"We will have all day to talk it through if he wants to. What time should we plan for dinner?"

"Let's shoot for six. I'll make dinner here, as I do every Saturday night." The look on her face told me that she would rather go out, but Paul had insisted on a night at home together. She went out the back door. I guessed it was time for her morning cigarette.

I had some coffee and waited for Paul to get up. After answering all my emails, and texting Jerome repeatedly, I got into the shower. There were more texts waiting for me, so I got dressed and called Jerome to short-circuit his inquisitiveness. We talked for an hour before I heard footsteps above me that I assumed was Paul.

When Paul came down to the kitchen for his first cup of coffee at nine o'clock, he looked no worse for wear. He had showered and was dressed for our day out. I gave him his space and waited for him to signal that it was time to go. I was just finishing a chapter in my book when he called down the hallway.

"Are you ready to go, or do you still have to do your makeup?"

I jumped up, pulled the door open, and stared down the challenge. Once I saw the grin on his face, I had to laugh, and then we were on the same wavelength for much of the day.

We hit the firing range and blew a bunch of money hitting defenseless paper targets with rounds from his matching 45 caliber pistols. He kept them in a holding safe at the range. Everyone seemed to know him, so I guessed it was a regular hobby for him. I did not ask any questions, but it did seem to bother him that I was a quick study, and nearly matched his scoring.

"How about some lunch?" He shouted over the noise. We both had silencing headphones that made us each look like the famous Florida Mouse.

"Ready any time!" I shouted back.

We checked the guns in with the cleaning service and left the noise behind us. My ears were still ringing from the repetitious hand-held explosions.

He drove us to a diner where again, they knew him by name. I was determined to let him have a great day, so I made no pretense of eating healthily. I matched his order, and we gorged ourselves on

Salisbury steak, mashed potatoes, and green beans. We had sweet tea to wash it all down. I could tell that he was in his element.

As I was mindful of his he-man construction boss persona, we only talked about the firing range and his new Lincoln truck over lunch. There were too many people around to get into personal issues. The watch on his wrist glinted in the sunlight. Mickey Mouse's arms held up the hour and minutes, which seemed to be a strange fashion choice for a construction foreman.

Back in his truck, he surprised me yet again when turned off the main road. There were no signs or houses for the ten minutes he sped down the two-lane blacktop. Finally, he pulled into a private driveway on the outskirts of town.

"Where are we going?" I ask.

"You'll see," was all he said.

The dirt driveway snaked through several stands of trees, and then the view opened to an old farmhouse. I could hear the howling and whooping of the dogs. There must have been dozens of them.

A woman came out on the porch, apparently alerted by her canine security system. She was gorgeous. Tall, beautiful skin, and eyes as big as saucers. I began to get scared that Paul was in deep.

As we got out of the truck, I tried to compose myself. It did not take long for me to be jolted back to reality.

"PAUL!" She shouted. "You finally came. I have been inviting you every week for months now."

He walked over and shook her hand. I could see the sculpted muscles in her arms.

He turned toward me and said, "This is my brother, Larry. Larry, this is Shirley, she works on my construction team."

I held my hand out, and she pumped my fist with the strength of two men. Another woman, almost as beautiful, appeared on the porch behind her. Shirley turned around when she followed our line of sight.

"This is Maureen. The dogs were her idea," Shirley said jokingly.

"Pleased to meet cha!" she shouted over the barking.

We got a tour of the shelter, which they ran on donations and their own money. They rescued cast-off hunting dogs and networked extensively to find them homes for their retirement years.

Back in the truck, he was somber for the first few miles home. "I have wanted a dog for years, but Joanie says she is allergic. Strange how her allergies don't affect her cigarette habit."

"I don't know what to tell you, Paul. Do you want me to talk to her about it?" I asked.

"No, I can show some backbone when I need to. I think it is time for me to find a four-legged best friend," he spoke softly, then smiled to himself.

After a few more minutes of quiet between us, I finally had to ask the question that had been bothering me since I had arrived.

"Paul?" I asked, startling him out of his silence.

"Yes?"

"I, uh, was just wondering...about your...watch."

"Yes?" He responded coyly, offering nothing more.

I let the silence work for me. After another full minute, he flipped his blinker on, changed lanes, and then turned into a ballpark run by the local leagues. Without a word, he killed the engine, got out and closed the door behind him. The keys were still hanging in the ignition.

I got out, tenuous with my line of questioning. He had stepped a few paces away from the truck and was looking out over the fields as the grounds crew prepared the fields for an evening game.

"I have never told anyone else this story. Consider yourself privileged, okay?" he asked sarcastically. I did not feel the need to interrupt him by responding.

"On one of those days while you were probably helping mom in the kitchen, isolated from the garage and dad's mercurial temper, I learned just how far our father was willing to go to shape me into his ideal son."

He bent down and picked up a tree branch leaning against the fence. Standing back up to his full height, he kept his shoulder turned away from me so that I could not see his face. Tearing the small twigs off with an uncharacteristic violence of rapid hand motions, he paused while I considered what he meant.

"That afternoon, after we had split and stacked wood all morning for Mr. Chambers, I reached into my pocket and got my new watch. I had slipped it into my pocket for safe keeping. It was the one thing I had always wanted, and I had used my paper route money to buy it."

The hand motions continued, belying his casual stance and measured speech.

"Dad was incensed. He told me that it was a toy and meant for girls or little boys. The only way I would ever become a man, in

185

his view of the world, was to put those things behind me and not look back."

He looked up at me. His eyes were steely, but there were some stray tears that had forced their way into his vision.

"I did not know what to say to him. As I stood there, waiting for more of his ire, he walked over to the workbench and got a ball peen hammer. When he tried to hand me the tool, I had no idea what I was to do with it. Eventually, after he stared me down, I took the handle, and let the hammer drop to my side."

He continued to throw small pieces of sticks and bark as he spoke. Before I had asked, I did not realize how much the watch had meant to him.

"He made me smash my brand-new watch into pieces on the work bench. I dared not cry, or I knew he would have whipped me right there in the garage. Once the watch was shattered, I cleaned up the pieces and dropped them in the trash. He never mentioned it again."

He threw the remainder of the stick off toward the woods, then turned to face me. "One week after we buried him, I bought this watch. I may have forgiven him, but I will never forget how he belittled me that day. That fourteen-year-old grew up to be a man, but from that day forward, I wanted nothing more to do with his notion of masculinity, or how I was to fit into his world."

"I am sorry. I did not know."

"No one did. Not even Joanie. She just thought I was trying to get attention. But you know, she has never belittled me for wearing it."

We pulled into the driveway at five. It had been a great day, despite my miscalculated question about his wristwatch. I was looking forward to dinner with the two of them, in contrast to my initial misgivings about the weekend.

Joanie met us in the living room with a big smile. "Have you boys had a good day?" She asked.

"Absolutely!" Paul responded.

"Can I get either of you a drink before we sit down?"

"Yes, two big scotches, please. Larry will indulge me if he expects me to be chipper for the festivities." He strode stiffly over to the sofa and lowered himself down on the end cushion. I could hear our father's grunt escape his mouth as he finished the motion.

I smiled and nodded. Joanie disappeared to get some ice.

Before I got a chance to ask the first question, Joanie was back with a tray. There were three drinks, and some snacks. She gave us each a highball, and then sat down with her glass of white wine. Each of our glasses had about three shots of liquor.

Paul finished his drink in record time then excused himself to shower. I helped Joanie finish the preparations for dinner. She had a simple meal planned. Paul was a meat-and-potatoes kind of guy.

The roast chicken was perfect. I doubt many home cooks could match her skill in the kitchen. The mashed potatoes were ready, as were the sweet corn and rolls. I searched my brain for a compliment that would not sound condescending or chauvinistic.

"It all looks wonderful. I hope you did not go to too much trouble," I tried.

"This is our standard Saturday night fare. Most other couples go out, but he wants to be at home after fifty hours a week in the trenches. He indulges me for our Friday night meal in town."

Paul appeared in the doorway to the dining room. His thinning blonde hair was still wet, and he had dressed in sweats after his shower. I was setting the table. It could accommodate twelve, but I had arranged the three places around one end, so we could be closer.

"Are you done discussing me with Joanie?"

I spun around and faced him. "Why would you say that?"

"Because that is why you are here. I am sure she has complained to you already that I am a slug that won't take her anywhere. Or that I am a couch potato every night, and all weekend long."

"Sounds like you have thought about this."

"I know she is worried. I am just coasting right now. It has nothing to do with her or how I feel about our relationship. There are just some things that are bothering me, and I need to work out a few details before I decide what I can do differently."

"Is there anything I can do to help?"

"Darn tootin' you can. I need another massage. I was afraid to go for one in town, some of those women are motivated by tips, and their extracurricular activities are never cheap," he laughed heartily.

"Well, Paul, I don't charge, and there are no extras. You get what you get. Also, I can do more than shoulders."

He raised an eyebrow and looked at me sideways. "Alright. Once we have digested dinner. It would be a nice finish to the night and may help me sleep a bit better."

"Are you having trouble sleeping?"

"Yeah, sometimes. I just can't turn my brain off. I turn over like a pig on a spit over a fire, just trying to get comfortable."

Joanie burst through the door with a platter of food. I took the tray from her, and she returned to the kitchen to get more. A few seconds later, she was back with the finishing touches for dinner.

Paul sat down in his usual place at the end. I waited for Joanie to sit, and then I took the seat opposite her. As recovering Catholics, our family often paused as if we would say grace, but then jumped right into the food.

"What have you been up to lately?" Joanie asked me.

"Work, and more work. I don't travel as much with this job, which suits me simply fine." I sipped my wine and put the glass down. "You may find this interesting; I have been helping a guy at work with his dating life. He met a former beauty queen, and he is smitten. She was Miss North Carolina a few years back."

"What do you mean, 'helping' him'?" Paul asked.

"He is almost forty, and recently divorced. He had not been on a date in twenty years. I coached him through the perfect date etiquette, what to wear, how to help her, and what to expect from a woman that might have, let's say, elevated standards."

"We really don't expect much, you know. All of you men sound like we have to be 'handled' like a fragile package," Joanie said, disgustedly.

"I did not mean it that way. It's just that he has been out of practice for a few years, and I wanted to make sure he did not step out of place. I think it is getting serious. There might be wedding bells in their future."

"Well, good for him. A man is not complete without someone to love him unconditionally." He touched Joanie's left hand. He knew I was building up to the announcement.

"I am glad to hear you say that. Our little sister is getting married!" I tried to sound enthusiastic.

"Sarah?" Joanie queried.

"Of course," I said.

Paul was silent. Just chewing. He sipped his water and put the glass down. Joanie and I were on pins and needles, waiting for his reaction, or any questions that might throw a wrench in the evening.

"You know, we had this gal show up on our construction site a few months back. To look at her, one might think she would be better suited for teaching elementary school or being a nurse. By the end of the first week, she was more productive than most of the men on the crew."

"And what is your point?" Joanie demanded.

"She had to keep to herself and put up with a lot of snide remarks. Everyone gets the standard HR spiel about harassment, so none of them went that far, but it was not a friendly environment at first."

"So, what changed?" I asked. "Are they getting along better now?"

"Yeah, the group is cohesive now, and quite cooperative. Not only that, but I also had to re-think what I expected out of my crew. She demonstrated that all my employees should be stepping up and cutting out the nonsense. She set the bar high, and some of the long-term workers were challenged to match the output, or risk losing out."

"You mean their jobs were in jeopardy?" I asked.

"Not really. But in a construction crew, the most productive people get to move on to the more rewarding tasks. They get to choose what they do next, and they take the better assignments. The slower ones are often stuck with menial tasks. We call that cleanup work."

"And what made you bring that up at dinner?" Joanie asked cautiously.

"Turns out this gal, Shirley, has a girlfriend. She was right up front about it. The men backed off, and they all have settled into their places on the crew. The girlfriend, I think that is the term they use, works in the mayor's office."

He looked up at me to see if I would keep our stop there a secret.

"Are you saying that you have a better understanding of our sister now that you have seen a woman outperform your guys on the site?"

"Absolutely. I could see this gal as the foreman in the next few months. Is that the right term? You know, that bothers me more than anything. I have to change all my terminology, just so I don't offend somebody."

"Does this mean you will come to the wedding for Sarah and Julie?"

"Is it in New Orleans?" He asked, suspiciously, raising one eyebrow.

"Of course, it is."

"Good, we could use a long weekend getaway. Couldn't we, Joanie?"

"Yes. Yes, we could!" She exclaimed. "When is it? We need to make the arrangements."

"I have the invite in my bag. I think it is the first or second weekend in November. It will be the standard schedule: rehearsal dinner on Friday night, wedding, and reception on Saturday. And a barbeque in the park on Sunday to wind it all down."

"Can you get us a room in your hotel, so we can stay close? I don't want to get lost in the shuffle down there," he asked.

"Certainly. I am planning to stay at the Hilton on the river." I said.

"Do you have a date for the event?" she asked, hopefully.

"No. For now, it is just me."

We finished dinner and I helped Joanie take the dishes into the kitchen. She would not let me help clean up, so I found Paul in the living room. He was stretched out in his easy chair, thumbing through a magazine.

I settled into the sofa and stretched my legs out from the cushion to the floor, with my butt on the edge of the seat. I was not too full, but the food was beyond good. I was relieved there was no dessert to pack on more calories, especially after the Italian feast the night before.

He looked up at me. I could tell he wanted to ask a question but maybe was not sure how to phrase it. He looked back at the magazine and cleared his throat.

"Is there anything I will be expected to do, in this service for Sarah? I know that I am the oldest, but I never expected to be a part of a ceremony for her, in Dad's absence."

"I have not heard of anything, but Sarah would love to talk with you. Perhaps you could ask her directly?"

"Okay, I will call her once I see the invite and make our hotel arrangements. Perhaps we could do that in the morning. I might need help scheduling flights, too."

"Sure, we can do it in just a few minutes' time." I patted my bag. "I have my laptop if that would help. I might need the Wi-Fi password, though."

He grunted and went back to his magazine. Joanie joined us quietly, settling into the sofa next to me.

I pulled out my computer. As they lounged on the sofa, I surfed for flights from Greensboro to New Orleans. "It is either Delta, through Atlanta, or American, stopping in Charlotte."

Paul looked up at me. "American, please."

"You want Friday, or late afternoon Thursday?"

"Friday, midday," was all he said.

"Return on Sunday night or Monday morning?"

"Monday," she said.

"Okay, it's booked. I will email you the confirmation."

"Thanks," they said, almost in unison.

A few more clicks, and I had booked them into a suite at the Hilton. I put a note in my reservation that I did not want to be directly next door to them, but on the same floor, if possible.

I stalled for time. Paul knew their home routine, but I was completely ignorant about how they spent their evenings. I did not want to start a deep conversation with Paul if Joanie was going to stay with us. It was just a few minutes later that she stood up.

"Good night, boys." she said and left the room.

Paul dropped the magazine on the table next to him and got up. He slipped out of the room without a word and returned with a bottle of cognac. I thought he was going to drink it from the bottle, at first, until I saw that she had put glasses out for us. He poured us each a snifter, handed me one and then sat back down. His sigh spoke to his fatigue, but also to his predicament. I let him compose his thoughts, sipping the brown liquid as slowly as I could.

"Sometimes I feel older than my elapsed years." He sipped some more of the brandy. "I want to grasp some excitement in life, but I don't want to upset the apple cart. We have a good life, even if Joanie thinks I am stagnating."

Not wanting him to think I was not listening; I cleared my throat and sipped some more cognac before speaking. "I believe most successful men go through a stage like you are describing. Sometimes life seems so easy, sticking to a routine, that we dare not try something different."

"I can tell you that it does not get any easier. Every year that ticks by is another reason not to change direction, even for simple tasks."

"Is there anything I can do to help? Perhaps plan a vacation for the two of you? I am quite good at it, you know."

He grunted. It was not what he wanted to hear. "I just have to tell you something. It is not easy for me to say, but please hear me out. Okay?"

"Um, sure. I will listen," I sputtered.

He cleared his throat, drank some brandy, then set the glass on the table next to his chair. After some fidgeting in the seat, he finally made eye contact and began to speak.

"I always resented you, Larry. Mom was so easy on you, while dad seemed to ride my butt like a bronco buster. Maybe it was because you were her favorite, and dad could not admit that I was not his favorite."

I felt as though lightning had struck me where I sat. He was not finished.

"It took me a long time to recognize that I had distanced myself from everyone around me, shunning any habit or mannerism that could be traced back to our father. When I hit thirty, and he died, I realized that I had become just like him, despite all my efforts."

I held my snifter and swirled the remaining brandy around in the glass. I drained the last gulp and finally put it on the table next to me before I crushed it in my hand.

"When mom died a year later, I actually felt relieved. I did not want to be burdened as the replacement of dad in her life. I think she died of a broken heart, but I simply cannot understand what she saw in him. No more than I can fathom what Joanie sees in me."

He finished his brandy and put the glass down. I waited for more information, knowing I could not interrupt if he had more to share.

"Now I am about to hit forty, and I am in a rut. I love Joanie dearly, but I have no idea how to make her happy. It's just that the man I have become does not know how to change and be a better husband. I worry that I will lose her before too much longer, but I am frozen to where we are now, afraid to make a change, and risking making it worse."

He got up and went into the bathroom. I waited in silence for him to return. When I heard the familiar squeak of the massage table, I knew he was prepping for another session.

He took the table and set it up behind the sofa. I dropped my bag on the ottoman. Before I could pull out my massage oil kit, he had poured us each another snifter. Now I was grateful that I had eaten so many mashed potatoes.

He had gotten towels from the downstairs bath. After draping them over the table, he stepped out of his sweatpants, and slipped his t-shirt over his head. Even being my brother, I could see what Joanie saw in him: trim, fit, muscular, and very well proportioned. His boxers clung to his skin, filling the cotton out with muscles that rivaled a Chippendale dancer's figure.

He drained his brandy and climbed up on the table, lowering his stomach to the cool surface, and sighing quietly. I spread some oil between his shoulder blades and began working his lower back over with my hands first. I added some forearm pressure, and the occasional elbow to release the tighter muscles. He grunted a few times, so I was sure he was still awake.

When I reached his shoulders, I added more oil, and hoped that I had his attention, so I got to talk uninterrupted.

"Paul, I don't know what the dynamics were between you and dad." I only paused when I had to exert more force in the massage. "But let me tell you about my relationship with our mother."

I waited for him to protest, but he was silent.

"Mom pushed me harder than any professor did in college, or more than dad did for you. Nothing I did was good enough. I never had the chance to come out to her. She told me, one teary night when dad was traveling on business. I could hear the disappointment in her voice as she revealed to me what she had figured out. She put into words, using harsh, unfeeling phrases to describe what I had been struggling to tell myself for years."

He turned his head to the side as I worked a sore muscle. I took the opportunity to sip more from my glass, nearly dropping it with the oil on my hands.

"Her distress was not out of concern for my safety, or my prospects for employment. She resented that I would not give her grandchildren, and a daughter-in-law that she could shop with, while the husbands worked. She never missed the chance to insert a verbal dig into our conversation, reminding me each time I spoke with her that I would never measure up. I was supposed to be an extension of her social life that she could show off to the neighbors."

Once I finished his shoulders and neck, I moved to his lower body. I oiled up my hands and worked his legs from the ankles to his knees, pushing the blood and relaxing the stiff muscles. I guessed that he probably stood up most days, from the tension I felt.

"I felt numb when dad died. I regretted not having made peace with his view of the world, and how I never felt as if I belonged in his family. I know, now, that the emotional distance between us was as much my fault as it was his."

I moved to his thighs, which were solid muscle, and as firm as any distance runner I had ever encountered. He spread his legs enough for me to get my hands between them. I kept a professional, and personal, distance from his well-rounded, muscular backside.

"I took care of mom, that year after he was gone. I knew she was not doing well, health-wise. The closer mom got to death, the angrier I became. I knew, as the time slipped away, her energy diminished, and her ability to apologize to me before she left us, was fading from reality."

I finished his legs. When I reached for the towel to wipe my hands, he grabbed my arm. There were tears in his eyes. "I never knew. I am so sorry. I thought you two were peas in a pod."

I had maintained my composure up to that point, but then I began to cry as well. I wiped my face on the towel when he let go of my arm. I made a spinning motion with my hand, and he turned over with the agility of an athlete.

Sniffling, and wiping my nose, I continued. "But in the long run, what she did for me was to prove that I did not need her, or anyone else's, approval. I had to love and respect myself, even when other people might condemn me."

Oiling up my hands, I began to work his pectorals and abs. He grunted a few times, and I moved down to his legs, starting at the edge of his boxers, and moving toward his ankles. It was the most thorough massage that I had ever given my brother. Before now, he would only let me do his shoulders.

"There, I think you should be relaxed enough to sleep through the night, but you might want to shower up before you lie down, so Joanie won't fuss about the oil on the sheets."

He did a full body crunch, swung his legs over the side, and jumped down as a gymnast would dismount for a panel of judges. He could have been a sixteen-year-old, for his limberness and agility. I turned around after putting the towels on the table, and he met me with a bear hug that took me by surprise. "I am sorry," he said softly. "Maybe you could help me figure out some stuff?"

"No, you jerk! You got oil all over my favorite t-shirt," I protested.

He refused to let go before he kissed my cheek. He always did that when we were kids, after he held me down until I gave up, and I cried uncle. It was the ultimate humiliation as a kid, but it was a poignant, and welcome, gesture as an adult.

He laughed and stepped away from me. As he was tugging on his sweatpants, and pulling his t-shirt over his head, I had to marvel at how well we were getting along. I put the table legs up and leaned it against the wall, careful to keep the surface covered with a towel to protect the door frame.

"Well, brother, tell me about your love life. Didn't you have a boyfriend for a while there?"

"Yeah, I had one, but it didn't last. I guess my expectations were too high."

"Any prospects on the horizon? I hear the online dating scene has really stirred the pot for digital cupids."

"I am more of an in-person kind of guy. I don't want to read a bunch of messages that may or may not be factual, and then find out they stole the picture for their profile from another website."

I sipped some of my brandy.

"I have one promising lead on a new catch, as it were. A friend at work, the one I helped with his dating manners, has a brother he wants me to meet. It might be a bit strained, since I am already close friends with the guy, and I see him every day around the office."

"You won't know if you don't try. I think it is time you settled down. Maybe your wedding will be the next event on our social calendar?" he asked.

"Okay, Mr. Cupid. Just because you married your high school sweetheart, does not mean we are all destined for domestic life."

"What are you afraid of? Sounds like you are denouncing the sour grapes before you have even made a serious jump for the vine."

"This guy, who may or may not be in my future, lives in Chapel Hill, several hours away from my job and home. Even if he were a great catch, and I am not sure that he is, it would put a strain on any relationship to be hours apart."

I finished my brandy and put the glass down next to me.

"The additional hurdle, for me, is that this guy has been estranged from his brother, and I am fearful of being the messenger. I don't want to find out that he has been holding a grudge for a very plausible reason, as that would make it awkward for me to stay friends with either of them."

He took a big swig from his glass and then looked me in the eye.

"Bullshit. I think you are already smitten with one, or both. If you finally find an adult male that returns your attention, you may not be the martyr anymore. Perhaps it is time to surrender. Move over to the winning side?"

He drained his glass and then poured us both more of the poison. I was too surprised by his statement to stop him.

"When did you become such a psychologist with romance insights?"

"Hey, I have heard your protests before. You always want to be in the superior role, the mature one, or the selfless idealist that gets left behind. You did it with Jeremy in college, and then with Jeffrey in law school."

My mouth must have been open.

"You may have thought that I was not listening to all of those family chats you had with Sarah, but I heard every word. I am not unsympathetic; I just think you should stand up to the challenge and go for what you want."

I drank more cognac, waiting for more of his lecture.

"Am I wrong?" he asked.

"No. I don't think so. It is just so difficult, sometimes, to know if they want me, or just someone to fill their time. I was devastated when Bernard left me. I really thought we had something, but he was only attracted to my wallet."

"I am sorry. Sarah told me you had broken up with him, but not what the issues were. You deserve better than that."

"Thank you." I paused to sip, then continued. "I am going to seek out Jerome's brother Sherman once I get back. Perhaps he will show some promise."

"I am so glad to hear that. Maybe you will bring the brothers back together and get laid in the process." He grinned, his glassy eyes shining in the darkened room.

We switched to small talk as we got more inebriated, whispering like teenagers about to be caught drinking by irate parents. He went up to shower about midnight, and I got settled in my guest room.

I stripped off my oily clothes, unpacked my suitcase, and brushed my teeth before getting into bed. As an afterthought, I filled the carafe next to the bed with water and put some Tylenol out for the morning.

I texted Sarah before I gave up on the day: *They are coming, Paul and Joanie. I think he knows what you will ask. He seems amenable. Will call you tomorrow morning.*

Finally, settled into bed, I wanted to call Jerome and tell him about my day, but I had to think about it before I could make any assessments. I turned off the light and tried to make myself comfortable in the strange bed.

Sunday Birthday

I awoke at six with a hangover. My phone had six messages from Jerome. I let him sleep for a while, then returned them all with one paragraph that summed up the weekend so far: *All is well. Brother was having existential midlife crisis. Paul is going to be promoted. Steak for brunch, then driving home. Wanna grab some dinner later?*

He responded with: *Yes. Six o'clock. My place.*

I padded into the kitchen on my sock feet to find Joanie sipping coffee in the breakfast nook. She raised her cup as a greeting, a smile on her face that betrayed her elation with the events of the weekend thus far.

"Good morning!" She said a little too cheerfully, but she had not finished a bottle of cognac last night.

I poured myself a cup, added some cream from the fridge, and then sat down with her. "You had no idea, did you?" I asked.

"None. I thought I might be losing him. I had heard him talk about Shirley, and I wondered if he was trying to give me hints about something untoward. I should have known better."

"There was no way you could have predicted it. I guess I did not understand how much he loved being on the construction sites."

Paul caught us talking about him. Standing in the doorway to the kitchen, I guess he eavesdropped to determine the nature of our discussion. We both looked up and he was smiling broadly.

"Yes, I will miss the day-to-day site operations, but I am on to bigger and better things. I might even get enough time off that I can take my wife on a much-needed vacation."

"Hooray!" she exclaimed.

I looked at her, and then we looked back at him.

"Happy Birthday!" we both said in unison.

Joanie tried to get him some coffee, but he would not let her. "I am not old and feeble yet, just forty," he joked. "No singing, please."

By ten o'clock, we were ready to leave for brunch. Only in North Carolina can one get a steak for brunch on Sunday, or coleslaw as a side with any meal. I let Paul drive, and the happy couple held hands while he expertly maneuvered the large truck around the quiet suburbs.

"Say, Paul, are you going to have to trade this pickup truck in for one of those foreign sports cars when you get the promotion?" I baited him with a smile on my face.

"Hell no. You will never catch me in one of those sissy-mobiles," he responded. We all laughed.

We got a table and ordered Bloody Marys all around. The hum in the restaurant was a country vibe that resonated with the locals. I felt welcome, but not at home. I am glad Paul and Joanie had settled here, but it would never be my local residence.

"Listen, Paul, if you play your cards right, perhaps you will get lucky on your birthday. I plan to head back home as soon as we are done here."

He eyed me with a scowl. "I got lucky eighteen years ago, when this lady next to me promised to be my wife for life." She smiled with watery eyes.

We ate quietly, listening to the country music playing softly over the speakers. When it came time for dessert, the waitress brought out a small piece of cake with a lit candle in the middle. We sang to him while he squirmed through the entire process.

I slipped him a card from me, and another from Sarah. He was not prepared for the emotion, given the public space, so he slid them into his breast pocket. I paid the bill and got us out of there before we had any more surprises.

The ride home was quiet. We went our separate ways in the house, mostly to use the facilities, and I took care of some last-minute packing. When Paul came back downstairs, I pulled out my phone, dialed Sarah and handed him the phone. He stepped outside and paced the backyard for as long as the conversation lasted. They had a twenty-minute talk, and he was a bit emotional at the end of it when he gave the phone back.

I grabbed my bags and put my massage table back in the trunk. I hugged Joanie, and, in a moment of low resistance, I hugged Paul.

"I will see you both in New Orleans," I said, my voice cracking.

"I want to see you there with a date. Promise me?" he said.

I nodded, climbed into the car, and sped off toward home.

Chance Encounter

It was a beautiful fall afternoon. I had spent an enormous amount of time choosing an outfit that would highlight my best coloring, and the body I had sculpted in the gym. I learned long ago that confidence starts with the right clothes, especially today, when my internal resolve was far from convinced that I was on the right track.

I found the coffee shop and tried to peer inside, but the windows were fogged with the moisture that had burped out of the Italian coffee machines. The autumn air was crisp despite the arrival of an Indian summer. I opened the door and looked around.

He was in the back corner, sipping from an oversized ceramic mug. Even without my history with his brother, I would have picked this guy out of a crowd as my ideal mate. He dressed a little better than Jerome and wore glasses that accentuated his eyes.

I got in line, ordered a coffee, and then waited my turn. The shop was crowded, with nearly every table full. By the time I got my drink, there were no tables left, and I was forced to find a seat with my target. I walked over and stood across from him. When he looked up from his phone, I flashed a smile that was bound to win over even a straight guy.

"Pardon me, but all of the tables are full. May I join you here?"

He must have been caught off guard. He quickly looked around the room to see if I was telling the truth. "Uh, okay. I guess so," he said. He tidied up the table where he had spread his keys, coffee, phone, and book.

My heart was hammering in my chest. I was torn between delivering the message from Jerome and pursuing this man at a full sprint.

"My name is Larry. I am only in town on business for a few days." I put out my hand.

He extended his hand warily. "I am Sherman."

We shook hands, making eye contact. He scanned me from head to waist and back to my eyes. His face reddened when he realized I was still watching him. His eyes dropped and I made myself comfortable at the small table with oversized chairs. I could not tell if he was shy or smitten. I was fighting a smile to appear more serious.

"Were you in the middle of something important, or could you spare a few minutes to talk?" I asked.

He looked up from his phone with a suspicion that I was trying to sell him something. The screen flashed and then went black. He had turned off his phone.

"Sure, we can talk. As long as you are not trying to sell me insurance!" he joked.

I had rehearsed this conversation for hours, yet I found myself struggling to put three words together. He looked down at my hands clutching my cup and then back at my face.

"Sherman. I really don't know where to start, and I don't want this to sound like I am ridiculous, but I sought you out, and I was just lucky that I found you here with this empty chair."

He shifted in his seat. I could only imagine the doubts he had about my presence.

"I will get straight to the point, as it were. I am Larry Brooks. I work in a large firm in the western part of the state." I paused, taking a breath. I continued with my winning, rehearsed line. "I am gay, I am single, and I am a very close friend of your brother."

As he jumped to get up, his thigh bumped the table and spilled his coffee all over the tiny surface. He sat down again quickly, and I did my best to mop up the hot liquid with the few napkins within my reach. We managed to corral the spilt beverage on the table, saving his book and phone in the process. There was a pool of caramel colored coffee in the middle, dammed by napkins around it. His keys were wet with the coffee, but they would survive. His right hand gripped the table with white knuckles.

"What do you want?" He asked through his teeth.

"I want to apologize for Jerome. He wants to reconcile with you."

"Why should I believe you? And what do you get out of this?"

"Sherman, I can only say that he feels terrible about the things he said, and he wants the chance to apologize in person." I stopped, took another breath. "As for me, I will get the chance to help my best friend through a very tough time."

The blank look on his face beguiled me. I suppose it was a lot of information to take in, just seconds after meeting a stranger in a coffee shop.

"Jerome is...your...best...friend?"

"Yes, we have become quite close over the last few months."

"Why should I believe you?" he demanded.

"He is hurting, and he wants to reconcile with you. Ever since Cheryl left him-"

"Wait, his wife left?"

"Yes. The divorce was final about a year ago."

"Oh my gosh," he said and dropped his chin to his chest.

"Yes, he is still devastated. I did not think I was ever going to get him to date again."

"You mean women, right?"

"Yes, one pair of jiggly breasts in the room and I have lost his attention for twenty minutes."

He laughed a little, but his business face resumed quickly.

"Tell me, how did you meet Jerome?" He tested me with a question.

"We work for the same company. I had seen him around the office a few times, but we did not really become friends until we spent a week together for a business seminar."

"And he knows that you are gay?"

"Absolutely. He even teases me about it when we go out. He likes to try to pick out the men I am looking at. I tried to do the same with him, but I always forget and look at the women's faces."

He laughed again. "That sounds like Jerome."

I stopped to sip my coffee. Sherman was just looking down since his drink had covered the table. I smiled when Sherman looked up from the mess in front of us.

"What?" he asked.

"You really are identical, aren't you? You even smile like he does."

"You are creeping me out."

"I am sorry. It's just that...we have spent so much time together; this is like some sort of weird déjà vu."

"How can I know that you are not just well informed from internet research and are somehow trying to scam me?"

"Well, I have only known him a few months, so I could not pass a test on his life story. I can tell you how he takes his coffee, that he adores barbeque in any form, and never gets cold indoors."

"Many people know those things about him. Anything else?"

"He has a shoe fetish. He has more footwear than any straight man I have ever met."

Sherman had a curious look on his face. "Okay, and what else?"

"He prefers dramas over comedies, and hates to watch violence, in any form." Sherman just stared at me.

"He told me about the scars that you have, and he does not."

"Now you are just getting personal," he griped.

"Sherman, please listen to me, just for a second. The Jerome I know is not afraid to cry. He is man enough to hold my hand when he is scared or upset. Or when I am. He feels terrible about how you came out, and that he was neither understanding nor supportive. I don't know what he said, or even why he said it, but I can promise you that my best friend, Jerome, knows that I am out, and has no problem with it. He pleaded with me to find you and deliver this message."

Sherman's face had softened from his anger-induced scowl, but I could not tell what he was thinking. "So, what happens now?"

"I would like to give you his card, and mine. If you decide to contact him, or if you want me to deliver a message, he would be receptive."

"And if I don't, or I am not ready to forgive him?"

"We will wait. If neither of us hears from you, then at least we tried."

"And that would be the end of this?"

"Jerome is my friend; I will do what he asks me to do. I can tell you that he is quite lonely and hurting. He could use some family around him to help him through a rough patch. I will support him any way that I can."

"What about our sister?"

"That is up to Jerome. He may ask me to reach out to Mandy if neither of us hears from you. That is his call, not mine."

An attendant came by with a cloth. He cleaned up Sherman's dishes, wiped the table, and made a point of making eye contact with me before he left. I smiled back at him, and he winked.

"Wait, did you say you were gay, and single?"

"Yes. That was Jerome's idea. He said you would lower your defenses if I tried to flirt. I thought it was a bad idea. I don't like that kind of a bait-and switch tactic."

"Don't you think that was a little cruel for him to suggest that?"

"Why?"

"You obviously have no trouble attracting attention. For him to think that you could get my attention with flattery just makes me angry."

"Sherman, I don't know you, but I know Jerome quite well. He is not cruel, and he thought it might give us common ground to start from."

"What common ground?" He demanded.

I sighed and steeled myself for a confession. "I fell for Jerome when I saw him. It was pure lust from the first day I spotted him. While I did my best to avoid him at work and make him feel like he was not being harassed, I really could have spent all of my free time stalking him."

"Why?"

"Because, to me, he is gorgeous. My sister says I have a gay Oedipus complex. I don't care what it is called, I know I like men that, well, what can I say...look like you...both do. Balding, sturdy, stocky. To me it is pure lust."

Sherman was clutching his phone nervously, as if he were planning to bolt from the cafe.

"I am sorry if I am too blunt, but if Jerome were gay, we would be married. There is no way I would let him get away from me."

"But?"

"I have hairy legs, and no jiggly breasts. He will always be my best friend, but never my husband."

Sherman tried to comprehend what I was saying. His face screwed up, and I thought he was going to cry for a moment. "This is a lot to take in."

"I am sorry. I am often more forward than I intend to be, I just don't play games well."

"Tell me again what is supposed to happen?"

"Ideally? You would contact him and allow him to apologize. I am convinced that he will make adequate amends, given the chance."

"And you? What am I supposed to...?" he trailed off, apparently afraid to finish the sentence.

"Nothing. Suffice it to say that you have an admirer in the world, but my first loyalty is to Jerome."

"I see," he responded.

"I neither want to lose him, nor will I let him down. He is my friend, first and foremost. I really did not come here looking for a date." I sipped my coffee. "In spite of how good you look in those glasses. I wish Jerome had some of your fashion sense. Maybe if he did not spend so much money on shoes..."

"Hey, that is not fair. Who are you to criticize his spending?"

I smiled. "It is good to see you defending him. Does this mean you are softening to the idea of his apology?"

"Maybe. I was just..." and he trailed off in thought.

"Yes? Care to share what you are thinking?"

"I was on the phone with Mandy last night. She asked if I was being too harsh about this. Given this new information, I wonder if she was right. I really hate it when that happens."

I finished my coffee and set the cup down. I waited for any further information from Sherman. "Was that it?" he asked.

"Yes, it was. Could I leave you his card? It has his cell number and email address on it."

"And yours? Would I get that too, in this deal?" He smirked.

I smiled. "If that is what it takes. Absolutely."

He watched me suspiciously as I pulled out two home-printed business cards. I made a point of putting Jerome's over mine. He ran his fingers over the type. I thought he was getting choked up at the thought of calling him.

"You can call, or text – or even email if it suits you. He usually has his phone around during waking hours, so if you just send him a text with a time to call, he will respond, I promise. And no, I will not be there for it."

"I am thinking about it," he snapped. "How often do you see him?"

"Me? Nearly every day when I am in town. We work in the same building, and we live two miles apart."

"He still lives in the same place?"

"I guess. It is the two-story colonial on Amster Street."

"You've been there?"

"I have stayed over several nights, and I have a key." I held up my keychain. "He has a key to my place, too."

"What in the world happened to him when I came out? He sounds like he has...been transformed."

"I am sure he would love the opportunity to share all of that with you. We have had some rather deep conversations, and I think you will like the man he has become. I know I love him, as much as I do my own brother."

I could see Sherman tearing up. I put my open palm out on the table.

"Please give him the chance to be your brother again. Please?"

He reached out but picked up the business cards instead. He stuffed them in his pocket. He grabbed his book and phone. Without another word, he stood up and walked out. I sat there for a few moments. I really did not want to leave without a solid answer for Jerome, but I could not sit there any longer with people waiting for tables.

Back out on the sidewalk, I never thought to look around for Sherman. He came up behind me when I reached my car. His voice startled me enough to make me drop my keys on the pavement. "Are you leaving town today?"

I picked up my keys and turned around to face him. "I have a room booked for one more night, but I may just drive back now."

"Why?" he demanded.

"I accomplished what I set out to do. The ball is in your court now."

"What will you tell him?"

"That I saw you, and delivered his message, along with his business card."

"But not mention your card?"

"Sherman, I don't have any secrets from Jerome. If he does not hear from you soon, he may ask me to tell him everything we said. I will, without hesitation, share this conversation from memory if it helps him to understand that I really did try."

He looked at me, watched my words spill out, but it was as if he was not hearing me.

"Sherman? Is something wrong?"

He was on the verge of an emotional outburst. I pulled out my handkerchief. He took it without a word. Several people passed by, and he looked visibly shaken by the sudden appearance of the pedestrians in our midst.

"Would you care to walk for a bit?" I asked.

He nodded.

The cool temperature was pleasant for a late afternoon stroll. He led the way, as it was his town. We turned off the busy

214

pedestrian mall and into a relaxed, gentrified neighborhood. I gave him the space to find his voice if he even wanted to talk to me.

"I know Jerome is a techy. He works as a project manager. What is it that you do at this big corporation?"

"I am in legal. I go over the contracts to look out for the company's interests."

"So, are you a paralegal or a lawyer?"

"The latter, but don't say it so loud, there are children nearby." I smiled at my own wit, but he did not catch the joke.

"Do you have any family?"

"Yes, I have an older brother and a younger sister. We have all the typical frictions. I am closer to my sister, but it helps that she likes women and I like men. I am not sure our brother understands us, but he loves us both...from a distance."

He was quiet for a few more strides. When he stopped, I thought he had more questions. Instead, he turned and went up the path. Then he climbed the steps. I watched him go, not knowing what was going on. When he got to the door, he turned around. "This is my house. Would you like to come in?"

"Uh, okay. I guess," I replied and closed the distance between us.

He had the door open by the time I got to the last step. He held it open for me, and then closed it behind him. The foyer was fitting for a home built in the late nineteenth century. The décor was impressive, and just what I would have expected of a home on this street.

"You have a lovely home," I stated matter-of-factly.

"Thank you. I had a decorator do it all. I am a computer guy, with not much style to speak of. I know it looks good, but I never would have had the intuition to put it all together. Some of the colors are downright odd, but are contemporary to the period, and they seem to work in these spaces."

"Could I use the bathroom?" I asked. "The coffee seems to have finished with me."

"Sure, down the hall, first door on the left."

When I returned, he was sitting in the living room. He had leaned back in a period chair, crossing his left leg over his other knee at a right angle. His position did not look comfortable, but neither did he.

"May I sit down?" I asked, trying to alert him that I had returned.

"Sure. That settee is original to the house. I had it recovered, but I find it to be a bit...stiff for my liking."

I sat down, expecting a firm cushion. I sank down in a surprise of gravity. I looked up at him, thinking he would apologize for the misdirection. He was not even looking my way.

The grandfather clock ticked incessantly as we sat in the quiet. I was good at waiting out clients for legal, but I had no idea what I was waiting for, in this instance. When he finally spoke, it startled me out of my thoughts.

"I came out late in life. I never understood the guys that knew what they wanted in their teens. It baffled me to think that there were any choices but women, and the traditional family route."

I worked on using my listening skills, without interjecting my opinions.

"When I found the courage to tell Jerome that I was dumping my girlfriend, he was disappointed. I thought he would have been more supportive. I had gotten the impression that he did not even like her."

"Sherman?" I asked. "When was that? Jerome has never told me that part."

"About two years ago. No, exactly two years ago. I even counted the months for a while, I was so angry at his intolerance."

"Oh, gosh. Okay."

"He said horrible things to me. I even made a special trip out to see him. I thought that would be easier."

"Was Cheryl there with him?"

"No, he said she was on a bachelorette trip with her girlfriends."

"I don't know what was said, or how the two of you expressed yourself, but he told me that Cheryl left him two years ago. I wonder if that was what drove him to be so ugly about your...announcement."

Sherman sighed just like Jerome does when he is confronted with news he did not expect.

"He could have been reeling from the loss of his marriage, but I don't know for sure. It just seems like the timing could coincide with your coming out."

"I did not know that. Mandy did not tell me, if she even knew."

It got quiet again as he processed the information.

"Have you really kept him out of your life for two years? That seems kind of harsh. Didn't he try to contact you?"

"Yes, he tried. The normal ways. Text, voicemail, email. Then he moved onto social media. I almost shut down my accounts to avoid him. I finally just blocked him and went on with my life." His voice was clipped and harsh but edged with emotion that bordered on tears.

"Sherman, Jerome seems like such a warm, caring guy. Was what he said to you so awful that you would block all attempts at reconciliation for this long?"

"You were not there, and you cannot understand how much he hurt me."

"I am sorry, I did not intend to diminish your pain, I am just trying to understand."

"Has anyone ever rejected you for coming out?"

"A few people have, but I was one of those guys that just knew when I was a teenager. I am comfortable with me. I don't tend to keep any people in my life that don't know up front and accept me for it."

"Fine. I see what I am up against," he huffed.

"Could I ask, if it is not too personal, have you had much luck, navigating the gay dating scene in this college town?"

"So, you are suddenly interested in fixing me, too? Am I just another project from this family that you want to take on?"

I stood up. "I am leaving, I see this is going nowhere. I will tell Jerome that I spoke with you, and that you have his card. The next move is yours to make."

"What? That's it? You are just going to walk out?"

"When you changed the tone to hostile, I no longer felt comfortable here. I am not here to debate, I wanted to ask you to contact your brother. I did that. Goodbye, Sherman."

I walked over to the door. He caught me before I could open it.

"Wait. I am sorry. This just has me all off-kilter. I don't know what to think anymore."

"Do you want my opinion?"

"I guess," he replied hesitantly.

"I think, in this case, that you came out and expected Jerome to celebrate for you. You needed him to validate you and your revelation. But you had deceived him, if not yourself, for years, and it shocked him. When he showed anger and hostility, you returned it, never considering that he may have had some monumental struggles, and a failing marriage. Now, after two years with no boyfriend, you are clinging to your anger at him, in a vain attempt to keep from dealing with your own issues and loneliness. Come out or not but grow up and make some choices. Stop holding onto empty anger at someone who does not deserve your ire. He really does love you. Give him a chance to show that."

His mouth was hanging open.

I let myself out and pulled out my phone to find my car. I was done with Chapel Hill.

It was getting late in the day, and I did not want to drive all the way home. I drove aimlessly for a while, then worked my way through two hours of evening traffic. I got back to my hotel around six. I was not hungry, although I knew I needed to eat something. I locked the car and walked to the nearest fast-food establishment. I rationalized that I deserved some level of pampering, considering what I had just gone through for Jerome.

When it came down to Arby's or Wendy's, I settled for the roast beef. I got my tray, found a table, and settled in to eat my protein-packed sandwich. I did not expect my phone to ring, and I did not recognize the number. The area code gave me pause, but I knew people in the capital region.

"Hello?" I answered.

"Hello. This is Sherman" the voice replied.

I sat up in my booth and reached in my bag for a pencil. "What can I do for you?" I asked.

He sighed, just like Jerome does to build up courage. "Can you talk, or are you with Jerome?"

"I am alone. I have not talked with him yet."

"Good."

More silence. I waited and could hear him breathing.

"Sherman?"

"I'm here," he responded.

"If you breathe any heavier, I may have to ask what you are wearing," I said, trying to break the ice.

"Sorry, it's just that I have been...sitting here since you left this afternoon."

"I see. Have you made any decisions?"

"Yes, I will contact Jerome. Please do not tell him - I would like it to be a welcome surprise."

"I am quite pleased to hear that. It's a deal. Is there something else?"

"Are you always so direct?" he asked. "It's just that..." and he stopped.

I waited for twenty seconds for him to finish. "Sherman?"

"I am sorry. My emotions have gotten to me," he sniffled.

He sounded just like Jerome, only it was muffled by the phone.

"To answer your question, yes, I am typically quite direct. I find it cuts through all the drama and excuses if I just say what I mean, and...I am sorry if I hurt your feelings, but I just had such an instant...intuition about how things were with you."

"I can certainly see why Jerome is so attached to you. We have never experienced anything close to that in our family dynamics. I haven't even had the nerve to call Mandy yet."

"Is that why you called? Do you want me to reach out to her, too?"

"NO!" he exclaimed, then laughed. "We really don't want to open that can of worms."

"Sherman, it is not that I am not concerned about you, it's just that my first loyalty has to be to Jerome. If there is any way that I can help - with that in mind - you just have to tell me."

"I really could use a friend."

"I am willing to explore that. Might I suggest reconnecting with your brother first?"

"He won't understand. Not the way you seem to grasp things, anyway. I might even need a shoulder to cry on."

"It is getting late, perhaps we could talk tomorrow, when our heads are clear?"

"Uh, ok, I guess. Any particular time?"

"I was supposed to be off tomorrow. I am open all day," I responded.

"Are you willing to meet me somewhere? How far would you have to drive?"

"Sure. I can meet you. I never checked out of the hotel, so I am just about fifteen minutes from anywhere in town."

More silence on the phone.

"Could I see you tonight?" he nearly whispered.

"I am not sure that would be a good idea. Why don't we both get a good night's sleep and then we can talk in the morning?"

"Please? I really could use some help."

"Will you answer some questions first?"

He paused. I waited.

"Okay" he conceded.

"Have you been drinking?"

"Just hot tea."

"Can we meet somewhere neutral?"

"I guess." He sounded defeated.

"Can you tell me where? I don't know the area."

More silence. "How about the..." and he trailed off without finishing.

"Sherman?"

"I am sorry, I don't go out much, so I had to think of a place. Did you pack a coat?"

"Yes, why?"

"Bring it. Meet me at the coffee shop where you found me this afternoon. It is a nice neighborhood to walk in, and I know a great ice cream shop nearby."

My gut was telling me no, but I did not want to argue on the phone. "I will be there in about fifteen minutes."

It took me twenty minutes in traffic. He was waiting outside the coffee shop. He was pacing, checking his watch. I honked as I passed by and then found a spot a half block away. He stayed where he was.

I walked back over to the cafe and waved when I got close. He had changed his clothes and had added a fall sport coat that made him more of a stylish gentleman than I had ever seen Jerome portray.

"Good evening, Sherman," I said.

"Hello, again, Larry."

We eyed each other for a few seconds. I did not know what to expect next.

"Where is this ice cream parlor? You have my interest piqued."

"It's this way." He turned and began walking.

I caught up quickly. He continued down the street past where he had turned earlier that afternoon.

"What is your drug of choice?"

"Hunh?" he asked.

"Your go-to flavor for ice cream. I love anything with strawberry in it, but I will settle for raspberry as a close second."

"Oh, that. I am a chocolate or vanilla kind of guy. Don't mess with the basics."

He stopped in front of a brightly lit shop with an enormous front window. Fanciful scoops of cartoon ice cream were painted on the glass. The door was propped open and there were a few people milling about, but none of them were in line.

"Shall we go in?" I asked.

He just stood there. "Sherman?"

"Sorry, I am in a muddle."

I led the way in, hoping he would follow. After perusing the menu, I chose a concoction called toast and jam from the list of gourmet flavors. He hesitated, again.

"Sherman? They are not psychic. You actually have to tell them what you want."

He smiled faintly. "I will have the same. Thank you."

I paid for the cones and sat down at a table more cramped than the coffee shop. The ice cream was incredible. The base was a rich custard with a taste of Bavarian cream. Specked through it were streaks of strawberry jam and crumbled, softened Lorna Doone cookies.

"I may just stay here tonight and keep eating until their supply of this flavor is gone," holding up my severely diminished cone.

He looked up at me as if I were speaking French.

"Sherman? Are you okay? It seems like you are in a fog, and I don't know what it will take to bring you out of it. Maybe we should have gotten espressos, instead."

"I am sorry, I just have a lot of stuff going on, and it is hard to put it into words."

"Take your time."

He licked at his cone, absent-mindedly. I paced myself, wondering if he would miss me if I got in line again.

"Larry, I am at a crossroads, and I could use some feedback on what to do."

I looked around the crowded shop. "We can walk and talk, if that would help."

"Yes, that would be better," he responded.

We got up and left. I had finished my cone and resisted the urge to take his by force. After fifteen paces of silence, I switched to my lawyer's 'deposition' mode.

"What are the particulars of this 'crossroads' that you mentioned?"

"Oh, that...right. I have had an offer to sell out my business to a conglomerate."

"Do you not believe the company will maintain your standards?"

"No, they have garnered accolades for their innovative practices."

"Will they retain your customers and treat them as you would?"

"I think so, their reputation is quite good in the industry."

"What is the nature of your hesitation? Is it too tempting of an offer to just say 'no' to them?"

"My main concern, for now, is just what I would do with my time if I no longer had to work."

I gave him a few more paces to sort out what he needed to say.

"I am very much a routine person. I cannot float through the days without a plan, a schedule, and a list of tasks to tackle."

"If you sold your stake, would you be barred from working in the same field with a non-compete agreement?"

"Yes, but only within a certain geographic radius. I could move and start over, but I am...settled here."

"Larry, you have a lovely home, and it sounds like a great offer, but I have to ask you the hard question."

He was silent. I counted five more steps that we took.

"Are you happy?"

He remained silent.

"If nothing changed for the next month, year, or decade, would you want to continue exactly where you are, how you are working and living?"

More silence.

"Sherman?"

"No," he croaked. He was crying, but I did not want to call attention to it.

I hesitated, then bent slightly and slipped my hand into his.

"Then you have your answer. You are in charge of your own happiness. If you don't pull the reins where you want the sled to go, your current track may end up being permanent. We could call that your burial plot."

We passed two college gals. They were holding hands, too. One smiled at me through her many piercings.

"Sherman? Are you still there?" I pulled on his hand.

He steered us over to a bench and plopped down. I dropped my hands to my lap.

"Do you have a lawyer you are working with?"

"Yes - a friend from undergrad. I have known him for years."

"Good, you need someone on your side."

"Do you have a bucket list? Travel plans? Hobbies?"

"I have always wanted to see Europe. I have never gotten around to it."

"What do you do when you are not working now?"

"I read a lot. As you so astutely guessed this afternoon, I have not done well on the dating circuit."

"What are you reading?" I asked, dodging the romance topic.

"I prefer fiction - mostly fantasy and sci-fi - but I dabble in history and technology."

"Tolkien or Lewis?"

"Tolkien."

"Bradbury or Card?"

"Orson Scott Card? I like his storytelling, but he was such a homophobic asshole that I won't pay for his books."

"I know. I check them out of the county library."

"Me, too," he added.

"What is your graduate degree in?"

"Software engineering."

"Have you considered teaching?"

"I never found the time."

"If you suddenly had no customers, I am sure you could work it into your routine, no?"

He smiled. "You are really good at this."

"Thank you," I said. "I have done some mentoring, and life-coaching. Funny, it never seems to work for me, though."

"Doctor, heal thyself."

"Thanks. I will avoid the potential malpractice if you don't mind."

"What is good for the goose, is -"

I cut him off. "When do you have to decide on this sale?"

"By the end of the week."

"Have you considered asking for a job in the new practice?"

"I did, but they resisted. Founder's syndrome."

"I thought that was just nonprofits?"

"Yeah, no, it happens in technology, a lot. The original players can hold a company back. They - we - can cause too much cultural resistance."

"So, it is all or nothing?"

"Yep."

"Is it worth it, financially?"

"I would not have to work again."

"It would not take me long to think about it."

"I am scared. I feel like I would be cut adrift."

"You know, I'll bet your siblings would love to help you through this transition."

He was quiet.

"I think your sister is a financial genius, based on my research. And your brother has adapted well to single life on his paycheck. They may even help you enjoy some of the proceeds."

He snapped his head around and glared at me.

"But you will have to call one of them before he even knows that you might get this windfall."

His head fell to his chest.

"What?" I asked.

"I just have not built up the nerve."

"Why not? You know that he is desperate to hear from you."

"It is not just the initial call; I have forgiven him. I feel like I would have to, I don't know...expiate myself, for treating him like this for two years."

"You will never know, until you reach out to him."

"I know that."

"Here is the bad news. While he may not call tonight, by tomorrow afternoon he will be lighting up my phone with questions."

"How long can you put him off?" he laughed.

"He will leave me alone for the drive home, but he has a key to my house. He may be waiting there for me when I arrive."

"I see."

"Before I left, he told me that he would be on a date tonight, so I will not bother him this evening."

"And in the morning?"

"He is at work by nine. He has been going to the gym each morning, so you could actually catch him before he is suited up to herd cats for the company."

Sherman smiled. "I guess that is a good description of corporate life."

"And accurate," I replied.

We settled into silence for a few minutes.

"Sherman, between the ice cream and the chilly air, I need to get inside. Can we walk back to my car now?"

"Shoot, I was just getting comfortable," he said. "Sure, we can go back now."

We stood up and began the walk back. It had gotten dark. I was glad we had not turned from the main road.

"You are going back to your hotel now?"

"Absolutely. I need to get inside, get warm, and then sleep."

"Oh, okay."

I stopped. "Did you have something else in mind?"

"I, uh, was just thinking."

"You might get us both in trouble with that kind of thought. I think it is better if you talk to your brother and smooth things over, first, don't you?"

"Are you saying that you are interested?"

"I decline to comment, either way. But as long as there is still a rift between you and Jerome, I have to put him first."

"Well, what are you doing tomorrow?"

"I was going to hit the furniture stores in High Point on my way home. My work here is done."

His face fell.

"Isn't it?" I asked.

"Yeah, I guess so," he said quietly.

I continued walking until I got to my car. I turned around to see him again. Sherman had gone back to his introverted, quiet state. I marveled at how gregarious his brother was, by comparison. "Sherman?" I said.

He looked up. "Yes?"

"Would you like to do something tomorrow? Maybe we could go out to breakfast somewhere?"

"Okay, that would be great." He perked up.

"How about nine o'clock?" I asked.

"You know, I could show you the furniture stores around here. There are quite a few in town."

"Let's talk about it at breakfast."

"Sure," he said.

"Okay, call or text me if something changes. Otherwise, I will pick you up at nine, at your house."

I had gotten so accustomed to embracing Jerome that I stepped forward and hugged him. He seemed surprised but returned the embrace. For me it was the familiar frame and pattern of breathing that had kept me on track for the last few months. I could not tell how Sherman perceived it, but he did not want to let go at first. I stepped back, clicked the button for my car door, and got in.

I waved through the window as I pulled away. He was so distracted that I did not even ask if he wanted a ride to his home.

Nor did I want the temptation.

Mission Accomplished

I arrived at Sherman's house two minutes before nine o'clock. I had checked out of the hotel and thrown my bag into the trunk. The quicker I could extract myself from this breakfast, the sooner I could get on the road for home.

I went to the door and rang the bell. The face at the glass side panel scowled with contempt, and my heart melted. He had not told me about his cat. I squatted down to touch the glass and the door swung open. I smiled, caught off guard by the figure towering over me.

"Good morning," he chirped. "I see you have met Onslow. He hates everyone, including me."

"I can see why. You have made no attempts at all to make him happy."

"No, I keep him in this three-thousand square foot cage. His bed is wherever he wants it to be, and there are more meals than he eats. I am surprised no one has called the SPCA."

I stood up and stepped into the house. Onslow had already disappeared.

"Are you ready to go?" I asked.

"Would you object to me cooking breakfast? I have some news to share."

"I guess not. Will it upset the homeowner?"

"No, he is fine until he throws up his breakfast. I give it about twenty minutes before we hear him retch."

I smiled despite the disgust I felt. "Cats are wonderful, but I don't want to be a servant to a tyrant, no matter how cute they are as kittens."

"Yeah, he hooked me at the shelter, and has been running my life ever since," Sherman mused.

He closed the door and led the way into the kitchen. He had already set the table, and the ingredients for omelets were on the counter.

"Coffee?"

"Yes, please," I answered. "So, what is your news?"

"I called my lawyer this morning and told him to put the deal into motion. I will be gainfully unemployed by the end of the month."

My face must have fallen.

"What?" he asked. "Oh, I called Mandy and filled her in on all the details of yesterday. She was gloating by the time we hung up at midnight."

"AND?"

"I called Jerome this morning. I got his voicemail."

"That's it? Really?"

"No, he called back about eight," he laughed. "We talked for a while, and I worked up the courage to apologize. He was really a gentleman about the whole thing."

"I am not surprised. Your brother is really something special."

"I know. And now I have some lost time to make up with him."

He poured the mug of coffee and set it down for me at the table. I seated myself and watched him crack the eggs. The khakis he had on must have been elastic because they showed every curve. It was hard to look away.

"Do you want an omelet? Or how would you like your eggs?"

He turned around and caught me looking. I blushed.

"Perhaps you would like to see the full menu, instead?" he asked.

"I am sorry, it's just that..."

"Don't be. I am glad to know that I did not try on ten pairs of slacks for nothing this morning."

"This would not be so difficult, if I weren't already so close to Jerome."

"Do you have another milestone in mind before I get to see more of you?"

"I did not have any particular goal post in mind," I said. "Will you be seeing Jerome soon?" Changing the subject.

"He said something about meeting up at the weekend. We have not solidified the actual plans, yet."

"Will there be a family reunion in the works?"

"Maybe for the next big holiday. What is that, Thanksgiving?"

"Where does Mandy live? I don't think Jerome ever said."

"She just moved to Charlotte but is always on the road. She is an executive in the financial sector."

"Do you plan on staying here in Chapel Hill?"

"I definitely want to keep this house. I have not asked Onslow how he feels about my relocating."

"That might be a tough negotiation. You will definitely need a good lawyer."

"Are you available?" he asked with a suggestive look on his face.

"For the right price, I would represent you. We will probably lose against the cat if court precedent is any indicator."

"Yeah, we have no chance at all. You have seen his face."

We both laughed.

Eating in silence, I tried to avoid his eyes, though he tried to catch me looking when he scooped more eggs. We had both settled into our thoughts, and a level of comfort that I would not have predicted based on the tension I felt yesterday when I introduced myself as Jerome's friend.

I helped him clean up the dishes and then he left to search for the latest expression of discontentment from Onslow. He returned with a smile on his face and the distinct aroma of mouthwash. I wish I had brought my toothbrush in from the car.

"Now, what kind of furniture would you like to browse for on this fine fall day? We have antique stores, craftsman's shops, chains, independent dealers and quite a few charity shops that seem to capture all the college kids' handoffs."

I smiled and waited for him to finish.

"Larry? Do you have a preference on furniture?"

"I certainly do. Why don't you show me what your decorator has put in your home? Perhaps we can take some inspiration from that."

"Oh, okay, but none of this is for sale, right? I am not willing to part with any of these items, some are one-of-a-kind antiques."

I nodded and waited for him to start the tour. He turned and went out the side door of the kitchen, and on into the dining room.

"I got this suite of furniture from an old farmhouse in Charleston. Well, actually, Susie did. She is my decorator. Everything else in that house was rustic and worn, but somehow this ensemble of honey oak was pristine and almost out of place there."

"It truly is a beautiful set."

He led me to the library, which had more books than most public facilities.

"I collect rare books on science and technology. My insurance for this room alone exceeds most primary mortgages," he laughed.

"Have you read them all?"

"Many of them, yes. But it is not as relaxing as one might think. I have to wear white cotton gloves and place the book in a neutral position to not damage the spine any further." He frowned. "I am thinking that I will donate them all to a suitable institution."

When I did not speak, he turned and brought the tour back to the parlor, where he had been confrontational the afternoon before.

"The pieces in here are an amalgamation of several estate sales that Susie and I attended together. She is particularly good at choosing quality items and spending my money in the process," he smiled brightly.

"It is all beautiful, and I feel oddly comfortable here, despite the formality of the setting."

"One of the best features of used furniture, for me, is the elimination of risk that the previous owners assumed. I no longer feel as if I must protect the brand-new, just-purchased patina that they must have fretted about. I also buy furniture to use and enjoy, not as an investment that might bring me a profit later."

He led me back into the foyer.

"I had originally tried to find stained glass for the windows that ran down the sides of the door. I thought it would make for a wonderful kaleidoscope effect on the oak floors."

"But you could not find suitable candidates? These are all clear."

"The idea was vetoed by Onslow. He needs to scowl at people to show his displeasure. I cannot impede his mission in the world."

We laughed, recognizing the truth of life with a cat.

He stopped and made eye contact. "Would you like to see the basement?"

"No, I am not much for dark and damp, no disrespect intended for your decorator."

"Well then, how about the upstairs?"

"Yes, I would like that very much."

His phone rang in his pocket. He grimaced.

"Why don't you go up and look around. I will handle this and find you once I finish."

I slowly climbed the wooden stairs, admiring the paintings on the wall, and the minute, detailed carvings on the risers. It was a surprise that the antique steps did not creak at all with my shifting weight.

I looked in each of the rooms upstairs, casually surveying the décor and style that was uniform and meticulous. The bathroom had an enormous footed tub with shiny brass fixtures.

I had to peek behind all the closed doors before I found the concealed shower stall. It was expertly hidden, with modern amenities and room enough for four adults. He must have sacrificed the better part of a bedroom or nursery to have accomplished such an extravagance. I really admired the attention to detail and attempt to keep the furnishings true to the period.

I went through the entire upstairs and stopped when I got to the attic stairs. I had no interest in cobwebs or old trunks, although he probably had a modern gym and a sauna, just disguised well with the antique door.

Instead, I found the master bedroom and marveled at the size. Even with the four-poster bed and all the heavy, ornately carved wooden period furniture, there was more floor space than I had in my chain hotel room. I had just finished counting the foot-lengths of the second dimension when I heard him clear his throat behind me.

I turned around, red-faced, and embarrassed. "I was just...measuring the room. It is enormous!"

"I combined two bedrooms, at great expense for the support beam and an architectural consultation. I wanted a sanctuary, and I needed a space big enough for all this furniture. It is the original, matched set from the governor's mansion in a southern state that I will not name."

"But is it comfortable?" I asked.

"As I said before, I thoroughly enjoy my possessions. I do not collect for looks alone. If it is not functional and pleasing to me, I tend not to keep it for long," he spoke with a sly smile on his face, closing the distance between us.

"I can't say that I believe you. Although I am not from Missouri, you will need to prove it to me. And I don't convince easily. Sometimes it takes several iterations of a solid argument to win me over."

I was glad that I had filched some of his mouthwash.

Back Home

I pulled into my driveway after the three-hour trip home in unusually heavy traffic. My first urge was to call Jerome and tell him about the trip, but I had to reign in my feelings about his brother, and the way that I had left Chapel Hill.

It was dark, and I was tired from the day's exertions. I let myself in, sorted the mail, and tried to find something to eat. It felt like midnight, but it was just after nine o'clock. I scrambled some eggs, made some toast, and capped the snack with some cranberry juice from the refrigerator.

I considered a drink, but I had a long-standing promise to myself not to consume alcohol before a workday, even if I had been on vacation - the best vacation day I could remember in my life.

I unpacked, changed to gym clothes, and settled in with a book. I had not finished the first page when my cell phone rang. The face on the screen was quite familiar, but I did not know it was Jerome until I saw the name at the bottom. I put down the book and answered the call.

"Hey, I thought you were going to call me when you got home today," he said, sounding perturbed.

Ignoring the barb, I tried to change the subject. "I understand that you reconnected with your brother."

"Yes, of course I did. You knew that. Why are you being so coy?"

"I don't know. It has been kind of a long day, and I had just settled in to relax before I go to sleep."

"Well, what did you do all day, then? I thought you were going to call me."

"Jerome, I spent the entire day with Sherman."

"That is great. You two must have really hit it off. Did you find a lot to talk about?"

"Not really."

The silence played out for a few moments. "I don't understand," he said.

"Look this is a bit awkward, okay. If it were anyone else, and I thought you were interested-"

"I am interested, dammit!" he shouted.

"I was going to say, if I thought you were interested in all the sordid details, I would be giving you a play-by-play account of what went down."

He was quiet, but I could hear his breathing. I pictured him looking off across his living room, taking in what I was saying.

"Are you saying –"

"Yes," I interjected. "How much detail do you want to hear?"

More silence.

"Jerome?"

"Yeah, I am here. Sorry, I was just processing what has happened."

"Is there a problem?" I asked, apprehensive about his response.

"Um, no, I guess not," he mumbled.

"Hey, do you want me to come over? We can talk about this – I don't want this to be a wedge between us."

"No, I was just getting ready for bed. I will see you later."

"Can't we talk about this first?" I demanded.

"No, please get some sleep and we can talk later." He severed the line.

He avoided me the next day. I could see he was online, but he had turned his status to 'busy, do not disturb' even though his calendar was empty. I waited him out, trying to focus on work.

He gave me the slip in the parking lot that afternoon and he did not answer his phone, so I just assumed he was on a date with Abigail. At least he was smart enough to not park in his own driveway, because I went by there a few times, scanning for movement in the house. I had a key but did not dare go inside.

A few more days of the same pattern nearly made me give up. I started to throw a tantrum on Friday afternoon when he left work early, but then I remembered that he had a weekend away planned with his new girlfriend. If I had not set it up, it would have felt a whole lot worse.

I dropped all attempts to contact him. My schedule changed as we worked on a contract with a firm in California. The time shift kept me off kilter and wondering if I could ever go back to east coast living. While I missed the connection with Sherman, it really hurt to be without Jerome, and I switched to planning for the wedding in New Orleans.

Wedding Bells

Sherman and I flew first class to New Orleans on the second weekend in November. Unlike the last flight, I did not have to ask my companion to hold my hand. He seemed to hesitate letting go, even for a moment. The clinginess was starting to bother me, but I needed to get through this weekend, and I could not afford to alienate him.

The alarm had gone off at three. We made it to the airport within the prescribed time frame and caught the very first flight of the day at seven. Sherman had told me that he flew for work, but I had no inkling that he was a timid passenger. I really did not mind holding his hand, even though it gave me flashback memories of the trip home with Jerome.

Sarah had insisted that we both be fitted for tuxedos, even though I did not want to force Sherman into the ceremony. We were still dating, technically, and I think the pressure of a wedding, with family and pomp, can put too much stress on people that are already committed. But after he surprised me and agreed quite readily, I ached to see him in the tuxedo. If a man must wear anything at all, there are few looks more appealing, with the singular exception of a uniform.

We got our rental car and went downtown to check into our hotel. The Cat's Paw was full up, mostly for the wedding and the celebrations. For that, I was greatly relieved, because there were just too many parallels to my week with Jerome. I used some travel points to upgrade us to a suite in the Hilton. Because it was my sister's wedding, I insisted on paying for the entire weekend's travel arrangements. I did not want Sherman to think that he would be dragged along just to foot the bill.

As we got to the correct address, there was a roadblock that messed up our directions, but we ended up being in the background of a commercial. The company was filming on location, and one of the lines in the ad was an instruction for the couple in the car (they were promoting) to turn right at the place where they could see a bear eating a man. There was a four-story mural of a grizzly with a full-sized man in his mouth as a playful advertisement for some other product. The final commercial only showed the wall for a few seconds, but it took some monumental labor to get it done.

We both started to wither in the car. I desperately wanted to go to Café Du Monde, but again, there would be another memory of Jerome that would have been awkward. We used valet parking and got checked into the spacious, yet sterile room. Setting our bags down, I turned to embrace him, and he tensed up.

"Is there something wrong, Sherman?"

"No, I am just a little tired from the early morning wakeup."

"I am not getting the impression that you are completely relaxed. Is there anything I can do?"

He paused for a moment, scanned the room with his eyes, and then turned to me. "You were here with Jerome, weren't you?"

"We were in New Orleans on our first trip together, yes. We stayed at Sarah's hotel in the French Quarter." I walked over to the easy chair and sat down. I needed to draw him out, and my proximity to him was just making him more tense.

"Oh, okay," he said flatly.

He sat down on the bed, staring at his shoes. He sighed. "What else did you two do here?"

I got up, walked over to the mini bar, and pulled out a cold water. Taking the cap off, I swigged a few reckless swallows to appear nonchalant, and then set the bottle down on the table.

"Sherman, I was sure that Jerome had told you this story by now. We met at a resort hotel for a conference we were supposed to attend in New England. As far as I know, neither of us knew that the other had registered for the same event. Arriving early, we had some time to get acquainted. When he finally confided to me that he was having a difficult time, we skipped out on the work commitment, and came down here, to Sarah's hotel. If you did not know, the property caters to women only. We stuck out like sore thumbs!" I grinned but he did not return the smile.

"I showed him around the French Quarter, took him to a few restaurants, and forced him to eat doughnuts in an outdoor café, several times. The one evening I spent dining with Sarah, he met Abigail in a bar."

"Is that all?"

"In a nutshell, yes. I was thrilled that he wanted so many massages." I regretted the words as soon as they were out of my mouth. "It did, however, help us to bond, as well as force me to be honest about my attraction to him. He was quite understanding, despite the close quarters." I tried to get a read on Sherman, but he was a blank slate.

"We grew attached to each other; we connected in a way I had never achieved with another adult in my life. We were fast friends, and it was the birth of our friendship." I sipped more water, letting it dribble down my chin to appear reckless. "Are you really jealous of my interactions with him?"

"To be honest, yes. I am, a bit. I realize that I would not be here, with you, if the two of you had not connected in such a profound way. But it still hurts me to think that I will have to share you with him."

"I doubt I will have much of his time if this infatuation with Abigail continues. Remember, Jerome has to see some cleavage to even get his attention. And she is winning that battle for now, so I am being relegated to second string, and very little locker-room talk."

He smiled. I walked over to him and put my hand out. He took it, and I pulled, gently, until he was standing. I embraced him and waited to hear more. He breathed deeply, not speaking for a few minutes.

"So, what, now?" he asked.

"We have to be at the restaurant by six. Until then, I am all yours. Are you hungry? Or do you want to rest for a while?"

"If I lie down, would I have to do it alone?"

"You never have to be alone in a hotel bed, if I am around."

He pulled out of the hug and began to unbutton his shirt. I waited for any more requests. "I believe I have won this battle," he said in a stage whisper. "That means you have to surrender your clothes."

"Yes, sir!" I responded, and quickly began to match his moves to disrobe.

We got a late breakfast in the café down in the lobby of our hotel. It was just some light salads and large drinks – New Orleanians are known for their consumption. After the early morning and hotel activities, we both wanted to nap for a while before we could begin to be sociable.

I texted Jerome a picture of our view from the terrace but got no response.

Back in the room, I wondered if we would get any sleep at all when Sherman emerged from the bathroom wearing just a smile. If I had to die of exhaustion, I was willing to take the chance, and forgo sleep until the grim reaper arrived to see the smile on my face.

The first evening was dinner for friends at an Indian Restaurant selected by the brides. We had a variety of dishes, most of which Sherman did not like at all. He was a good sport, especially considering that he was struggling to remember the names of all the family members, as well as overcome his introverted nature.

Sarah and Julie invited us out for a night on the town after the meal. Sherman was already withdrawing into his isolation mode, so I suggested breakfast together instead. They agreed, and we got a cab back to the Hilton.

In the car, on a side street, I thought I saw Angie, our rickshaw driver. I wanted to speak with her, but it would have been awkward, so I turned away before she recognized either of us.

Sherman was silent for the elevator ride and the initial fumbling around the dark room, searching for the light switches. I had resigned myself to a night of television and fitful sleep. I left him alone to sort out his bedtime routine and took a quick shower to relax my muscles.

When I emerged from the bathroom, Sherman was gazing out over the river. The reading light above his place in the bed was the only illumination in the room, and his furry skin glistened more beautifully than the most elaborate constellation in the night sky.

I approached him quietly, taking him by surprise, while still telegraphing my intentions. We stood together, with my arms around his chest and my chin on his shoulder, watching the water below us, solemnly flowing toward the Gulf of Mexico.

"I am getting cold," I whispered.

"I have a surefire way to fix that," he responded.

Breakfast Battle

The four of us met at Brennan's at ten o'clock on Friday morning. Julie and Sarah looked luminous, as the brides-to-be. Sarah had pulled some strings and gotten us a private room. Sherman looked a bit tired, but I am sure we both had missed enough sleep to appear a bit rough around the edges.

"Shall we have some hair of the dog?" Julie asked us to break the ice.

"Absolutely!" Sherman replied. "But I need some caffeine with it, if I am going to make it through the day."

"Irish Coffees, all around!" Sarah exclaimed.

"Sarah, tell me again how you two met," said Sherman.

She smiled, looked sideways at Julie, and then at me. "We were in a coffee shop. I got a large drip coffee with a shot of espresso, and Julie, who took my order, did two things: she spelled my name with the silent 'H' at the end, and told me, in a stage whisper, that professionals call it a 'red-eye' when a shot is added to a coffee." Sarah stopped to blot her lips with the napkin.

Julie continued the story. "Then, she returned every day for a week. After her first visit, I never had to ask what she wanted. I hoped, by the end of the week, that she was seeking more than coffee. I wrote my name and number on her cup, just below her name."

Smiling and slightly embarrassed, Sarah picked up the story. "I called her that very evening. We made a date for the following weekend, which went very well, indeed." She nudged Julie with her shoulder. "And then, as lesbians do, I brought my U-Haul on our second date, and moved in."

We all laughed as the server entered our room with a tray of waters and large mugs of fragrant, potent coffees.

"How long have you two been together?" he asked after the drinks had been shuffled around the table.

"Five years," they said in unison and began to laugh. They were both giddy with excitement, and it was wonderful to see my sister so happy.

I sipped my coffee, trying to forestall the next questions, and enjoying the rush of warmth from the whisky.

"And how about you two? What was the event that brought you together?" Julie asked.

Sarah shot her a sideways glance and I said nothing. I waited for Sherman to speak first. I really needed to hear how he interpreted our first encounter.

"Coincidentally, we met in a coffee shop as well. Larry did not have to ask my name, as he was already on the prowl for someone that looked just like me and had my name."

Julie looked terribly confused. I let the silence play out.

"At a fragile point in my adult life, when I had reached one of the more difficult crossroads I would face, this gorgeous man followed me into a coffee shop. He forced his way into my glum afternoon, took a seat at my table, and then surprised me in more ways than I thought were possible." He finished, looked toward me, and waited for the next question.

"Wait, no, he already knew your name?" Julie asked.

"I work with Sherman's brother, Jerome. He asked me to reach out to Sherman. They had fallen out, and I was attempting to reconcile them." I paused, sipped my coffee, and continued. "Because they are twins, I knew exactly what he would look like, and of course, his brother had told me his name."

"Oh my gosh, you have an identical twin? I wish you had brought him this weekend!" Julie almost shouted. The coffee and alcohol combination were working.

"I need a little distance from my brother, at least until I get to know Larry better," he blurted out. The truth was that neither of us had a choice about the distance from Jerome at that point.

When he saw the expression on the ladies' faces, he continued. "We still have some things that I need to work out with Jerome. Larry and I have only been together for a short while, and I reconnected with Jerome on the exact same day that I fell for your brother. There has been a lot of change in the last few weeks."

"I am sorry, Sherman, I just meant that he would be welcome. You are so darned cute; I cannot imagine having two men around that look like you," Julie added.

"Well, I believe that Larry, here, would like nothing better. He fell for Jerome first. It was only my dumb luck that my brother is straight."

The server appeared at my shoulder to take our breakfast order. We ordered some appetizers to share. Each of us got one of the egg dishes on the menu, and another round of drinks. None of us were planning to drive anywhere.

"I am sorry, Sherman, I certainly did not mean to stir up any anxiety. I had noticed that the two of you are very well paired. This could be the match you both have been waiting for," Julie said apologetically.

Sarah put her hand over Julie's.

"If I have my way, we will never be apart," Sherman stated plainly. "But I have always been a hopeless romantic." He shyly glanced in my direction to see my expression.

I could not contain my smile. "That is a relief to hear. When we skipped the wedding and charged right into the honeymoon, I was wondering if we could ever get back on a track to make things permanent." I took the box out of my pocket and placed it on the table between us.

Sherman teared up, and the ladies cooed until he opened the black velvet cube with trembling hands. Inside were two identical bands, one for each of us. The interior glowed with the candles above, the rose gold highlighting the reflection from around us. The exterior white gold had a beveled edge that only exposed a hairline of the pink lining.

"I have been waiting for the right time to ask you." My voice hitched with emotion. I forced myself to continue. "Would you please marry me? It would make me the happiest man on the planet."

He nodded, brushing the fuzzy box with his fingers. I leaned over to kiss him while the girls applauded.

With tears of joy, I looked up at my sister. "You may have beat me to the altar, but I am not going to let you be happier than me, dammit."

"Gosh, you are so competitive! It's not a contest, you know!" Sarah exclaimed.

"We would like to keep this quiet until after the weekend. I have no intention of upstaging your moment," Sherman offered.

"Would you mind if I mentioned it in the toast at the end of the reception?" Julie asked, cautiously.

"That would be lovely," Sherman said through his tears.

The server arrived with the appetizers, which saved us all from more of our emotionally laden conversation, for the moment.

I started eating before we had any more questions thrown at us.

"What did it take for you to convince our brother to come down here?"

"Oh, crap, that reminds me. I agreed to pick them up at the airport at four. I had better back off on the alcohol." I pushed the half-finished mug of Irish Coffee away from me, and switched to water, to be safe.

Sherman finished his coffee and then he started working on the remainder of mine. The smile on his face was worth any tears we had shed in the process.

As they picked at the scraps on their plates, and had another round of drinks, I told them an abbreviated story of Paul's Birthday weekend.

"Where are they staying?" Julie asked timidly.

"I got them a suite at the Hilton, but I made sure they were a few rooms away." I sipped some more water. "We have the same departure time on Monday. After driving us all to the airport, I will turn in the rental car. We have the same flight, so we will say our goodbyes in Charlotte."

My companions were full and looked kind of sleepy. "I will get us a cab, what can I arrange for you, ladies?"

"We only have a few blocks to walk. I have arranged to dress at a friend's house for the rehearsal. We can go crash there until it is time to boogie," Sarah said, with Julie nodding as much from tipsy sleepiness as agreement.

I paid the bill, and we got out into the bright sunlight. We waved goodbye to the ladies and looked around for a cab. The one person that I did not want to see suddenly came into view.

"Angie!" I exclaimed. "Are you still scaring people with that contraption?" I asked coyly.

"Well, if it isn't the honeymoon couple. Have you come back to repeat the damage from last time?"

"Last time?" Sherman asked.

I turned my back to her and made eye contact with Sherman to get his attention away from the boisterous rickshaw driver.

"Jerome and I took several rides when we were here. One of them was when we were very drunk. I guess she thought we were a couple, the way we were giggling."

"Wait, no, this is the same guy! Don't do that to me."

I spun around to face her.

"Angie, this is Sherman. The other guy was Jerome, his twin brother."

"Eww, that is kinky!" She said and laughed to herself.

The look on Sherman's face must have matched the horror on mine.

"Could we just get a ride to the Hilton Riverfront, please?"

"Um, sure. Climb in," she said, averting her eyes.

We got in and she started to pedal. I tried to hold Sherman's hand, but he pulled it away from me. I thought that we might have a long afternoon ahead of us.

She dropped us at the hotel, and I paid her in cash. Before she had a chance to apologize or give me her card, I turned and followed Sherman into the lobby. I let the silence play out between us, simply because I could not defend what I did not know. He hit the elevator button and kept his back to me.

I desperately wanted to talk to Jerome and reminisce about our experience in the rickshaw. I was tempted to text him again, but I knew he had no interest at that time.

When the doors opened on the top floor, we walked over and keyed ourselves into the suite. Just as I stepped through the door, I had an instant realization.

"Sherman. I must go back to the restaurant. I forgot to pick up the ring box," I said in a flood of words.

He reached into his coat pocket and produced the box. I searched his face for a hint at what he was feeling. Without a pause, I knelt in front of him and looked up at his face, a forlorn puppy impression for each of us.

"If you will let me put the ring on your finger, I will be yours for the rest of our lives. I cannot bear to quarrel with you."

He was silent, raising his chin so I could not see his eyes. Perhaps he was thinking. I slowly reached up and took his free hand in mine. I gently tugged on it, hoping to propel him forward with a level of forgiveness for the mistaken identity.

When he looked down again, he was crying. "I am sorry. I just cannot get past the time you spent with Jerome. There is no doubt, for me, that nothing sexual happened, but I just feel as if...you have already had so many experiences with him that I am going to be playing catch-up forever."

"He is my best friend, and a really great guy. But you must remember that I have no breasts, and that he probably forgets both of our names when Abigail takes her top off for him."

He smiled and nodded. With no further prompting, he lowered himself to his knees. We were eye-to-eye on the tile floor. He stuck out his left hand and wiggled his fingers. I slipped the ring onto his finger and kissed him passionately. He pulled away, grabbed the second gold band, and put it on my ring finger. We were engaged. We both cried, holding each other like frightened children who have finally found comfort.

Slowly, I raised myself up, and pulled on his hands for him to join me. We embraced again, and the tears had stopped. He was the first to break away.

"I think you need to take a quick nap to refresh yourself before the drive to the airport."

"That is a good idea. Would you care to join me?" I asked.

He nodded slowly, and we walked hand-in-hand over to the bed.

I awoke at two that afternoon. We were tangled together in the bed. Neither one of us wanted to stir, but I kept running my hands all over him.

"What are you doing?" he asked.

"Does it bother you?"

"No, it feels wonderful. I was simply curious."

"I am doing inventory. I want to have all of this committed to memory. I will know the instant something changes, because I am going to do this every day for the rest of my natural life."

He turned over and stretched out on his stomach. I continued my labors, enjoying every motion of the process. He drifted back to sleep.

At half past two, I sat up and rubbed my eyes. I put my hand on his back and ran it down toward his buns.

"Sherman?" I asked him quietly.

"Yes...?"

"Can I ask...did you want to go with me to pick up my brother?"

"Not sure. What are my options?" he asked, with his voice muffled by the pillow.

"You can get dressed and be my co-chauffeur for the ride out to the airport. Or you can stay here, like this." I ran my hand over his body again, "and I will do inventory again the minute I am back in this room. Or you could get up and meet us in the lobby for a cocktail when we arrive from the airport."

He raised his head from the pillow. "What do you want me to do?"

"If we are going to be married, we will make decisions together."

"We're not married yet," he laughed. "What do you want me to do?"

"I suppose, under the circumstances, that I will go, alone, and pick them up. When we arrive back here, we could all have a quick drink in the bar, and you could meet them briefly. They will probably need to change for the rehearsal, and the dinner to follow. We will only have a few minutes at the bar, so the pressure would be slight, for you."

"And if I want to go with you?"

"Then I would have to insist that you get dressed. I am not going to share this..." running my hand over his backside again, "...with anyone else, ever."

He made no movement and no sound. I ran my fingers lightly down his very ticklish side, and he doubled up, pulling away from me. His feet hit the floor and the powerful shower head began to make splattering sounds in the glass enclosure. I took the opportunity to join him.

We dressed for the rehearsal dinner. Our plan, initially, was to cater to what Paul and Joanie needed, since they were just getting into town. I had already arranged for a porter to take their bags up to their room the moment they arrived, and the suite was prepared for their entrance.

Friday afternoon traffic snarled us at every turn, and we barely made it to the terminal in time to save them from getting into a cab. We had even pulled over and switched drivers so that I could try to communicate with one of them, but neither of them had their cell phones on.

I jumped out of the car and ran over to the taxicab where Paul was negotiating rates. "Paul!" I shouted over the street noise. "Your phone is not on! I have been trying to reach you for thirty minutes."

He took his phone out of his pocket, finally realized it was on airplane mode, and shrugged. Given his history of non-responsiveness, it probably stayed that way for months without him knowing it. Our comfortable lead time for the rehearsal was gone, and we had to get them to the church for his part of the ceremony.

"Where is Joanie?" I demanded.

He pointed to his left. "Smoking. She thought you had forgotten us. It stressed her out."

I grabbed their bags, waved the next customers in the taxi line over to the waiting cab, and dragged it all over to our waiting rental car. Sherman was already arguing with the crosswalk police. He had stopped the vehicle in a bad place. All our stress levels were now at peak stages.

Sherman took the lead in getting the car moved to an appropriate place. I sought out Joanie, and Paul waited at the curb for the two of us to return, before we went in search of our driver. Our new chauffeur had put the bags in the trunk and kept the engine running. I grabbed the front seat, the anxious couple piled into the back, and we sped off in search of the correct church.

I pulled up the address on my phone and started barking directions. Sherman drove admirably, considering the heavy traffic and aggressive local drivers in competition for each of the lanes. Once we were heading in the correct direction, I turned around to face our new arrivals. They looked frightened.

"Don't worry, he is really good at this. The last time we had to rush at this speed, there were only minor injuries for the passengers, but we got there on time," I said with a smile. Neither of them smiled back.

Sherman merged into traffic on a three-lane road, and it was his chance to slow down and match the speed of the traffic lights. He never flinched once, despite the chaos all around him.

"Paul? Joanie?" I asked, to get their attention. "This is Sherman, our driver. He also happens to be my date for the wedding. Larry Brooks plus one?"

"Which came first, the position as our maniacal chauffeur, or your date?" Paul answered back, slyly.

Joanie did not get it, at first, and then she understood. Perhaps she saved her laughter for another time.

Paul reached forward and put his right hand on Sherman's shoulder. "I am so pleased to meet you, and to learn that you are working for the common good. Please let me know if my brother causes you any problems, and I will tell you all his embarrassing childhood secrets. They might come in handy later, for any spats you might have."

Sherman smiled at the thought, while I grimaced. "Thank you. We are almost there, and I am sure Larry has alerted Sarah that we will be there." He glanced over at me to see that I was texting feverishly, hoping to catch someone at the church before the dry run began.

The drive from the airport to the garden district parallels the river and increases the congestion as the local Friday afternoon traffic gets caught up in early weekend revelers. The thirteen-mile drive to the rehearsal took us more than thirty minutes and deposited our frantic passengers at the door of the church the very minute that the delicate-step practices were starting.

My perfectionist sister was insistent on rehearsing the nerves out of the planned ceremony. Paul knew, when he accepted his place in the wedding party, that it might mean casualties in the line of duty, as she drilled us like a military platoon. By the look on his face, Sherman was not prepared for the experience. The only thing missing was a whistle for her to blow when she was dissatisfied with the results.

Given the drama of the planned procession, I was sure that everyone in attendance would be duly impressed with their forethought, and planning. The minister was patient, and notably hesitant to disagree with what the lead bridezilla wanted. Perhaps he had learned from past attempted interferences, that his opinion was just not welcome.

Reverend Hyde came over to speak to me about an issue, and I was surprised at how close he stood next to me. Before he finished the first few words, his hand was already on my back, and his lips were nearly touching my ear. Perhaps it was his way to gaining attention for the importance of his request, but it left me wondering about his motives.

"Larry, is it? I might have some problems with the way they are marching up the sides, is this something that I should speak to Sarah about, or the wedding planner."

"I am sure that Sarah can take your suggestion and relay it to the others, for those who would benefit from the information."

His hand had slipped down further on my back, nearly reaching my right flank with his long arm. He never pulled back from his rather intimate pose at my ear. I had a gaydar sense that this was not his first time speaking in this manner.

"What in particular, reverend, should they do differently?"

"I believe the couple, that is, Julie and her father, might trip on a loose piece of carpeting on that aisle. We will try to secure it before the service, but just in case, please let them know." His hand had slipped further down my back. It came to rest at the top of my buttock.

Imagining that I had to extract myself before he checked my inseam with the other hand, I nodded vigorously and excused myself.

When we finally performed the entire march adequately twice in a row, Sarah allowed us to retreat into our civilian lives. The wedding party was dismissed for our family gathering at a local establishment. Once again, Sherman drove the four of us admirably well, and we arrived only moments before the brides.

We were in a private room for the twenty of us. The room had two large round tables, with twelve place settings at each. Wine was flowing, and the staff was setting up the buffet for salads and soup. The entrees would be delivered, based on guest preference.

As Sarah and Julie arrived, we stood up and applauded. The evening began with a toast from the father of the other bride. He was tall, dashing, and looked quite dapper in his sport coat, waistcoat and bow tie. When he stood up, the podium was nearly dwarfed with his shoulders towering above it. I could see where Julie got her height.

He sipped from his glass, cleared his throat, and put on his reading glasses. I had never met the man and did not know what to expect. None of us did.

"For those of you that I have not yet met, I am Julie's Father, Bill Armstrong. I am here with my wife of thirty years, Madeline. She has granted me permission to speak for the two of us. It is only the second time in our marriage that I have been entrusted with this responsibility, so I had better do it quickly before the alcohol in this town goes to my head."

There was polite laughter in the room.

"Tomorrow, we will gain another daughter, in a ceremony of love and commitment that has been on our wish list for Julie since she finished her undergraduate studies. As her father, I may be slightly biased, but I see a light in her that radiates out to the people in her life, making us all happier, better, more enlightened people. When she came home to tell us that she had finally met the 'one' she did not have to say a word. We could already see the exponential radiance that she was emitting, just having the love of Sarah with her at the time.

"When we finally met Sarah, we were as enamored with her as Julie is. We were convinced, at least I was, that these two lovely women would make a happy life together, giving us all a beacon of bliss that we could hold in our hearts, even when we were a thousand miles away."

He stopped, sipped more from his glass, and wiped his eyes with a brashly loud red handkerchief.

"As I stand before you this evening, my tears of joy are also echoed by a sense of loss, for my little girl, who now holds a doctorate, and has a great career, has found someone that can make her happy. The fact that this person is Sarah Brooks, only makes it that much sweeter, as we already love her as much as anyone else in our extended family."

He wiped his eyes again, and then held up his glass. "Please join me in toasting these two wonderful women as they begin their life together. May we always look to them as the paragon of what is right with this world, no matter what anyone else might say."

There was rustling as we all grabbed our glasses and stood for the honor.

"To Sarah and Julie!" he said with gusto.

"To Sarah and Julie!" the crowd echoed.

We clinked our glasses, drank, and then clapped while the other well-wishers stood to say their bit. The servers poured more wine and cleared plates for the buffet starters.

The remainder of dinner was sedate, at least while the food outweighed the volume of alcohol. That balance is difficult to maintain in a town that loves to frolic.

I am not sure why we stayed on, long past the witching hour, but we were having a great time, and none of us wanted it to end. The restaurant asked us to pack up and go just after eleven, so we moved, in a caravan of three taxis, to the Hilton hotel bar.

The twelve of us were the only people in the small nook of a room off of the main lobby. Perhaps because it was just family, it was easier to stay in the secluded area and continue carousing than it was to admit defeat and march off to bed. The brides-to-be communed with us, The Brooks Brothers, our dates, and Julie's parents. The last four were assorted college friends, who were locals to New Orleans, and probably accustomed to seeing the sunrise before the end of a party.

By midnight, the crew dwindled from a dozen down to six, and then by one o'clock, it was just the four of us from North Carolina, as the brides went up to their room. Each time we lost a few more, the conversation grew a bit quieter and yet more abandoned, with the alcohol lubricating our tongues, and diminishing our inhibitions.

Fortunately, none of us had sufficient memories beyond the outrageous final bar bill that we agreed to split. I doubt anyone said anything inflammatory or insulting, either. It was as if the happiness of the wedding couple had permeated all our lives, if just for the weekend of bliss that we experienced together.

Wedding Preparations

I struggled to open my eyes, embarrassed that I was more dehydrated than a frat boy after his first kegger. Padding across the room silently, I slipped into the bathroom and started my recovery regimen. Two Tylenols, and two glasses of water were my tonics for such mornings. I gargled with some of the mouth wash on the counter and quickly returned my cold, bare feet to the warm carpet.

Raising the covers ever so slightly, I slipped in behind Sherman, and cuddled up to his warm mass. He shifted slightly, then relaxed enough for me to match the curve of his fetal position. The hairs on his back tickled me in the most delightful ways. There wasn't anywhere else I would rather be, headache or not.

"Hey," he whispered. "Did you really..."

"Don't even start with me! You do know that I have your brother on speed dial. I can match you fifteen to one on embarrassing anecdotes from your adolescence."

"A lot of good that would do you now. He does not want to respond to me lately," he said.

"Perhaps he is just busy with Abigail," I said, covering for my best friend.

He giggled and then turned over to face me. "Your brother is really a great guy. I expected, maybe with the construction background, and small-town lifestyle, he might be less, I don't know, accepting."

"I broke him in a long time ago. I just wish I had intervened before he picked his current wife, but I guess we all have our burdens to bear."

"Do you not like her? She seemed harmless enough."

"It's just that she...I don't know, seems so placid. Like a Stepford wife. Only, her drug is tobacco."

"Yeah, I guess I can see that. Not bad, though. She could have been a high-maintenance gal, like Jerome got."

"Abigail has the two things Jerome most wants in a woman. And they both just barely fit into her expensive push-up bra."

We giggled together for a few minutes, relishing the joke at their expense.

"Okay, we have to pick up our tuxedos by eleven. We can change into them at the church. How much time does that give us for the most important task of the morning, my getting a hangover-cure for breakfast?" I asked, tickling the hairs on his chest with my breath.

"THIS is the most important task of the morning. I would want to be nowhere else."

"You are going to make a great husband. I am not sure what I ever did to deserve you," I said, pulling him closer.

"You know," he whispered, "flattery will get you everywhere."

If the rehearsals did nothing else, they did allay some of the anxiety of walking slowly in front of a large crowd. We got to the church early. The minister's stoically plain wife met us at the door with a scowl on her face. Sounding much like a spinsterly school matron, she instructed us to change into our tuxedos in her husband's study as quickly as humanly possible.

Wearing nothing but our boxers and some thin black socks, I was surprised to see the reverend peek through the door. From his view, Sherman's face was still hidden, but there was a lot of skin exposed in the mirrored closet door behind us both. The door swung open, and the elderly man came in with a tray raised high above his shoulder, balanced on one large hand. Deftly, the door whisked across the thick carpet and closed behind him, which he accomplished while balanced on one foot. He seemed unfazed that we were not quite dressed. He cleared his throat, as if we had not noticed him make his entrance.

"Gentleman, I know this may sound odd, but I find that these ceremonies can add a lot of stress, and there is only one way to deal with the pressure, in New Orleans." He lowered the tray to his waist, and we could see the six shot glasses, perfectly balanced and brimfull of golden liquor.

We looked at each other, then back at him. He took one of the shots, held it up, and waited while we delicately gripped the small vessels of elixir. He made a toast "to the happy brides!" And then gulped the shot. We followed suit. The whisky burned but neither of us complained. He put the empty glass down and retrieved another. We shrugged and did the same.

He held the glass high, looked at Sherman, and then at me. "If I were any younger, I would want nothing less than to be at the altar with either one of you beautiful men on my arm. Since I am not, I would be honored if you would consider me for your commitment service when you two are ready to tie the knot." With that, he looked at us each again, and then downed the shot. Sherman smiled broadly, and I suppressed a laugh. We drank down the whisky and returned the glasses to his outstretched tray.

"Thank you both for indulging me. There is mouthwash in my bathroom, just behind you." He took a few long steps, and then closed the door behind him as he left. We broke into gales of laughter, falling onto the small sofa together. We were still cackling when Paul made his entrance. His tuxedo was on a coat hanger, with his hand extended away from him to keep it from touching his jeans.

"Well, it sounds, and smells, like you have already been celebrating. Do you think you could sober up before the service?" he asked rather curtly.

We erupted into laughter again. Sherman almost toppled over on the Persian rug when he tried to stand. I grabbed his arm to stop him from falling forward.

"Geez, you really have shocked me, here today. I thought I had two upstanding citizens in this wedding party, but all I see are some immature frat boys. I guess I am going to have to take charge here." He scowled at us. "Or would you prefer I get the minister in here to crack the whip?"

"No, please! Not him," I stammered. We stood up, clenching our teeth, and swaying with the laughter roiling within us. I felt as if we were called into the dean's office after a campus prank gone south.

It took all my willpower to stop the shuddering hilarity and start getting dressed. Sherman would not even make eye contact, or we would have broken up again.

Shirking all pretense of modesty, Paul stripped down in front of us, all the way to his boxers. He checked to see that we were making progress, and then began dressing himself in his tuxedo. We did our best to match his progress. Almost finished, Paul and I came up short when it came to the bow tie. Sherman had his deftly tied, without using a mirror, in less than a minute.

"Shit. I cannot get this blasted thing tied," Paul swore to himself.

Sherman crossed the room and put his hand on my brother's shoulder to get his attention. He reached around each side of Paul's neck and gently took the loose ends in his strong hands. They both faced the mirror and my gorgeous fiancé tied Paul's bowtie in one try, as if it were as simple as shoelaces.

He tied mine next, and then we put our coats on. Lining up to see ourselves in the mirrored doors, it was worth all the efforts we had expended to arrive at this moment, just to behold the three of us in black and white.

I felt choked up and had to find my handkerchief to stop my tears. "If I didn't realize how great looking you were before this, I can honestly say I would follow you to the ends of the earth to say our vows, if I can just see you in a tux for our wedding."

"What?" Paul said.

"Oops. Busted," Sherman muttered.

"Is there something you have not told me, Larry?"

"Yes, I am sorry. We got engaged yesterday. I wanted to keep it a secret, so we did not steal the limelight on Sarah's special weekend."

"You jerk! What other secrets are you keeping from me?"

I looked at Sherman, made eye contact, and shrugged. When I turned my face back to my brother, it was serious and grave. I spoke in a low tone.

"Just one other thing. Um...we are broke, so we are going to have to move in with you and Joanie, at least for the first year or so, until we can get back on our feet."

He grimaced. I could see the stress in his face processing what I had said, and then he came back with one word. "Good!"

It was then I knew he got the joke. He grabbed me and gave me a bear hug, risking Sarah's wrath if he wrinkled our suits. Once he let me go, he grabbed Sherman and did the same. It was not over for my betrothed until my brother kissed him on the cheek. We were both still stunned when the minister barged back in to get us.

Using a timer on his digital camera, Reverend Hyde had no compunction about posing for a quick picture with us. It was not until much later in the evening, after the alcohol had been flowing for a while, that I learned the truth about the photo op. The preacher had grabbed the butts of the two men closest to him. I suppose that I was too far away, or that he only had two hands.

We all got some mouthwash, gargled quickly, and then quietly entered the sanctuary. Julie's Father was in his place, and Paul strode confidently over to his. Sherman and I arrived at the entrance hall, just as the wedding planner was getting everyone into procession order.

The ceremony had Broadway-quality choreography, down to the attendants, and the decorations used in the service. When we watched the video a few weeks later, everyone was impressed with the theatricality.

Sherman and I entered, together, stepping forward as somberly as we could manage after the experiences of the past thirty minutes. The flower girls followed, three of them dropping petals on the crush covering the carpet. The ring bear, in a traditional furry, brown grizzly costume, growled at each designated point, delighting the pews full of well-wishers.

Finally, when the music changed to the wedding march, Paul and Sarah placed themselves at the side aisle, while Julie, and her father, made a mirror image on the opposite wall. They marched forward, in unison, with the ladies in matching white gowns on the inside. Their escorts, in black tuxedos, were on the outside, making a symmetric movement, and turning with military precision toward the central altar at the end of the aisle.

Without the video to capture it all, I would have forgotten the entire event in a wash of happy memories. Sarah had gotten two professional cameramen, and a director to stitch it all together on the fly.

The ceremony and vows were beautiful and touching. I only hoped that I could do as well when our time came. Repeatedly, I tried to catch Sherman's eye during the most poignant parts, but he would not look at me. I could tell from the sheen on his eyelashes that he was choked up. We both held together until the end when the minister made his pronouncement of the day.

"These young ladies have matured into women, they appeared before us today, transformed as brides, and now will enter life together as loving spouses. May they walk in unison with all of the blessings of this congregation for the rest of their lives." He stopped speaking, as the music, and our tears, began.

The recession out of the church led us into a stark, sunlit afternoon. While the guests moved on to the reception venue, we spent the next hour taking picture after picture with every conceivable combination of the wedding party, family relations, and scenic shots. The randy minister pushed his way into as many photos as he could, but always with the gentlemen of the wedding party. We tried to read their faces later in the images as he no doubt took liberties with the placement of his hands.

Leaving the two brides behind to finish their pictures, we sped off in a limousine to the hotel ballroom. Paul let us in on a secret plan he had to surprise Sarah, and we promised to keep it to ourselves.

The party was in full swing when we arrived. One of the best things about a celebration in New Orleans is the quality of the music. And the ladies had not skimped on the entertainment. The hottest band in town was rocking the stage next to the spacious dance floor. I grabbed Sherman's hand and dragged him out to the center of the room. The gorgeous introvert in my arms never knew what hit him.

Leading him through several dances I knew, he finally loosened up by the fourth song. We even took a break for a glass of champagne. It was a short rest, as I did not want to miss out on any more of his moves. Seeing him bending and twisting in his tuxedo was the greatest thrill I could remember from the entire wedding day. We tossed our jackets on a nearby chair at the next break, and slow-danced while the world around us disappeared.

The band went silent when the ladies of the hour arrived. The entire room erupted in applause as they entered, arm-in-arm. They made a tour of the venue, hugging friends, kissing relatives, and basking in the moments of glorious happiness.

With a crash of cymbals and a raucous drumbeat to get back into the mood, the band let loose with another one of their hits. The party continued, with drinks flowing and food spread around, as lavish as any Roman feast might have been. I held my breath when they started with the speeches. Paul had promised a surprise, and I was on the edge of my seat for his turn at the microphone.

"Good evening, everyone. I am Paul Brooks. Sarah is my little sister, and I have a few things I would like to share with you while you enjoy this fine wedding cake." He held up the plate of perfectly cut layers, the lemon cream oozing out of the chocolate layers. Even the white fondant rose was intact.

There were murmurs and forks clinking on glasses to quiet the crowd. He waited to begin, and when the quiet overtook the room, he politely cleared his throat with the microphone held away from his mouth.

"As I said before, I am Paul, Sarah's big brother. As the oldest, and most responsible member of the family, I am tasked with telling you something about our clan, giving you some context for our dysfunction, and finally, providing some thoughtful advice for the road ahead."

There was some nervous laughter, and I was sure that my face was red with excitement, if not a little irritation about the dig. Sherman reached over and put his hand over mine.

"I always thought we had the quintessential middle-class homelife, with me breaking our parents' will down to make it easier for my little brother, Larry, and my even younger sister, Sarah, to get away with everything. As the oldest, I never got to be the favorite. Larry was the apple of mom's eye, and Sarah, she could always light up our father's face just by entering the room. Everyone knew that she was his favorite, and none of us complained, because they were so close that it was the perfect father-daughter dynamic."

He paused, sipped from his glass, and looked around the room. "This will get interesting, I promise," he said to a round of polite laughter.

"Unfortunately, their dynamic came to an end when our dad passed away just after Sarah finished her undergraduate degree. Dad had such grand plans to marry her off with all the bells, whistles, and fanfare that he could manage. But he never got the chance. We lost our mother a year later. She died of a broken heart, lost without her anchor. She told me that very fact."

"I assumed the reins of the Brooks clan. Steering our small cadre of misfits, I tried to establish an order by which we could continue our parent's legacy. All that fell apart when they both moved away. Larry is but two hours from me, give or take a full day's frantic drive through North Carolina traffic. And Sarah ended up down here, in the Big Easy, running her own business. The best part of her move, for me, was that New Orleans was where she found

Julie. We all know how that turned out." He raised his glass and the guests all applauded.

He stopped, as he appeared to get choked up. Wiping his mouth with his dinner napkin, he continued, but his voice was not as strong.

"As I prepared for this evening, I considered how little my words might mean to a crowd of people that barely know me. While I adore Sarah, my only sister, and want the best for her, the only person that could possibly convey what we all want her to hear would be our father. As he cannot be here, I will have to resort to the next best thing."

His voice hitched. He sipped his drink, wiped his mouth, and then pulled out an envelope from his pocket. Clearing his throat again, he struggled to continue.

"I have here, as the oldest son of the family, a hand-written letter from our father, to his favorite daughter, Sarah. He made me promise to read this at her wedding, and I intend to fulfill that promise now."

The tears were streaming down Sarah's face. Her left hand was curled between Julie's two fists, and her right hand was clasped in her new father-in-law's prayerful embrace.

He opened the brittle envelope with his steak knife. The paper that slipped out was crackled with age. A hush fell over the crowd. In a show of vulnerability that I did not expect, he put on a pair of reading glasses, peered at the first page, and then began reading aloud.

"My dearest Sarah, I am so very sorry that I could not be there for your finest moment, when my little girl becomes a woman, and flourishes in the love that will carry her through the rest of her life. What I want you to know, most of all, is that you were the light of my life. Having a daughter that saw me as a hero and let me be her guardian protector made me the man I was meant to become."

Paul paused and wiped his mouth.

"While I may not have always understood your tom-boy tendencies, I knew that you had gotten your sensitivity and warmth from me. Your mother's genes supplied the toughness I saw in you with so many of your endeavors. Now, as you charge forward into married life, please take my advice on three important issues."

He paused, wiped his eyes, and sipped some water. There were no dry eyes in the venue, even the band was choked up.

"First, it is always better to be happy than it is to be right. Compromise is the cornerstone to a happy marriage. Second, set your priorities for life together; once you have those in order, nothing can come between you. And lastly, never let a day go by that you do not let the people in your life, that you love, know it. If I have any regrets about my life, it was that I did not do that enough for my family. Thank you for hearing this old man's words of wisdom. Dad."

He dropped his hand to his side and covered his eyes with the napkin. Joanie reached up and took the letter from his hand for safekeeping. The crowd transformed from weepy and touched to enthusiastic applause in a few seconds.

Everyone held their breath as Sarah composed herself. It was her turn to speak. She stood, wiped her mouth with a napkin, and then blotted her eyes.

"I cannot say, in the time we have left, how much you all mean to me, and how honored I am that you chose to be here with us, on our special day. For me, I will take dad's words to heart, and I intend to begin today. I love you all. Nothing material in this world can replace the feelings I have for my wife, our family, and our friends." Her voice hitched, and she held her napkin to her mouth.

"Just when I thought this weekend could be no better, for all our planning, orchestration, and preparation, I have been entrusted with a secret that, somehow, made it all pale by comparison. As you already heard from my older brother - thank you, Paul - I would like to put the spotlight on our brother. Larry, could you please stand?"

I was taken by surprise but rose to the occasion. My left hand was firmly in Sherman's.

"Just yesterday morning, I was witness to a marriage proposal. My brother, Larry, has asked his boyfriend, Sherman to marry him."

I pulled on his hand for Sherman to stand with me. "He said yes!" I shouted to the crowd.

The applause was deafening, and overwhelming. I could feel the tears escaping, and I was unashamed, as I knew that my path to happiness with Sherman was rock-solid. I just wish I knew if we could count on his brother to endorse the relationship.

On cue, the band started up, and the speeches were over. I pulled Sherman into a tight embrace, and then kissed him as passionately as I dared in front of the crowd.

To my surprise, he took my hand and led me onto the dance floor. We were in reverie for the rest of the evening. The champagne flowed, the guests danced, and the party continued through the late hours.

Sunday

It was after four when we finally breached the doorway to our hotel room. I had never been so tired, yet so full of joy. I spun Sherman around once, dance-floor style, and then held him in my arms while he struggled to get away.

"Now that you have seen what kind of party my family puts on, have you thought about what you would like to do for our wedding?" I whispered into his ear.

"Um, no," he responded. "Besides, I may have a competing offer, so I need to see what happens with that before we make any concrete plans."

I pulled back from our embrace. He was pensive and his brow was furrowed. "I have to seriously consider the possibility of Harold over you. I am sorry."

"Harold WHO?" I almost shouted.

"Harold Hyde." He swallowed hard. "You know, the gorgeous minister that performed the ceremony this afternoon. I am sure that he would never ask me to dance in front of all those people," he finished, then grinned so big that I could have killed him.

"Okay, I will give you thirty seconds to think it over. I will bet you that he does not know half the ways to please you that I do."

"I cannot say that I believe you. Are you willing to prove it to me?"

I nodded slowly. "Every single day, for the rest of my life."

"Okay, but we will have to start now, so that I can give him my answer by morning."

"It is morning," I said and began removing his tuxedo with all the restraint that I could muster.

We finally looked at the clock at five minutes past eleven. I sat up, stretched, and marched across the room to the bathroom. The shower head sprang to life as I turned the lever on the faucet. By the time I had brushed my teeth and swallowed a few Tylenols with a tumbler full of tap water, the steam was escaping from the glass enclosure. Gently pulling the door closed, I saw that a familiar hand appeared on the frame. Making room for Sherman, we shared the shower in a ritual that I had grown quite fond of.

Once we were out of the shower, I texted Paul: *we are up and ready to go, how about y'all?*

He responded immediately: *Of course, we are ready! Where have y'all been all morning?*

I sighed and squelched my first instinct to respond with sarcasm. Instead of cleaning the room sufficiently to allow the maid to identify the carpet and bed under our mess, we left the Do Not Disturb sign on the doorknob as we stepped into the hall.

Sherman was still amused by the additional hang card that said, "Refill My Mini Bar" and backed with "Please Collect Laundry" but I would not let him linger over the implications of leaving either sign up for the maid.

Paul and Joanie met us in the lobby. They looked perky and refreshed.

"Nice to see you both alive on the planet," he said, far too happily.

"Good Afternoon!" she chirped.

"Good Morning," I said flatly. "I suppose you both slept well?" Secretly, in my hungover state of mind, I plotted their deaths.

"Absolutely," he said. "and I am too young to stay in bed all day."

"I am sorry we kept you waiting," Sherman said, trying to douse the flames that I was actively fanning.

Shaking the car keys in my hand, I led the way to the rental car. After clicking the remote, the doors unlocked, I tossed the keys to Paul, and I hopped into the back. He was a better driver, anyway.

"Should I know where we are going?" he asked.

"I will pull it up on my phone," she said.

We were quiet in the back. I was just pleased that we did not have to be fighting the traffic and recovering from our evening of wedding party mayhem. The irritating voice emanating from the tinny cell phone speaker led us directly to the picnic shelter reserved for the wedding party.

Even though it was an outdoor barbeque, it had been catered. When Sherman went to the car for his sunglasses, I snapped a picture of the logo on the food boxes with my phone. The text message to Jerome had one image, and one word: *remember?*

We began to gorge ourselves on some of the best barbeque on the planet. When I started interacting and eating, I had not considered how I was supposed to maintain a conversation with the people around me, continually text Jerome with updates, and keep Sherman in the dark that I was reliving our wanton week at the Cat's Paw. I doubt that he ever looked up from the cheerleaders on his big screen television to notice the messages.

The casual park atmosphere seemed more than natural. We were in our element, as a family, and happy to be together again on a day that usually meant hasty departures after the big event. When the brides finally left us to start their honeymoon, we settled back into our chairs, and resumed our conversations. Joanie and I took the lead on cleaning up the tables and securing the reusable supplies. Paul drove us back to the hotel, where we parted company to rest before any evening activities.

I left my phone unlocked, laid it down on the desk, and went into the bathroom. Sherman picked it up and asked one question: "Have you been texting him all day?"

"Yes," I admitted. "I sent him a picture of the BBQ logo, and few other reminders of our week here."

He looked bewildered, as if I had admitted cheating on him.

"He is still my friend, even if you are the main man in my life. You cannot be jealous of a few texts," I said. "Are you?"

He went in the bathroom for a long time. When he emerged, his demeanor was different. "I am sorry," he said. "It is still a tender point for me."

I crossed the room and took his hands in mine. "Please tell me what I can do. I just cannot stop trying to converse with him. Outside of you, and family, I don't have anyone else to talk to."

"It is not that I want you to leave him behind, or stop, it just seems to come up more often than I would expect, when you are spending time with me."

"What am I to do?" I asked. "I cannot please both of you. Of course, you are my primary concern, but how can I manage a friendship if you are jealous of the friend?"

"It is not that he is my brother. Well, not just that. It is that he always gets precedence of your attention. I would be jealous of anyone in that role."

"What if it were Sarah or Paul that took my attention away from you? You think you might feel differently?"

He looked at me, then his eyes went up and to the left - a clear sign that he might reveal himself in a lie. "No, I guess not."

I was shocked. He told the truth, but it cost him.

I wrapped my arms around him. "How about this? I let him know that we will be going to silent mode for times that I will spend with you, devoted to you. I need to manage his expectations because I don't want to hurt him. Okay?"

"Um, I guess. Yes, let's try that."

I picked up the phone and sent the message: *Going offline for the evening. Talk at you when we get back into town tomorrow night?* And hit send. Then I turned the phone off.

Is that better? I asked hopefully.

"I suppose."

"Does that mean I won this round?"

"Why do you ask?"

"Because I think it is time for you to surrender your clothes..."

He smiled and began to undress. I raced him to the finish. Then we both won.

At dinner that evening, we had jettisoned all but the core family from North Carolina. The four of us went in search of a small meal to cap off a spectacular weekend.

As we walked along the riverfront, I proposed a deal for my dinner companions: "How about this?" I asked, haltingly. "We have a light dinner, perhaps go for a walk along the riverfront, and no one gets snockered tonight, me included?" I laughed.

"Sounds like a reasonable request," Joanie responded. The other two said nothing. I doubted they were in any shape to argue.

We found a small café on the river, shielded from the breezes yet open enough to bless us with a view of the river.

Once we were settled in with soft drinks and menus, I asked my question.

"So, tell me, Paul, how are things with your girlfriend, Shirley?" I asked.

He pulled his menu down to show his smile. "She is kicking butts and taking names. I suppose all those nights managing those stray dogs gave her the skills to manage those construction flunkies."

We all laughed heartily.

Monday

The four of us met for breakfast in the hotel café. Beginning with strong coffee for each of us, I timed my first question to coincide with the second cup for the quick drinkers. Sherman, possibly emboldened by the long weekend's exposure to my family, beat me to the punch with the question I had been holding for two days.

"How long would you have held onto the letter from your dad if Sarah had not gotten married?"

He looked up at Sherman, considering carefully what he would say. "I had instructions to give it to her after fifteen years, or my death, whichever came first." He sipped his coffee and then continued. "Honestly, I did not know how long I would have to wait and had nearly forgotten the promise. Your surprise visit for my birthday reminded me of it, brother."

"I don't suppose you have one for my wedding? From either of our parents?" I asked, tenuously.

He looked at me and shook his head. "No, I am sorry, I don't. However, I would be honored if you would allow me to say a few words at your ceremony. Have you set a date yet?"

"No, not yet. First, I wanted to see if Reverend Hyde was available for the timeframe," Sherman responded.

Paul and I lost all our composure. Our hysterical howls of laughter upset the table and had us under livid scrutiny from everyone else in the restaurant.

"I thought he conducted a beautiful service. What has gotten into the two of you this morning?" Joanie asked.

Just as we had settled down, Sherman, with a sly smile on his face, spoke up. "I loved his attentiveness and the additional, I don't know, um, personal touch."

We lost our composure again, and then left the room together to get away from the source of our consternation. Paul and I were hanging on to each other, laughing hysterically in the lobby while Joanie pretended that she did not know us. Sherman would not even look at me. It was only when we saw our food arrive that we were brave enough to rejoin them at the table.

We checked out and I drove us to the airport. Leaving the three of them at the curb for baggage check, I returned the rental car and then met them in the first-class lounge.

The flight was uneventful. When the plane landed in Charlotte, we huddled up to say our goodbyes. Sherman and I were going to drive home, but Paul and Joanie had one more short flight, to Greensboro.

I hugged Joanie and kissed her cheek. She permitted Sherman to do the same, kissing the other cheek. Sherman shook Paul's hand heartily, looked him in the eye and thanked him for a great weekend. Paul pulled him into a quick hug.

When my time came to speak to Paul, I pulled him away from the group. "Listen, thanks ever so much for making this weekend a great experience, for both of us."

"Sure, no problem at all," he said.

"While we have not set a date yet, you will be at the top of our guest list for our ceremony, okay?"

"I certainly hope so. Just don't do one of those exotic destination weddings."

"It will be remarkably similar to Sarah's, I promise. I may even hire her to arrange the whole thing."

"Great! Was there anything else? We have a plane to catch."

"Yes, there was one other thing. Do you think, if I give you enough notice, that you could write me a letter from one of our parents? Maybe our mother?"

He blinked a few times, surprised. "Of course. It would be my honor." And then he grabbed me in a bear hug. I could feel myself tearing up, but I did not care. He let go and turned to leave for his gate without looking at me again.

Tuesday Reckoning

I had almost put Jerome out of my mind, but I did try to call him on occasion to see if he had softened his attitude. Each time the voicemail kicked in, I left a silly sing-song message, or some nugget meant to appeal to his nostalgia for when we met. He never returned the call, nor did I know if he was even listening to them anymore.

I realized that Sherman's two years of avoiding his brother came from the same gene pool, and I was just getting a small taste of what my friend had experienced, even though I knew neither was justified. Sherman sympathized with me, even as he wanted to bridge the gap between us, as I had for him and Jerome. My departure from the good graces of his brother had effectively cut him off again, as well.

Finally, weeks after the inciting phone call that nearly severed our relationship, Jerome decided to answer my call.

"I am glad I finally caught you in. I almost felt that you were avoiding me."

"I am sorry, this has been a difficult time," he offered.

"I would think you would be happy. Two birds with one stone!"

"Larry, you are an adult. Make your own choices, but don't rub my nose in it."

"I don't even know what that means."

"Don't you think, maybe, that it was a bit fast. You had just met, what, that day?"

"Well, yeah, that was why it felt so right. There was an instant spark."

"What was that noise?" he asked.

"My car door. I just pulled into your driveway."

Jerome came to the front door, left it ajar, then retreated to the living room. I followed, closing the door behind me. He had ended the call.

"I thought you just might be happy for me," I said.

He looked up at me. His face a wash of emotions that I could no longer read.

"I had just made up with him, and I have a lot of baggage to jettison. You just added to my load, thank you very much," he groused.

"But why? He is delightful to talk with, and he is nearly as gorgeous as my best friend."

"Har, har, har," he said sarcastically. "You have worn that joke out, counselor."

"Jerome, please look at me."

He raised his chin. His eyes were steely, but I could tell he was not angry.

"I found someone that I could love for the rest of my life, and you are acting like I am dumping you, even though you and I were never a romantic item."

"It is not that, it's just that, I don't know, I thought I would have more time with you before I had to adjust to both of you...together."

"What is that? Jealousy? And which one of us are you jealous of?"

"What is that supposed to mean?" he demanded.

"Are you concerned that you would lose me as a friend or that you will have to compete with him for my attention?"

"Larry. Stop. Please. Just listen for a second," he nearly shouted. "I had just gotten in touch with my brother. I had not heard from him for two damned years, and I have a lot of guilt about that. I know it was my fault. But I never expected to get him back and lose you in the process. It hurts to think that you, of all people, would want to be with him."

My blood pressure was rising, and I must have left my mouth open, aghast at his thought process.

"Well, what do you have to say for yourself?" he commanded.

"Jerome? I don't understand. I found someone. He is gorgeous, I like his company, I wanted to get to know him better, and neither of us wanted to delay that spark that pulled us into the fire we found from the first moment together. I held out until he had at least called you with the olive branch. Was I just supposed to walk away after that?"

"I don't know. I just wish...you had waited. This has complicated things, and I am just not sure where I can go now for advice. I feel like I got a second chance with my only brother but lost the connection I had with you."

"Why? I will always be your friend, as long as you want me around."

"But don't you see? I cannot confide in you if I have any problems with him or even with Abigail. You are with him now, and that puts me in the backseat. I am left with just a girlfriend who does not seem to understand what I am going through. I had almost created a life that provided everything I wanted in it, and now I am going to have to start over."

"Now you are just being maudlin. We are both tired. Get some sleep and we can talk some more at lunch tomorrow." I prodded for a commitment.

I stood up to leave and he stayed seated. There had not been a day we had spent together since we had returned from New Orleans that I had not hugged him. It hurt to stand there, waiting for my best friend to decide he still wanted me in his life. After a long pause, I turned to go.

He caught up to me at the door. "Wait!" he said.

I turned around and he stepped into our familiar hug. I held him for a while, but I could feel him pulling away emotionally, before either of us tried to separate from the embrace.

I stepped back, but kept my hands on his shoulders, as I often did.

"I am sorry if I have hurt you, Jerome. But I have waited so long to find a man this attractive and who has any interest in me. You must understand, I know you have said the same about Abigail."

"Yeah, but I did not realize it would happen so fast. In one single day."

"But you must admit, my dear friend, it is all your fault," I announced.

"What? How can you possibly mean that? You jerk!"

"It is simple: if you were gay, and liked hairy legs instead of jiggly breasts, we would already be married, and I would be staying here with you, tonight."

"It is just like you to blame me when it is your fault. I think our marriage would have been a disaster. You have terrible taste in men."

He opened the door, and neither of us could hide our grins in the evening lights. I left him to lick his wounds, and I went home to recover after weeks of anguish, and a few painful words from my dearest friend.

Epilogue

A little more than a year to the day that I had first been assailed by Jerome in the pool, I attended his wedding. He married Abigail, the former beauty queen who he had met in New Orleans while I was being interrogated by my well-meaning sister over dinner that night. I agreed to serve as his best man, although I thought his brother would have done a splendid job. To see the two of them in tuxedos for the event would have set my world on fire.

I married the second most gorgeous man in the world on Valentine's Day. He bristled at the title, simply because he was the older of the twins. It took a lot of convincing for me to believe that *all* his furniture was comfortable. We still spend weekends there when we need to get away from the newlyweds.

Sherman teaches at the local community college, and he mentors young scholars through their academic careers. Many of them are completely oblivious that the full-tuition scholarships they receive come from his generous foundation, or that his only involvement in the scholarship process is the academic advising that he does, after-the-fact.

My weekly massage appointments with my best friend have been canceled by his new bride, but I was able to find a suitable replacement for the time slot, with a few more scars to examine in the process. I have let my license lapse, and I no longer feel constrained by the professional distance I once observed so carefully as a certified masseuse.

Sadly, Onslow did not agree to the move. He still scowls angrily when he is forced to commute between his two homes, and we are in danger of international animal cruelty violations each time we force him to do something he does not like. We both defer to his sense of disgust with the world, even if we don't agree with it.

I will never regret shamelessly following Jerome to the conference in New England where we finally connected and became friends. Now, I only stalk Sherman around our shared homes, and I am never disappointed with the results.

Author's Note

When I first set out to put this story into words, my motivation was simple: how far can two guys push a 'bromance' and still be friends if there is no possibility of a romantic relationship? I had considered all the elements in different combinations – and this one just seemed to work.

I am gay and have many straight friends. Most of the men that I call close friends, simply don't fit the stereotypical male roles. They cook, they shop, they are not uptight about their sexuality, and can laugh about our differences. I have willingly gone along with bachelor parties, and trips to the fast-food chain known for its beautiful servers – just as they have indulged me in a few interests.

While this is a work of fiction, I must admit that there are some elements of truth in it. I am just not willing to say which components. Writing should be based on real life experience, or it can never ring true for a reader. The characters exist only in my imagination; they are not based on any person, living or dead, but may have traits we all recognize in our own environment.

Stalking, as known in the news of our modern time, is a serious crime and I certainly do not intend to diminish the pain of those who have been harassed by an unbalanced, or unwelcome, admirer. Nor would I defend someone who had made another person's life uncomfortable through repeated attempts to force a relationship.

With that said, there is a middle age understanding that I have acquired in life that would lead me to believe that any one of us could suddenly suffer from an irrational obsession with someone they find attractive. It would not matter if either party were already attached to a significant other.

I suspect that, as we age, our psyches can push us to suspend reason to connect with someone that we have no business pursuing. The human sexual response is one of the most powerful urges we can experience, and we cannot simply turn it off when it no longer serves the purpose of the initial coupling instinct.

It is not difficult to be monogamous and faithful. I have done it for several decades, with no regrets or after thoughts. That does not mean that I am not going to notice a spectacular specimen of masculinity on occasion. It does mean that I will take that appetite home with me, where it is welcome, and even encouraged.

Thank you, Clifton, for thirty-seven years!

Made in the USA
Middletown, DE
29 August 2023

37492017R00170